A DEREK MASON MYSTERY

Scalping THE Red Rocks

Greg Lilly

Cherokee McGhee

Williamsburg, Virginia

ISBN 978-0-9799694-6-1
0-9799694-6-8

First Edition 2010

Cover illustration by Braxton McGhee
Author photograph by Mike Blevins

Published by:
Cherokee McGhee, L.L.C.
Williamsburg, Virginia

Find us on the World Wide Web at:
WWW.CHEROKEEMCGHEE.COM

Printed in the United States of America

Dedicated to the memory of

Rochelle Brener Weis

poet and writer, Senior Poet Laureate of Arizona

My teacher, my muse, my friend.

Scalping THE Red Rocks

Greg Lilly

CHAPTER ONE

The psychic foretold love and loss for me in Sedona. Couldn't the bitch just give me a break? Love, that would have been worth the fifty dollars, but no, she had to add loss.

⚜ ⚜ ⚜

I steered the Ford Explorer off Dry Creek Road and into the condominium's parking lot. The buildings had a low adobe style and courtyards scattered with prickly pear cactus and juniper. In the seat beside me, Aunt Ruby fiddled with her purse strap.

"This one doesn't seem right, Derek," she said. "Maybe we shouldn't even look at it."

The real estate agent's Mercedes waited in the driveway. Parking the SUV next to it, I turned to Ruby. "You haven't even seen the inside. These condos are great."

I had to admit I liked the style and location the best of all the condominiums we had seen. The place was perfect for Ruby: One level, no stairs, a garage, no yard maintenance, close to shopping and the medical center. Not that she needed a medical center, but as she aged, the proximity comforted me.

Ruby had gotten the itch to move to Arizona after visiting some friends in Sedona. She wanted a new start, a complete change from her old life. Not waiting for any more protests, I climbed out of the Explorer and walked around to open her door and helped her down. Now in her early seventies, Ruby valued her independence, her youthful appearance, especially her ruby red hair, and wanted no form of old-lady assistance, except for her L'Oreal 74 Copper hair color. She would accept my hand to help her from the passenger side of the SUV as my gentlemanly act, not as a sign that she needed help.

"These things are so hard for a lady to gracefully exit from," she complained and tried to hold her skirt down as she slid from the seat.

"Moving to the West, you need to give up some of that Southern gentility," I kidded her. "We will buy you some jeans."

"Lord, I can't remember the last time I wore slacks, let alone a pair of Levi's." She held my arm as we walked up the sidewalk toward the mission-style front door. The morning sun hadn't peaked over the roof, so the front of the condo was cool and shaded; the air held the clean sweet smell of sage.

"See," I said and opened the iron gate to the low-walled courtyard, "you could have your morning coffee out here and look at those views of the red rocks." The condo's front courtyard defined a small area around the entrance to the home, not so much for privacy, but more for the Southwestern style. Sage grown tall and thick, almost to the roofline of the adjoining condo, created a nice hedge from the neighbor's driveway. Something scurried in it, shaking the thin branches. "Wildlife at your doorstep," I said. But she didn't respond, only stared at the front door that had been left open.

"Aubrey shouldn't leave the house exposed to the desert creatures," she mumbled. "Why, a scorpion or a rattlesnake could just waltz right in there and spring on me."

I pushed the door open wide and a key in the lock brushed my hand. Surprised that her real estate agent Aubrey Garner had been so forgetful, I dropped it into my pocket to give back to him.

Inside, the entry floor was tiled with deep-tan Travertine and the walls were bright white. The place was empty of furniture, but an arched niche by the door and the ceiling beamed with vigas— exposed rafters made from peeled tree trunks—assigned a distinct Southwest style to the interior. "A blank canvas," I said to Ruby, "for you to paint your new adventure."

She ran her hand over the polished wood of the door then pushed it closed. "Nice," she said. "You know how we have to pull up on the knob to close the door back home? Nice to have new things that work."

"Aubrey," I called to announce our arrival.

No answer.

Ruby opened the coat closet and scanned the size. With a few strides in, I glanced around the great room and the kitchen. "Aubrey, it's Ruby and Derek."

Again, no answer.

"Maybe he's out on the back patio." I left Ruby as she surveyed the kitchen. The glass doors to the back courtyard displayed a panoramic view of Thunder Mountain's towering height just blocks from us and the long, flat, tree-topped plateau of Mogollon Rim to the distant east. I unlocked the patio door and slid it open. The air in the West always amazed me with its purity, at least in the more rural areas. Possibly the lack of humidity or the airflow across the mountains, but in the high desert of Arizona my breathing seemed easier.

Aside from the air, I attributed that to being away from my family. The trip to Sedona came at the perfect time for me. Aunt Ruby had decided to move out of North Carolina, I had a business errand, and everything converged in Sedona just like the New Age rhetoric claimed.

But then it hit me: sulfur. The smell the Baptist preachers warned about, brimstone, hell, burning flesh. It was just a flash as the wind whipped it by. But the odor seemed to lash by again as if a ribbon of sulfur bound the atmosphere of the patio.

A fire pit on the edge of the patio held fluffy ashes that stirred in the breeze. Someone had left small stones circling the cemented rocks that formed the fire pit's border. Assuming the condo was uninhabited might have been a mistake—I glanced around for anyone nearby. I seemed to be alone. I sniffed at the ash and found the source of the sulfur odor. The placed stones looked to be arranged as some sort of a compass since they lined up with the sun's path. Someone had made the fire recently and burned something nasty. I wondered if it had been Aubrey or another agent, since there weren't really any other signs of a transient squatting in the place. With a quick aim from my cell phone camera, I snapped a picture of the ring—I was curious and wondered if the rock circle was a Sedona thing. Our rental house had several books on Sedona and its New Age rituals. I stepped away from the smelly fire pit and stared at the towering crimson rocks and the black ravens gliding on the air currents.

Sirens screamed. The sound of a large truck raced by the front of the condo, fading away up Dry Creek Road. When I looked back for the ravens, they had left and a gray plume of smoke snaked up behind Thunder Mountain. *Construction fire.* I had read in the local newspaper about fires set at new building sites.

When I reached for the door's handle, the fact hit me that I had unlocked the patio door, so I knew Aubrey hadn't left out the back.

Inside, Ruby continued her inspection of the kitchen cabinets, her frown easing into a satisfied grin.

"How does the kitchen suit you?" I asked.

"Nice," she said. "But I miss ours in Charlotte. I knew where everything was and how that old oven tried to burn on the right side."

"After all those years in that same house, I'm sure you knew it well."

"It knew me too," she added. "I feel odd going to a new place, like I'm cheating on the house in Sedgefield, being unfaithful."

"Best to let some young couple buy it and raise their family there." Ruby and Walterene had lived in the same house since they were in their twenties. In a quiet old neighborhood called Sedgefield in the heart of Charlotte, North Carolina. They made their life together in that house, cousins who had never married or showed any signs of interest in the male of the species, the old maids of the family. I never thought much about their sexuality, but after Walterene died I realized that my aunts had been a couple—no truer marriage existed in the family, no union more loving or supportive than Walterene and Ruby's. Now that Walterene had passed on, Ruby seemed lost. I could see the hurt in her eyes. Getting on with her life, moving to Arizona, selling their house and buying a new condo just for her—without Walterene—must have felt like a betrayal of Walterene's memory. A new life away from the environment she shared with Walterene must have scared her. I admired her for the first steps and wanted to support her along the way.

"Where's Aubrey?" she asked from the kitchen.

"He's around somewhere. Might have stepped out for a moment."

She narrowed her blue eyes to squint at the hallway. "Something feels wrong here. I can't explain it—I'm just not comfortable in this place."

"Could be that there's no furniture," I said. "The other houses we saw still had people living there. It's hard to imagine how cozy this could be with just bare walls. I like it. You could place the couch there." I pointed to the long wall across from the fireplace.

She raised a painted eyebrow and nodded a noncommittal agreement.

Trying to lift her enthusiasm, I suggested we check the bedrooms down the hallway but as I walked into the master suite the air chilled at the door even though the warm April sun beamed through the east window. No sound or cool current wafted from the central air vents but the room definitely seemed colder than the rest of the house.

"Ruby, stay there for a second," I said not sure why, but I had joined her in thinking that something was askew.

I turned the corner and saw it from the open bathroom door: A man's body lying on the tile floor. Motionless, feet together, arms extended out. Blood covered the tile, blood that had gushed from the top of his head.

His scalp had been cut away.

CHAPTER TWO

The police swarmed the little condo, confining Ruby and me to the kitchen where a detective asked questions. Murder didn't happen often in Sedona, and the entire police force seemed to converge on the scene.

"That's all we can tell you," I concluded the retelling of our arrival at the condominium to a police detective. Turning to Ruby, I could see the nervousness in her eyes. She hadn't seen the body, but knew that Aubrey had been killed. The promise of the place had been displaced with the terror of a violent murder, and I had to admit, it shook me a bit. *Okay, more than a bit.* A body with the top of its head peeled off was a gruesome sight. Blood covered the bathroom floor and I had stepped in it, tracking it back through the carpeted hallway and on the kitchen tiles. Ruby had noticed my blood-stained path back to her side, staring at it as if the footprints would take on a life of their own.

"Can we go?" Ruby asked me.

"May I take my aunt home?" I asked the detective.

With a shift of his eyes to the Sergeant and back to us, he asked for our cell phone numbers and released us. "We'll have more questions, so I'm asking you not to leave town anytime soon," he added and stuffed his notebook in his back pocket.

Ruby held onto my arm, her touch trembling. We climbed back in the SUV. For a moment, we both just sat there, not saying a word, letting the activity of the police surge around the exterior of the car, the sun-warmed steel cocoon, safe from the upsetting scene.

"Why," she finally asked, "why would anyone do that?"

The bloody scene stuck in my head. Aubrey's body had been laid out, that's what bothered me. He had been arranged and posed in a certain way by the killer, a killer who didn't seem to mind taking the time. *If Ruby and I had arrived earlier, could we have intervened?*

Could we have saved him or would our bodies be arranged next to Aubrey's?

"Let's get out of here." I felt too close to this. I needed distance. In the small town of Sedona, no place was more than a few minutes away, but distance was relative. Our rental house perched on a hill near Coffee Pot Rock was only two miles east, but seemed a safe shelter from the horror of Aubrey's death.

We rode in silence until we approached the road that led to the grocery. "Stop at the store," Ruby said. "I want to cook some cornbread and fry a chicken." Cooking helped Ruby distract herself.

Inside the Safeway, she loaded her cart while I scanned the shelves of the liquor aisle deciding how to dull my senses, my own form of distraction.

"Derek?" a voice asked over my shoulder.

I turned to find Myra Greer, the local banker, holding a deli platter. Myra had helped Ruby set up her Arizona accounts. "You moonlighting as a caterer?" I asked attempting to seem light.

Myra smiled. "No just picking up something for a celebration tomorrow."

Celebration? I couldn't comprehend celebration at that moment. Although I held Stoli Vodka in my hand, I didn't intend to party. The sight of Bloody Mary mix on the shelf behind Myra's shoulder turned my stomach. I glanced down at my shoes; traces of Aubrey's blood still clung to the edges of the soles.

"Are you feeling okay?" she asked. "You look pale." She shifted the deli tray to one hand and reached up and touched my forehead. "You're clammy."

Pulling myself out of the bloody memory, I focused on Myra's warm hand on my temple. Not everyone in Sedona was so motherly; Myra, we had discovered, came from Charlotte too. That's one reason Ruby wanted to bank with her. About seven years older than me—maybe thirty-five or thirty-six, Myra had the confidence of a successful business person and the grace of a woman comfortable with herself. She had curves which I had always liked in a woman; not a sexual thing, but I liked women to look like women and men to be strapping and handsome. Being a liberal gay man didn't mean I couldn't be a traditionalist when it came to body-types.

"Do you need to sit down?" She led me toward the deli's tables and chairs.

"I'm fine, just a bit frazzled."

"What happened?"

Should I tell her? The story would be in the paper when it came out on Wednesday, and she knew Aubrey Garner from working with him on a real estate development project. The police detective hadn't said not to tell anyone. *Could Myra keep a secret?* I knew I rationalized because I wanted to tell someone, to talk it over. Ruby never talked of such unpleasantries and she would busy herself with cooking as soon as we returned home. "Would you like to come over for dinner? Ruby is off collecting ingredients for cornbread, pinto beans, and fried chicken. How about a little Southern cooking? I think we've been house hunting too furiously and need a break."

"That sounds wonderful. Although," she began, but hesitated for a moment, "I had plans with my friend Topher. Could I bring him?"

"Oh, if you have a date—"

"No, he's a long-time friend. You might even know him from Charlotte," she said. "You probably ran in the same circles."

"Can't say I know anyone named Topher."

"He's a great guy and my best friend since we were in high school."

"We're happy to have you both. Ruby and I haven't had time to socialize since we arrived." I saw Ruby turn the aisle corner with a full grocery cart. "Ruby, we're having company for dinner: Myra and her friend Topher."

Myra said hello to Ruby and thanked her for the invitation, then excused herself to get back to work.

As we watched her leave, Ruby said, "I hope I have enough."

The task of preparing dinner for other people would keep her mind off Aubrey and the events of the morning. Now, I knew the Stoli would have to be limited until the guests arrived.

✂ ✂ ✂

Back at the rental house, we organized the groceries, and I poured us both a little vodka and mixed in just enough cranberry juice for a shade of pink that wouldn't remind me of blood. The drink and I went outside to the deck for a cigarette. The view from the deck encompassed Thunder Mountain, Coffee Pot Rock, and to the east, Ship Rock. The range of hues from maroon and crimson to rose and coral colored the rocks, spires, and ridges of Sedona—the landscape that attracted millions of tourists. The limestone had weathered into amazing shapes that had acquired fairly practical names: Coffee Pot Rock *did* look like a large old-fashioned coffee pot. As I stared at it, sipped my drink, and inhaled the sweet smoke of the cigarette, the shock of finding Aubrey's body slipped away—just a bit. I relaxed for the first time, although the image kept creeping back into my mind.

Almost as a reflex, I flipped open my cell phone and called Daniel. On-again-off-again, Daniel and I had a few years' history. We'd met when I moved back to Charlotte after Walterene's death and I felt Ruby and my sister Valerie needed me there. A hard-driven man, Daniel's principles made him a tough reporter and an opinionated one, which made journalistic impartiality difficult for him. We shared the same ideology, but differed on approach. He tended to rush in like a bull and worry about the effects later, while I had become more cautious. He was a crusader. I was a mediator—not always, as Daniel would often remind me—but I liked to think I had mellowed as I closed in on thirty. Daniel, although well past thirty, seemed to be getting more righteous as he aged—hence, the on-again-off-again status of our relationship.

"Derek, how are you?" he asked as he answered the call, sounding excited to hear from me.

"Howdy from the Wild West," I said.

"How's Rudy's home search?"

"Hit a bump," I said. "Actually, there's been a tragedy. Her real estate agent was killed."

He began to fire the questions of a reporter: who, what, where, when, how. I told him all I knew, which as I repeated it, wasn't much.

"Are you okay?"

"Fine."

"No, you're not fine. Really, are you holding up?"

"Yes, Daniel. I still have my head."

"Do the police think the killer might still be around? What are they doing to catch him? You and Ruby aren't in danger are you? Maybe I should fly out there."

"No to all those," I said. "I'm calm and safe. The killer must have been long gone by the time we arrived." I liked the way that sounded as I said it and decided to tell myself that over and over.

"How's Ruby? Did she see the body?"

"No, I'm thankful for that. It was gruesome. Why would anyone cut the skin off the top of someone's head?" The image still bothered me.

"It gives me chills to think of it," he said.

Chills from the thought? Hell, my hands hadn't stopped trembling.

"Didn't the Native American warriors do that to their enemies?" he asked, and I could almost hear the snap as he switched into reporter mode. "Was the scalp a trophy or a warning to others?" He typed in the background. "I just searched the Internet on 'scalping.' Hmm, not necessarily a Native American rite, white trappers and bandits did it too. Some generals put a bounty on scalps of certain troublesome tribes to get whites and other tribes to eradicate them."

"But," I said, "why would that happen to a real estate agent?"

"That place is crawling with agents trying to make money off the housing market—tribe against tribe, and what about that Harris Construction deal?"

"Don't go there," I warned. Daniel had never cared for my family's business. The whole extended clan had ties to Harris Construction. After leaving California's Silicon Valley, I found myself back in Charlotte and being courted by my cousin Mark—in more ways than one—but he did convince me to join the company as an information systems planner. In the past few years, I had

moved the company into state-of-the-art systems that had improved
the profitability and efficiency of our construction projects. Kudos
to me, but what Daniel didn't like was the reputation the company
had of capitalizing on opportunities. The booming Southwest was
an opportunity. Officially, I helped Ruby find a house. Unofficially,
I had Harris Construction business.

"All I'm saying," Daniel began, "is you have more going with
that guy than just finding Ruby a condo."

"*Had* more going," I corrected him.

A raven flew to the far end of the deck and cocked its head at
me. The talk of business began to bore me. Daniel had a way of
doing that lately. I wondered why I had called him, especially at the
newspaper office. That tended to be the time his bulldog of a brain
would clamp onto something and not let go.

"Harris Construction has a stake in that Apache Trails project
that not only affects Sedona, but also people back here in Charlotte,"
he said. "And you could be in danger too if the murder had to do
with his business dealings."

"Let me call you back later," I cut him off. "Ruby needs
something. Love ya. Bye." I slapped the phone shut. *Yeah, Ruby
needs something all right: A nephew with a buzz and I ain't getting
one talking to Daniel.*

The buzz came and hovered just below my stress point. By the time
the doorbell chimed, I was relaxed and helping Ruby with supper
preparations. I opened the front door to Myra and her friend Topher.
She hugged me and introduced him. Nice, I thought, real nice.
Topher Langston stood an inch taller than me, had the bluest eyes
I had ever seen, dark hair—receding at the hairline just enough to
be attractive, and from what I could tell by his slightly open denim
shirt, snug jeans, and boots, he had a *hot* body. When we shook
hands, I lingered a little longer than needed and flashed my best
smile. Then I pointed them in the direction of the den and kitchen
so I could follow and check out Topher from the back. Maybe it
was the vodka... Maybe it was the stress of the day... But I was

"in lust" with Topher, and only on my third drink. I claimed to have become more cautious as I aged, but that concerned delicate situations, business dealings, career moves; in the line of love, I was still a fool and I did rush in.

We settled outside on the deck around the table where Ruby planned for us to eat. She had set out some deviled eggs and I'd added chips and salsa. I delivered beer to Myra and Topher, more vodka and cranberry for me and Ruby. All four of us sat around the table making small talk. Myra glowed and I wondered what made her so damn cheerful. "What's this celebration tomorrow?" I asked remembering the deli tray she'd purchased that afternoon at the store.

"A new phase of a big real estate development is closing in the morning," she said. "It's my largest loan."

My hands started to sweat. I knew exactly which loan it was since Harris Construction lingered in the background of the deal, and it was one of the reasons I had accompanied Ruby to Sedona. To make it more startling, Aubrey was the developer. With him gone, the project would take a dive.

"Myra," I started, but couldn't think of a sensitive way to phrase the news. "Aubrey is dead."

She stared at me from across the table, not blinking or breathing.

Topher rubbed her shoulders to get her back with us, but it was he who spoke first. "Are you sure? How do you know?"

Odd questions, I thought. *Not 'What happened?' or 'When?' But then, I wasn't the authority on the appropriate questions.*

"I just saw him yesterday afternoon," Myra said.

Ruby excused herself and went into the kitchen.

"Ruby was with me when I found him," I explained.

"You found Aubrey?" Topher asked.

"Yes, we had an appointment to see a condo. Aubrey's car was parked in the driveway, but we didn't see him inside, until I went in the master bath, and there he was."

"Oh, God. A heart attack?" Myra asked and leaned across the table.

Sitting back in his chair, Topher sighed and shook his head. "He was murdered."

We both looked at him as if he had blood on his hands.

"How did you know?" I asked and held onto my glass waiting for his answer.

"It's a small town. There hasn't been a murder here in years. I heard the rumor at work, but didn't think it was true." He turned to Myra. "That's why I didn't say anything. I just thought it was a rumor—or wishful thinking on some people's part."

Now he had my total interest. "Wishful thinking? Aubrey had enemies?"

Myra rubbed her temples and took a deep breath. She sipped her beer as Topher allowed her to answer. A sign of years together: They knew when it was more apt for the other one to respond. "This development is not popular. A large ranch that borders national forest came on the market, and Aubrey saw an opportunity. He sold as many of his holdings as he could and mortgaged a few of his other properties to buy the land, then recruited investors to develop estate-style homes on it."

"So? That happens all the time," I said.

"Not here," Topher added. "Sedona is surrounded by national forest, limiting the amount of available land. Think of it as Aspen or Manhattan where land is at a premium. People here are satisfied with that. Property values stay high; growth is limited; the place keeps a small, resort town feel."

Myra stood and walked to the deck's railing. "Follow me and I'll show you what was happening," she said. Topher and I trailed her, drinks in hand, down the steps to the red dirt, cactus, and juniper behind the house. The rental house backed up to forest land, so we could walk up to a slight ridge to view the western part of town. She pointed toward a formation of rock at the outskirts of Sedona. "That is Cockscomb. The northern side is ranch land, privately owned."

The waning daylight made the beautiful landscape enthralling. Gentle rolling hills of juniper, pinyon pine, and red dirt, stretched into acres of wilderness just beyond the houses and condos of the town. Rising in the middle of the terrain, a short ridge jutted up from the ground, deep red rock formations that resembled the comb of a rooster. I glanced back to the developed part of Sedona to see every hill and ridge covered with houses, multi-million dollar homes, all clawing to top the rise and capture the best views—views that other houses and development slowly ruined. "You mean that land isn't protected?"

"Part of it is," Topher said. "The north part is the ranch. Aubrey and his partners plan to develop, pave, and build it up for wealthy snowbirds just like the rest of Sedona."

He sounded bitter, and I guess my face revealed my reaction.

"Human nature," he explained. "After you move here, you want the 'door to close,' no more growth. Even in the few years Myra and I have been in town, the place has changed significantly. Most people I work with can't afford to live here—they live in nearby Cottonwood or Camp Verde and commute in."

"What kind of work do you do?" I asked, since Myra hadn't mentioned his occupation.

"Marketing Director for a Jeep touring company," Topher said. "When Myra and I moved here, I wanted to pursue my painting, but I also needed something to pay the bills. I bartended for a while. Then I drove a Jeep as a guide. When the owners found out about my background in marketing, I was promoted."

"You live in town, right?" I thought he must make good money.

"Yes, but neither Myra nor I would have been able to afford a house here if we moved today. We got in just before prices became outrageous and the real estate agents went wild. It seems like everyone you meet in Sedona has their real estate license."

I had to smile to myself at the attitude toward the agents. Every town seemed to have their scapegoats for whatever problems there were. Politicians, gays, blacks, rednecks, Jews, Catholics, Baptists, retirees, college kids, real estate agents—whatever the issue, there would be a group blamed for it. I placed my hand on Topher's shoulder as we looked across the landscape, "Do you really feel they're the root of all evil?"

He laughed. "Well, a little bit. They're just more visible at selling off the town, scalping the land like a hot ticket to the Super Bowl."

Myra watched the landscape to the west as if lost in her own thoughts. The breeze picked up as the sun lowered toward the horizon and ravens floated on the updrafts around Sugarloaf rock.

"Let's get back," I suggested. "Aunt Ruby will have supper ready."

At the house, we sat on the deck and ate one of Ruby's delicious meals of crispy fried chicken, pinto beans, mashed potatoes smothered in butter, baked cinnamon apples, plus cornbread to sop up any leftover juices. The mood turned away from Aubrey's death, as we discussed our time in North Carolina.

"Ruby, will you miss living in Charlotte?" Myra asked.

"Lord, yes," she said. "I lived there all my life surrounded by family. It will take some getting used to being out here."

"But it's good for her health," I added. "The humidity in the summer and the icy winters were more than she could take. Besides, she has some friends out here."

"Who?" Topher asked. "I might know them."

"Oh, just some ladies I met years ago when Walterene and I used to visit Palm Springs."

Myra smiled as if she read right into Ruby's hidden identity. "These women," Myra started, "how long have they lived here?"

"Oh, twelve or fifteen years, I think. Retired teachers and a real hoot—that's what I like about them. They love to cut up," Ruby said with a laugh. "People back home are so solemn. It's nice to be around active people my age."

"You might even find romance here in the Red Rocks." Topher lifted his beer glass to Ruby as if to toast the idea.

I immediately joined the toast, nodding to Topher. *Yes I might find some romance here too.*

Chapter Three

y ringing cell phone woke me the next morning. A detective with the police department asked, or more specifically summoned, us to the station for more questions. I pulled on jeans and found Ruby sipping her coffee on the back deck. "Tell them I can be there in an hour," she said. "I have to finish my coffee and fix my hair and put on my face."

With Ruby appropriately coiffed and caffeinated, we entered the police station. "Should I have an attorney here?" I asked Detective Sarras as he sat me down in a small room without Ruby.

"Why would you say that?" He looked at the table and arranged his papers. His brown eyes avoided me. Probably in his fifties, he didn't seem to have the confidence of a man with years of experience on the police force. I wondered how long he had been a detective.

"Just wondering if you separated me and Ruby for a reason."

He shifted on the metal chair and stretched his neck and adjusted the collar of his polo shirt. "Don't want group-think to taint what you and Ms. Harris can remember about yesterday morning."

"Fine. What more can I tell you?"

His shoulders stiffened as if I were his opponent and we were about to spar. "How did you know Aubrey Garner?"

"He's the agent helping my aunt find a home here."

The detective nodded. "And how else?"

I leaned forward. "What do you mean?"

"It's a simple question. What other involvement did you have with Aubrey Garner?"

We locked eyes for a long moment. I assumed he referred to my family's business. Not that it was a secret, but we didn't publicize Harris Construction's involvement with the Sedona venture; I wondered where he found this link. But I gave him points for it. "The company I work for is involved in a development project he's heading." I corrected myself, "*Was* heading."

"That would be Harris Construction, headquartered in Charlotte, North Carolina?"

"Yes."

"Apache Trails?" he asked as if to confirm the fact.

"Yes," I said again with a little more volume.

"How did Harris Construction come to be involved in a project so far from North Carolina?"

"We're an international company with satellite offices all over North America," I said. "Our business development executives seek out opportunities. And this was an opportunity."

"Are you a business development executive?" He kept his eyes on his notes.

"No, I head up the strategic technology department."

"What knowledge do you have of Native American rituals?"

"Excuse me?" *Did I hear him right?* "Like Indian rituals?"

"Yes. Navajo, Apache, Kiowa, Cherokee." He drew out Cherokee.

"Not that much." Not only did he know about the company, he had done some personal research—extensive investigation on the Harris history, but not the things we hid. No one knew those except the family, and they would never be part of any public record. But, he had found some information on lineage, nothing shocking now, but a hundred years ago, it would have never been stated. "Yes, there is Cherokee blood in our family, but no one admits it. It goes back many moons." I smiled.

The detective shook his head. "Such a wise ass."

"Listen, what are you getting at? I didn't scalp Aubrey because my great-great grandmother was a Cherokee. I know he was scalped—I found the body. What other rituals are you talking about?"

"Just an eagle feather and a medicine wheel," he said off-handedly.

Could I get him to tell me more? I turned on the charm. "You're good. Did you notice the fire pit in back, fresh ashes?"

"Yeah, that was the medicine wheel."

I made a mental note to look up "medicine wheel" in the books at the rental house. "Not much else seemed out of place," I said. "The condo was empty. By the way, where do you work-out? I need to find a gym while I'm here." I knew the man was straight as wing-tip shoes, but everyone has a bit of vanity.

He stretched again, puffing up his chest. "We have a weight room here at the station." He extended his right arm as if to get a kink out of his shoulder and flexed his bicep. "Who made the appointment with Mr. Garner?" He relaxed in his chair and crossed his leg over his knee, wiggling his foot against the table.

"I did."

"Who else knew about the appointment?"

My mind raced to remember if we had told anyone about that particular viewing. "Just the receptionist at his office who scheduled it."

"What about Topher Langston and Myra Greer?"

My hands quivered and I placed them firmly on my knees. *How did he connect us with them? Was I being watched? I had just met Topher the night before.* "Now wait, why are you bringing up Myra and Topher? I hardly know either of them." The carefree attitude of Sedona seemed to be giving way to a police state of secret surveillance. He knew too much about me and Ruby.

He scribbled in his notes.

I waited and let the silence fill the room.

Glancing up as if expecting me to go on talking, he raised his eyebrows. But, I just continued to stare at him. I knew how to shift the balance and make him feel uncomfortable with the quiet.

"Did she ever mention her husband?" he finally asked.

Husband? I hadn't even considered Myra was married. "No."

My answer lingered in the stuffy air waiting for him to respond. But my curiosity squeezed out the next question. "Who's her husband?"

The detective hesitated as if he shouldn't reveal any more information, but he continued. "A couple of years ago, a man fell from Devil's Bridge. Ms. Greer and Mr. Langston were there.

Langston had sustained a gunshot wound. Officially, the death was an accident."

"Unofficially?" I asked.

"You know, everyone in Sedona is on a second or third life," he started. "People move here for the natural beauty of the place, and then try to find work, usually nothing like what they did in the real world. But for me, I was able to put concept into practice. Before I joined the force," he said and tapped his pencil, "I spent 25 years teaching criminal justice in a small California college. In theory, a man falling from a cliff with other people around—other people with whom he had an altercation—just doesn't add up to being accidental."

I read his name badge to remind me of his name: Sarras. A former professor turned police detective, which explained the extensive research on the family. But, he also seemed to have a deep interest in Myra and Topher and wanted to associate them with Aubrey's death. "Detective Sarras," I addressed him by name to show respect, "is there a connection between the accidental," I made sure to label it *accidental*, "death of Myra's husband and Aubrey's murder?"

Sarras sat back in his chair.

I hoped he would continue talking. He had piqued my curiosity. The college professor in him must have preferred the more conversational line of questioning rather than the bright-light interrogation of television.

After a few seconds, he answered. "Just interesting that some people seem to draw death."

My mind made the correlation of Myra working with Aubrey on the development financing, but I couldn't make a link from Topher to Aubrey. Had they known each other at all? Obviously, Topher had heard about Aubrey's death at work, so there was recognition. Could there have been a romantic relationship there? No, I thought, I can tell if a man is gay and Aubrey hadn't been gay. *What other connection did Topher have to him?*

"Thank you again for coming in." Sarras's words broke me out of my absorption. He stood across the table with his hand out to shake.

"I'll let you know if I can think of anything else." I grabbed his hand in a hardy shake and walked out the door. Odd man, I thought, but someone to watch out for. The level of personal information he had on me disturbed me. *Narcissistic on my part?* A little, but he had revealed he had the data at his disposal, and for some reason, I just didn't like strangers to know that much about me.

❈ ❈ ❈

Ruby had coordinated with Myra on casseroles and main dishes to take to Aubrey's family, but a call to the real estate office confused her. "Here we make all this food," Ruby said as she poured sweet tea into a plastic jug, "and that girl at his office doesn't even know who is having the gathering." She raised her spoon that she'd stirred the tea with and pointed it at me. "Now, I know when you lived in California, folks didn't take food. But, those California people are an odd bunch to begin with."

"I don't think Aubrey had much family here," I said. "There might not be a funeral."

"No funeral? Why, I never heard of such a thing. People got to mourn." She grabbed the phone and punched numbers.

Was there anyone to mourn for Aubrey? We weren't that well acquainted for me to know his personal life. I was sure Detective Sarras knew all about it; I could imagine Sarras at his computer late into the night searching out details on people Aubrey interacted with—his paperboy, the mailman, the woman at the dry cleaners.

"Myra," Ruby talked into the phone. "That silly girl at Aubrey's office couldn't tell me where the gathering is." She listened a moment. "I know." Leaning against the kitchen counter, she held a pen in hand ready to jot down information. "An ex-wife?" She raised an eyebrow at me. "And a girlfriend?" Ruby clucked her tongue, "Well, that man certainly spread himself around. What church did he go to?" Shaking her head, she said, "Don't surprise me one bit."

She scratched some notes on a pad and said good-bye to Myra.

"What's up?" I asked.

"Myra will find out from his ex-wife where the gathering will be," she said. "No visitation, of course. They couldn't do an open casket." Apparently, Ruby had recovered from the initial shock of us finding him and had shifted into gear as the unofficial funeral/social director of Aubrey's passing. "She said that sometimes families don't even list in the newspaper's obituaries. Can you imagine that?"

"It's the wild West," I said. "They just dig a hole and dump them in."

"Hush," she admonished me. "That's disrespectful of the dead. They could be watching you."

The thought hadn't occurred to me in years. When I was little, my mother would warn me that Papa Ernest, my great grandfather and lord of the family, watched over all of us. If he had seen what my cousin Mark and I did with each other on camping trips...

Only Aubrey could tell us who killed him, so if he did observe us from some other dimension or parallel plane or fluffy cloud or brimstone basement, maybe he would drop some hints. Sarras didn't seem to have a suspect. And his mention of Myra and Topher had disturbed me. Myra connected Ruby with just about everything in Sedona, and she was fast becoming more than her banker, the two were becoming friends. And as for Topher, he seemed to be a settled and rational man. Of course, that was one dinner, and I had encountered many a psycho who appeared normal on a first date. And I couldn't help but wonder: Am I a suspect in Sarras's mind? Mark and I had discussed some "issues" with the way Aubrey was handling the development project—Apache Trails. The luxury homes had the potential to be one of the most expensive and exclusive neighborhoods in all the Southwest. Certainly people would pay the projected two million for the lots. The estates built out there would be as awesome as the views of the Red Rocks and sunsets. So, yes, I was probably a suspect.

❈　❈　❈

The gathering was held at the real estate office, after it had closed for the day. I helped Ruby unload some covered dishes she had insisted on bringing. With arms full of plates hosting stacks of ham biscuits, tubs of potato salad, and a couple of casseroles, we maneuvered the steps carefully. Topher ran up from the parking lot and relieved Ruby of a couple of dishes. I turned to see where he had parked and saw a Jeep, with *Blue Jeep Tours* stenciled on the side, starting to pull away.

"Wait up, Hawk," Topher yelled back to the Jeep driver. The man in the Jeep stole my focus now because apparently Topher had ridden with him. Tall and rather large framed from what I could see. A cowboy hat shaded most of his face and a long dark ponytail snaked from under the back of the hat. Not particularly handsome, but my viewpoint wasn't so good. "Derek," Topher called holding the door open with his foot. "Come on and set down these plates."

Ruby organized her spread to the disapproving eye of a paid caterer with a tray of stuffed mushrooms.

"Come on out and I'll introduce you to Hawk," Topher said.

I followed him back outside to the parking lot. A couple of cars pulled into empty spaces and the Jeep had moved out of their way, pointing toward the exit as if he couldn't wait to escape from the place. We approached the idling Jeep. *The boyfriend?*

"Hawk," Topher said and the guy turned around to face us. Stoic. That's what I'd say of his face. A Native American, tall, heavyset, round face, dark eyes, but something about those eyes... I'm not sure, but I felt sorrow from them, the pain of regret. "Hawk, this is Derek Mason," Topher said to him. "Derek, Hawk is one of my friends."

He smiled at that, not a full-teeth Miss America smile, but more than a grin. I must have given the full pageant smile since Topher said *one of my friends* instead of boyfriend. I shook his hand, firm grip, and Hawk nodded to me. "Pleasure," he said in a low deep voice.

"Go," Topher said and patted the Jeep's door to send him off.

"Man of few words," I commented.

"Yep. He's a bit shy around new people. Odd thing is he's not shy giving tours. He's one of our best guides. I think it helps when he has a script to follow."

Topher explained that Hawk had dropped him off after work. "I wanted him to come in," Topher continued, "but like I said, he's not into crowds of people."

We returned to the real estate office. Now a few more people had arrived. Such a bizarre feeling to be standing among desks and file cabinets comforting the family of the deceased, a man it seemed that few people had liked, since no one actually wanted to host this assembly of mourners in their own home.

"Is this an indication of Aubrey's life?" I asked Myra, who had helped Ruby set out the food. "Few friends, everything based in the office?"

In a midnight-blue dress that hugged her curves, she looked rather sexy for a funeral. Her russet hair lay in loose waves and cascaded to her shoulders. "Yes, I understand that he worked most of the time, a bit driven by Sedona standards. That's the story on why he and Tricia divorced."

Topher stood near her side. A few buttons open on his black silk shirt exposed tan taut skin and an amethyst owl fetish, strung on a leather cord, nested in his dark chest hair. I wanted to reach out and touch it—the owl...well, maybe his chest too. But it didn't seem the place or time to grope him.

"But Aubrey had a girlfriend, didn't he?" I asked.

"Oh yeah," Topher said. He nodded across the room to a middle-aged woman in a flowing purple skirt and a peasant blouse that slunk off one pale shoulder. Her blonde hair could barely be contained by the black scarf she had tied around her head. "That's Clarity Received."

"Excuse me? What's a Clarity Received?"

"That," he said and nodded toward her again. "She owns part of a New Age bookstore and runs a retreat center."

"You mean her mama actually named her Clarity Received?" I had never heard such a thing, not even in San Francisco.

He laughed. "You can take the boy out of the Carolinas...

No, her *mama* didn't do it. It's her Sedona name. I have no idea what her family name is. Some people take new names—spiritual names—when they come to Sedona. Apparently, she became lucid once entering the city limits."

"Or she completely lost it," I said.

"She has done well for herself here," Myra said. "Along with the retreat center and bookstore, she owns a tour company called Native Visions."

"So, if that's the girlfriend, is the ex-wife here too?" I asked.

Topher searched the room, then smiled. "Tricia is across the office at the conference room door. Looks like she has set up court to receive condolences in private."

Pretty. Fortyish. Polished. Something in the way she held herself neglected to give me the impression she mourned Aubrey's passing. She held her head high and her expression lacked emotion, which could have been Botox or a recent face lift. I could spot surgical enhancements from twenty paces and this one had the works, as did the man standing by her side. He looked to be in his late forties, but with the tight jaw-line and raised brows of a twenty-year-old.

"Who's the Dorian Gray next to her?"

"Kimbo Blue," Topher said and pulled me to the side of the room and Myra followed.

"That name sounds familiar," I said.

"For one," Myra began, "he's Topher's boss. He owns Blue Jeep Tours. Secondly, he's a former child star. Grew up in Hollywood, but outgrew his adorable pixie presence."

"What did he do? I can't really place him."

With his hand on my shoulder, Topher kept his voice low. "Kimbo is a great guy. I like him, but he does expect people to know who he is. He played Jodie Foster's brother in one of those Disney films back in the seventies. Then he was on that television show 'Rascal.' It lasted about six episodes." Topher seemed to review Kimbo's screen credits in his mind. "Oh, and he played a friend of Willie Aames on 'Eight is Enough.' Besides a bit of theater in L.A., I think that's it."

"Looks good, nice work on both of them," I said. "So, are they a couple or are they fag and hag?"

"Now, Derek," Myra began, "I hate that term 'hag.'"

Topher shook his head, "Oh, fine, and 'fag' is okay?"

"Excuse me," I said interrupting their quarrel. "Could one of you answer my question: Couple or not?"

"Tricia and Kimbo have dated for about a year, since she divorced Aubrey," Topher explained. "Kimbo may look of vane but he's a shrewd businessman. Kimbo has secured the best drivers and the most scenic Forest Service trails for exclusive use, which pisses off his competitors, especially Clarity who can't get her tours onto the same trails. He may look like Kimbo the Bimbo, but the man has a sharp mind."

Nothing about the ex-wife, her boyfriend, or Aubrey's girlfriend sounded like motive for murdering Aubrey, although the prime suspects are usually the people closest to the victim.

"Come on." Topher took my hand. "I'll introduce you to Kimbo and Tricia." He led me toward the couple standing by the conference room. Myra joined Ruby at the food table, by the copy machine, where Ruby stayed busy serving the covered dish casseroles, while the caterer carried a tray of hummus-topped cucumbers around the office—two competing factions vying for the stomachs of the mourners.

Tricia appeared to be both composed and wilted at the same time. Her eyes, rimmed in red, showed a bit of age, but the rest of her face look perfect. The cool expression warmed a bit when she talked to people, but I could see the weariness in her demeanor. Kimbo had the look of an aged pixie, just as Myra had described. I could see the shadow of boyish good looks in the man.

"Kim, this is my friend Derek Mason," Topher said to his boss.

As we shook hands, Kimbo cocked his head. "Don't I know you?"

"I was thinking the same thing," I said.

"Yes," Kimbo said, "Harris Construction in North Carolina."

Then the recognition came to me too. He and a delegation of Sedona business owners had flown to Charlotte to discuss the Apache Trails project—the same development that Aubrey was about to start—although, unlike Aubrey who had secured a partnership with us, these business owners wanted us to pull out.

"Right," I agreed. My cousins Mark and Mike had refused to abandon the project based on the stated concerns: the ruin of ridge views, irresponsible water usage, the pavement of Jeep trails, and the destruction of wildlife habitats. After being in Sedona for a while, I understood their points, but when they presented those concerns to the Harris executives, nothing had a concrete, bottom-line liability. I remember how the fact that business owners came to us with a lot of fuzzy facts and no hard numbers surprised me. Corporations like ours couldn't kill a project just because a coyote might have to move his rabbit hunt a mile into the wilderness. The owners of the old ranch wanted to sell, Aubrey wanted to buy, and Harris Construction saw plenty of profit in the investment. Of course, the ranch would not be developed by Aubrey. Someone had seen to that.

I said it before I could censor myself: "Looks like your coalition stopped the Apache Trails project—one way or another."

Tricia's back stiffened.

Kimbo's face blanched.

Topher choked on his wine.

CHAPTER FOUR

Kimbo's eyes flashed like lightning across the desert sky. He didn't look to Tricia or to Topher, but focused on me.

As soon as the words had come out of my mouth, I knew I'd pushed too far. Hell, I didn't even know why I said it. The logical trail of thought from where I had met Kimbo before and where we were now just fired off a few synapses that didn't connect in the most polite manner. Not that I thought a group of small business owners in a resort town could kill a developer… Or did I? From Kimbo and Tricia's reaction, they seemed to have something to hide. Topher seemed more shocked by the comment than his two companions. Apparently, he didn't think I would say such a thing to their faces.

"For you to imply that *anyone* in this town would commit murder," Kimbo said in a staged offended tone, "is an outrage."

"Probably, a transient," I said. "Since no one in Sedona could do such a thing. I bet it was the same person who has been setting those arson fires at construction sites."

"Excuse me." Tricia broke in. "I prefer not to discuss this at my ex-husband's wake. I am the widow here." She walked away from our little group to greet an older woman by the receptionist's desk.

Kimbo shot me a dismissive glare—as much as he could with a forehead full of Botox—and followed Tricia.

"Guess I hit a nerve," I said to Topher.

"Shit, you accused Kimbo, if not the Sedona Gentry, of murder."

"And arson," I said.

He yanked me out the door to the front steps of the office. I pulled out a pack of Marlboros and offered him one as an apology.

Reluctantly, he accepted.

"What is the Sedona Gentry?" I asked after taking a drag on my cigarette and holding the lighter for Topher.

"That's a group of local businessmen that fund projects for the community. They formed back before the town was incorporated and had acted as the city officials." Topher leaned against the stair railing, glancing back at the door to the real estate office.

"Sounds a bit like a small town Mafia," I said.

"No, not at all," he said and exhaled a curl of gray smoke into the air. "When the town needed funds for a library, these guys pooled money and got it started. They funded organizations that offer services to the elderly and kids. Actually, they do more for the community than the city council and mayor."

"Lots of influence?" I asked since they didn't have it when they visited Charlotte, I wondered how that had affected the egos of these men.

He nodded. "When they band together on something, it's basically the most prominent men in Sedona supporting the cause."

"Aubrey wasn't part of the Sedona Gentry, was he?" I knew the answer before I asked.

"No, and they fought the Apache Trails development," he said. "But these men aren't capable of murder. They're businessmen and philanthropists. In fact, Aubrey wanted to join the Sedona Gentry, but money alone doesn't get you in."

"What kept him out?"

"Attitude... And rumors." Topher offered no more.

"Okay." I leaned on the rail next to him, so close our shoulders touched. "You got me now." I whispered as if someone might hear, "What rumors?"

He took a drag on his cigarette as if he needed time to decide if he should repeat the small town gossip, then sighed and said, "Frequent trips to Nogales."

Maybe that meant something to him, but it baffled me. The urge to touch him won out now that we stood alone outside. I reached up and rubbed the back of his neck while pulling him closer to me. Our faces inches from each other, I asked, "Nogales means what?"

"It's a border town in southern Arizona. The main industry is the border, whether it's tourists wanting to walk into Mexico, senior citizens going over to buy their medicines on the cheap, horny straight guys looking for sex, or drug and migrant trafficking through tunnels."

Not that I knew him that well, but Aubrey could have been there for sex or the trafficking. "And what did people think Aubrey did in Nogales?"

"The Mexican Border isn't a destination for most people." He frowned. "Aubrey was profit minded, and he wouldn't drive south if he didn't see money to be made."

"So, he went to smuggle in drugs to deal?" I asked, since Aubrey didn't seem the type to take drugs.

Topher shrugged. "All I know is that people say he went to Nogales frequently. What that means differs from person to person, but none of it seems good. He wasn't feeding the poor or vaccinating children down there."

The door to the office swung open, and in a sinuous sweep of her plum skirt, Clarity emerged and scanned the horizon with frantic eyes. "Oh, it's not time yet." Her alto voice a bit more calm than her movements.

"Actually," I said glancing at my watch, "it is 6:53. What time are you looking for?"

Still searching the sky, she scratched her head above the scarf and didn't respond to my question. Not a bad looking woman, but she wasn't who I would have guessed Aubrey dated especially after meeting his ex-wife Tricia. For everything Tricia apparently was, Clarity apparently wasn't. Tricia seemed to personify sophistication, style, and control, whereas Clarity exuded zeal, simplicity, and exploration. Tricia wore tailored dresses paired with fashionable heels that couldn't be practical in the rocky landscape, but she looked perfect in them. Loose and flowing garments veiled any hint of Clarity's figure and a pair of sandals revealed un-pedicured toenails. In physical appearance, the two women couldn't be more different. Obviously, Aubrey saw something in both women that attracted him.

"Oh, Topher." She seemed to just notice him and grasped his hand while he ground out his cigarette with his boot. "He was such a lost soul," she continued. "But, there is a convergence of energy today—a perfect time for him to rejoin the Great Spirit—a full lunar cycle after the Vernal Equinox, which should occur in a few more minutes. Everything should be back to its rightful place." She searched the sky as if expecting something to arrive and take Aubrey's body away.

"Actually, Aubrey is still at the coroner's office in Phoenix," I offered.

She freed Topher's hand and regarded me for the first time. "You," she said, "have an old soul." Then with a longer look into my eyes, she added, "You have the key."

Not quite sure what to make of that, I said, "Thank you."

"You're welcome, and Aubrey isn't in Phoenix. Aubrey isn't in that body anymore. His spirit was released, and it hovers and mingles with our energy and the earth's energy." She swept her hands in the general direction of the Airport Mesa.

"Purgatory?" I asked.

"The Catholics didn't have it all wrong." She glanced at the sky as she talked. "There is a time after death that the spirit lingers, and when the energies of the earth converge with the energy of the soul," she explained and looked me in the eye, "we reunite with the Higher Power."

"This is one of those times?" Topher asked.

"Yes!" she almost squealed. "What a wonderfully harmonic moment. Can you feel the energy building?" She took a deep breath and walked down the steps past the parking lot and into the red dirt and junipers. "Come, boys. Hold my hands and let's encourage the energy."

Topher nudged me with his shoulder. "Come on, you old soul, she just lost Aubrey. The least we can do is an energy convergence with her."

"I usually don't converge energy until I've known someone for a while, or at least until they buy me dinner," I kidded him.

We joined Clarity in the area off the pavement that abutted the hill to the Airport Mesa. Luckily, we were out of sight of the real estate office, hidden by a pinyon pine and a manzanita. Standing in a circle facing each other, we joined hands and lifted them toward the crystal blue-violet sky.

"Feel the energy swirl up from the ground and start in your base chakra," Clarity instructed.

First off, I had no idea where my base chakra was or even what a chakra looked like. Hopefully, I had a base chakra and it twirled with energy. My mind concentrated on an image of a churning gear. I opened my eyes to see if Clarity and Topher were doing anything that I should be doing, but they only stood with their eyes closed holding my hands up in the air. A fit of laughter threatened to break the solemn silence. I tried to think somber thoughts, but the image of three grown people standing in the desert off a parking lot converging energy to help a soul return to—well, wherever it had an appointment—just seemed comical.

"Now feel the energy of Aubrey join us as we flow through the sacral and solar plexus chakras." Clarity's voice brought my mind back to my spinning gear that moved Aubrey up a conveyer belt. I squeezed Topher's hand and opened my eyes to check his reaction. He only smiled and squeezed back.

The process of going through chakras took awhile, but I began to follow her better especially since the chakras took on names I could locate: heart, throat, third eye, and finally the crown.

"The energy surges out the crown chakra," she announced, "pulling the lost souls to the loving embrace of the Higher Power." At that, she said a blessing and dropped her hands. "Thank you. Aubrey is now complete. We can all rest easy." She hugged us both and headed out across the desert.

"What did you get me into?" I asked Topher.

"Don't you feel it?" he asked with a serious tone.

Maybe I should have felt something from this New Age experience, but I had to admit only silliness lingered in me. "Not really. Do you?"

"A bit more grounded," he said. "I know that was bizarre for you, but think of it as a meditation, a time to relax your mind and focus on the natural surroundings. I don't know if we helped Aubrey's spirit find its way, but what a noble effort if we did."

Maybe he was right. The time to hold Topher's hand, to smell his scent... Oh, and the time to fill my senses with the world around me. All good stuff. I did feel grounded. And Aubrey... Aubrey was more than a real estate salesman, a would-be developer, a man that wanted to rape the land to make a profit, a guy struggling to become a millionaire at any cost — that was a lot to overcome. He was a person, bad and good. Two women had loved him. He didn't deserve to be murdered in an empty condo with his scalp sheared off.

The sun finally dropped below the mesa and cast long shadows across the parking lot. The red rocks below the Mogollon Rim to the east glowed in scarlet hues from the reflection of the setting sun. "Now that I think about it, I am feeling something." I took Topher's hand and pulled him close and wrapped my arms around his waist. He did the same. The press of his body next to mine triggered emotions that I hadn't felt in a while. Thoughts of Daniel invaded the moment, but I ignored them and focused on the man in front of me. We were a bit awkward for a second. I wasn't sure if I was going for a hug or a kiss. Then, there in the shelter of the pinyon pines, junipers, and manzanitas, just as he leaned in and our lips *almost* touched, Myra's voice carried across from the real estate office.

"Topher," she called in a pleading voice.

He pulled back and answered, "Over here."

Breaking our embrace, we tramped through the brush to the building.

I muttered, "Bitch, bitch, bitch," with each step. *How I hate to be interrupted.*

"Topher, the police took Hawk," she said.

"What? What for?" he asked.

She grabbed Topher's arm. "Aubrey's murder."

CHAPTER FIVE

As if stunned, Topher sat down on a stucco retaining wall at the base of the steps. "No way. The last person in the world likely to commit violence is Hawk."

"Hawk? Who just drove away?" I asked.

"He was here?" Myra asked and looked toward the road. "We have to do something. Oh, Derek, he's the nicest guy."

"Yavapai-Apache," Topher added, "and not someone who would lift a hand to anyone." He looked to Myra. "No, he wouldn't even to get back what was his."

"Of course not," Myra said. "Someone came in and said they saw the police pull him over on the highway. And put him in the back of the police cruiser."

Topher began to pace. "My fault. We shouldn't have gone." He muttered to himself as he turned away from us.

Not sure if I should reveal it, but Topher seemed upset that Hawk might be a suspect, so I started slowly, easing in to it. "One thing the newspaper didn't report was Aubrey had been scalped."

Topher turned back around. He and Myra stared at me for a moment, as if trying to decipher what I'd said.

"He didn't do it," Topher announced. "Not Hawk, he's too gentle. He doesn't believe in violence."

Maybe that was what I saw in his eyes: gentleness. "Why do you think the police have him?" I asked.

His narrowed eyes stabbed at me as if I had told the police to pick up Hawk. "Prejudice. Hawk's an Indian. Not a wealthy Californian. He did not do anything —I know it."

The outsider in his own home, so typical of what I had gone through all my life. People had told me I was bad; teachers, ministers, family treated me as if I were broken, not fully one of them, *not him, he's deviant.* So, here I saw prejudice for a Native

American. I wondered if he had tolerated the mockery of kids at school, the name-calling, the bullying that gay kids do, just because he wasn't white, just because he wasn't like them. My fingernails cut into my palms and I realized I had clinched fists.

I heard a deep sigh from Topher and his calm helped relax my mind. Frowning, he seemed to mull over the reasons. "You said Aubrey had been scalped. But, that doesn't necessarily mean Indians."

"Right." I remembered what Daniel had said over the phone. "Not all tribes did that. Trappers and soldiers did it as much to the tribes as the tribes did it to each other. It was more of a trophy or proof that the person was dead than a way to kill someone."

"I wish we knew more about Aubrey's dealings," Myra said. "I think it was more professional than personal. He had a lot of deals going. As I gathered the paperwork for his loan for Apache Trails, I found he had Limited Liability Companies all over the place. It was just a web of funding—deals, partnerships, and sketchy legal alliances."

I glanced back at the door to the building. "Aubrey's office is downstairs." I nodded to a hallway entrance at the bottom of the parking lot that led to suites under the main office. "If we could get to his computer, we might find something." Would I really go through his computer? Well, if the computer was signed on to his account, it wasn't so bad, a bit like an open diary.

Topher looked to Myra. "I don't know that much about PCs, I'm a Mac guy."

"Don't worry. When you talk Information Technology, I'm the man." I took off toward the lower entrance with both of them following.

"How will we get in?" Myra asked. "It's bound to be locked."

I pushed on the door. She was right. "There is a way around this," I said. Both Topher and Myra stared at me as if I had been chosen as the leader of the club, or maybe we had become *the Hardy Boys* with *Nancy Drew*, or they just needed someone to give them a glimmer of hope that their friend Hawk could be proven innocent.

"We have to do something," Topher said. "Should we try to pick the lock?"

"No, that's breaking and entering," I said like I was some expert on the law. "If we do it, we have to do it electronically."

"Hack into his computer," Topher said part as an answer and part as a plea.

I was paid to stop this type of intrusion on the Harris corporate network, so the real estate office would be easy for me to penetrate.

What? No way. My conscience slugged me.

Do it. The adventurist in me prodded, taunting my technical pride, testing my network skills. I worked out the plan in my head.

"The main office is wide open for the wake," I explained. "If I can get to a computer without being noticed, I can open a port on their router that will allow me to tap in from the Internet. We can do all the searching we want from the privacy of my laptop."

"I know we can find something to clear Hawk," Topher said.

"We won't know until we try," Myra said. "But, this is akin to breaking and entering like you said, even if it is over the Internet and not physically into his office."

They both watched me as if waiting to see if I had any objection. I would have wanted someone to do it for me if I were in Hawk's place. "It seems justified to save Hawk, right?" I wanted them to both be with me totally, since I was the one hacking into the office network.

"I'll get you to a computer," Topher said.

Inside, people still milled around. Aunt Ruby was down to just a few ham biscuits and a couple of remnants of casseroles. The caterer had left, probably defeated by the popularity of Ruby's home-style cooking. Tricia still held court at the conference room. Topher inquired about Kimbo's whereabouts and was told he went to the police station to see about Hawk. The expanse of cubicles didn't allow much privacy, but Myra found a computer in a nook near the water fountain. The PC's screen blinked to life when I moved the mouse. I clicked on the Web browser and the damn machine played a little Irish ditty loud enough that I dropped to my knees and scooted under the desk, sure that I had just alerted the entire office to my covert activity.

"Shhh," Topher hissed. "Turn down the speakers."

"Someone is coming," Myra whispered.

Already under the desk, I didn't want to pop out like a gopher just as someone walked up, so I stayed in the dusty dark.

"Hi, Doris," Topher said.

"You need something?" the woman asked.

"No, Myra just wanted a drink from the water fountain."

I heard Myra slurping like a thirsty camel. "Poor Aubrey," Myra added after hydrating herself. "What a terrible way to die."

"I will miss him," the woman, Doris, said in rather a formal tone.

The conversation lagged and no feet moved, which was about all I could see from my vantage point. For motivation, I ran my hand up the back of Topher's calf.

"Whoo," he said and jerked his leg away from my touch. "You know, I'm feeling a bit light-headed, too much wine on an empty stomach I'm afraid. I better just sit down here for a minute." He plopped into the desk chair and almost hit me in the eye with his knee.

Doris said her farewell and left us.

"You two are the worst actors," I said and rolled Topher and the chair out of my way. "Now watch and let me know if anyone else decides to head this way."

With Topher and Myra as look-outs, I worked quickly. Luckily, most small businesses never changed their router passwords, and I logged on and opened a port to allow access from the Internet, and just to be sure I didn't open it to every high school kid in the country, I set a password.

"Okay, that's it," I announced. "We can log on from the house. Let's get Ruby and head back."

Does committing a crime justify clearing someone of murder? Yes. I knew I shouldn't worry about it. All those years of securing computer networks allowed me to find the best way to hack into one, but I thought, once we check Aubrey's files, I'd close that port back up and no one will be the wiser. The computer geek in me couldn't go off and leave the network open.

Topher and Myra helped me load the Explorer with the fragments of Ruby's triumph of feeding the mourners of Sedona.

"I swear," Ruby said, "I never saw people eat like these people. You'd think no one ever has real food. Why, that little girl passing around a tray of cucumbers was wasting her time. A cucumber wouldn't fill up anybody." She settled into the passenger side of the Explorer. "Myra, you and Topher come on over, and we'll have some supper. I noticed none of you ate a thing."

"We'll be there," Topher said. "Derek has some things to show us on his computer."

"Can you believe that?" Ruby shook her head. "He drags a computer with him everywhere, and now you kids want to sit around and play with it on a beautiful night like this."

The night sky had darkened and the stars popped out to reveal a sight more spectacular than any city skyline of lights could ever match. I wondered if Aubrey made it to where Clarity hoped he'd gone. Then I thought of the man behind bars for a murder that Topher swore he could never commit. Maybe I could help set things right. I was going to try.

CHAPTER SIX

With supper over and the dishes put away, Topher, Myra, and I sat down at the dining room table with my laptop computer. Aunt Ruby retired to the den to watch her favorite television show. Not only did the rental house have digital satellite television, it also boasted a high-speed wireless Internet connection, which helped me get some work finished for Harris Construction, and now allowed us to tiptoe into the real estate office's network.

The workgroups set up on the network easily identified each real estate agent's team. Aubrey's group included three computers: his, the receptionist's, and the file server. The receptionist had turned off her computer for the night, but Aubrey's appeared to be up and running; apparently, no one had touched it since his death. A click on his name brought up a screen with the standard shared directories. "My Documents" smiled at me. Knowing what little I did about Aubrey, I guessed he was the type to let the computer tell him where to save everything. A double click revealed hundreds of random files, none organized into subdirectories or into any naming conventions.

"What a mess," I said. My wallet poked my right butt cheek as I sat on the hard wooden chair at the table, so I stood and pulled it out of my back pocket and emptied the keys and change from my front pockets onto the table. "That's better," I said and sat back down and cracked my knuckles and flexed my fingers.

Myra peered over my shoulder. "Aubrey was a busy man. Look at all those files."

Wondering how to best dig through all the files, I decided to sort them by last revision date to see the documents he had worked on most recently.

"Copy them to your laptop so we have time to look without being connected to their network," Topher said.

He had a point, but that would be actually stealing. So far we had just broken in and looked around. My hands hovered above the keyboard. *I should do this. Daniel wouldn't think twice about it. Don't be a pussy. Do it.*

What were Topher and Myra getting me into?

Apparently sensing my hesitation, Topher leaned in and put his hands on my shoulders. "Man, it's like being a virgin, either you are or you aren't. We've penetrated the network. Might as well go all the way."

"You boys are getting me all tingly inside with this techno-sex talk." Myra fanned herself. "I agree with Topher, let's copy the files. That way we're in, we're out, and it's over—just like sex when I was married."

The married comment reminded me of what Detective Sarras had said about Myra's husband's death. I wanted to ask exactly what had happened, and how she and Topher had been involved, but it wasn't the time. I took a deep breath and pressed Control-A then Control-C, moved to a subdirectory on my laptop and dropped the files in with a Control-V. "Wham – Bam – Thank You, Ma'am. It's done."

"Great," Topher said and squeezed my shoulders. "Now pull out and thank her for the ride."

"It's lucky you both are gay," Myra said. "With an attitude like that, you would never hook-up with a woman."

With the files copied to my laptop, I disconnected from Aubrey's computer. The list of files looked like a jumble of letters and numbers, nothing making sense at first glance, but he must have had some system of naming them.

"Open the latest one," Topher said and sat down in the chair next to me, pushing the heap of keys and my wallet away so he could set down his wine glass.

A word processing document opened and revealed a letter to a local construction company where Aubrey tried to finalize the road pavement details. The entire project wasn't to the stage that had been represented to Harris Construction.

"Has any construction started out at Apache Trails?" I asked, since the letter made it sound as if grading had just begun.

"The dirt work is done, utilities and guttering, plus the initial road work," Myra said. "I had just finished the loan for the next phase, a large phase, and Aubrey was supposed to sign that next day."

"So, if the killer's motive was to stop the destruction of that land, then he was almost out of time," I said as I scanned down the list of files. The word "gentry" embedded in a file name caught my attention, and I opened it. "This is interesting."

Myra stared over my shoulder. Topher leaned in from the side. The spreadsheet listed each member of the Sedona Gentry, their net worth, their previous year's income, broken down into investments, salary, LLC profits/losses, and real estate holding valuations. Aubrey had accumulated quite a cache of data on these men.

Odd, I thought, not one of them had much liquidity. Most had money tied into long-term investments like real estate. These men would have been able to help raise money, but to ask for cash in a crunch, I doubted the twenty-five of them *together* could have put down fifty thousand within a week. Lots of influence, lots of assets, but little real cash—that was one thing that Papa Ernest had preached to his children and grandchildren: Keep liquid—be able to pay your debts. The list of these men and their cash flow had me wondering exactly what *was* the Sedona Gentry. If they embodied the goodness and benevolence that Topher claimed, then I couldn't see how they could fund any project. Although, they did own quite a chunk of Sedona's land and commercial buildings, and therefore, had a huge stake in the success of the community, its tourist-driven economy, and the raw western landscape that drew visitors.

"What would be worse for the economy: A murder in a small town or the destruction of a scenic ridge line?" I asked.

"The murder would soon be forgotten, and most tourists would never know," Topher said.

"But the development of houses over the ridge would ruin that view," Myra said. "A view that is to the west, a view that is seen all over town when people watch the sunset—that event would affect more people for a much longer time."

Moving in closer, Topher looked at the spreadsheet again. "What are you thinking?"

"I see it," Myra said. She grabbed the wine bottle and refilled our glasses. "The Gentry has their money tied up in this town. If uncontrolled growth spoils the red rock views, their investment is shit."

"Have some more wine, Miss Myra," Topher kidded her. "Your vocabulary seems to be improving with each sip."

She raised her glass to him. "I'm still wound up on the news of Hawk's arrest. I wonder if Kimbo was able to see him at the police department."

"If they arrest Hawk, they might as well arrest me too," Topher said. "He's about as likely as me to commit murder."

Myra chuckled, but the words caused the hair on my arms to rise. *How likely would it be for Topher to commit a murder?* I tried to dismiss the thought and stay focused on what the police had on Hawk.

The arrest puzzled me. Hawk wasn't part of the Sedona Gentry, although he worked for one of them—Kimbo Blue. *What could the police have to justify his arrest?* The list of file names from Aubrey's computer didn't seem to have anything related to Native Americans, but of course the word "Apache" showed up over and over.

"I need a cigarette." I pushed back from the table and headed out to the deck. Topher and Myra followed. The stars stretched across the dark sky twinkling into infinity. Nothing could compare to the western skies for the clarity. I blew a column of gray smoke and watched it twist and rise. "Tell me about this Hawk guy," I said to no one in particular.

Topher answered, "For awhile, Hawk ran his own tour company. It was called Native Visions. He focused on taking people to see the Sinagua ruins around the area. Seems like he did a few tours to the Hopi Reservation too."

"How'd he end up working for Blue Jeep?" I asked.

"He couldn't pull enough tourists to have steady income, and then a couple of years ago, the Forest Service closed the national forest for a few months to all traffic—everything: hiking, camping,

Jeeps—because of summer wildfire danger. The drought made the place a tinderbox." He leaned over my shoulder and took the Marlboro pack from my lap, pausing as if asking my permission to bum one. I nodded. He shook out a cigarette and lit it. "Like I said before, Kimbo is smart. He had a contingency plan and had secured exclusive rights to some private land to continue running his Jeeps, but the other tour companies, including Native Visions, had to shut down or drive the tourists around on the highway."

"That's when Hawk went out of business," Myra said. She stared at Topher's cigarette. "I thought you quit."

"I did," he said.

A frown darkened her face, but she said no more on the subject. "Didn't Hawk work for Clarity after that?"

"What?" I asked.

"Oh, yeah. Actually, she bought the tour business from him and hired him to drive. In a small town, the workforce tends to get a little incestuous," Topher explained.

Heat came to my cheeks, so I was glad we sat in the starlight, and they couldn't see. The word "incestuous" always brought back... awkward memories.

Topher continued, "He used his Jeeps and did some healing excursions for her. Clarity is quite a businesswoman. I'm sure that was one of the attractions she held for Aubrey."

"So, Hawk sold his tour business to her," I said leading them back to the subject of Hawk.

"Right," Topher said. "He made some money from the sale and rolled it into real estate. You see that a lot here, real estate is safer than the bank."

"Hey," Myra protested. "The market can dive again." She wagged her index finger at him. "Banks are safe."

"Anyway," Topher said and took a drag from his cigarette. "Hawk played up the Indian side of the tour. I think he used that big medicine wheel up off Schnebly Hill Road."

There was the mention of a medicine wheel again. "What exactly is a medicine wheel?"

"A tool that most Native American tribes use," Topher said.

"The medicine refers to improving your connection to life. Maybe a power, a way of understanding." He searched for the words. "A process that heals you and your relationship to all of life. The wheel itself is a method to do this. Lots of ceremonies use the wheel, and the tourists really love it. A bit like the Stations of the Cross in Catholicism."

"Is it always used for healing, or could it be used for something more...sinister?" The image of the medicine wheel on the patio of the condo where Aubrey lay scalped inside didn't appear as a healing tool to me.

Topher shrugged. "No idea, but Clarity could tell us. She incorporates Reiki therapy into the wheel."

"Again, I'm not up on the Sedona lifestyle. What's Reiki?"

Myra took a sip of her wine. "It's a way to balance the energy centers of the body, and some say the world in general."

"Hold on." I propped my cigarette in the ashtray and went inside to the bookcase in the den to locate the book I'd seen on medicine wheels. I flipped on the outside light so we could read.

"Whoa," Topher said and shielded his eyes. "Bright light, bright light."

"Here's a book." I handed it to Myra.

The book displayed several diagrams and a lot of text. Myra flipped through it. "Says here that the circle is used by a lot of different cultures and that each position on it has symbols that can mean different things to each culture." She looked up. "That's the hard thing about Native American customs, each tribe did things their own way and seldom documented the ceremonies. Legends and ways are taught by the elders in an oral tradition."

Topher reached for the book. "I know there are some common meanings to the positions."

Myra smiled at him.

"What? Yes, I do listen, and I used to explain the Medicine Wheel off Schnebly Hill Road when I was a Jeep driver. I never did any ceremonies, but I pointed it out." He found a diagram of a circle with just a couple of lines, like crosshairs in a target. "Everything is cyclical: the day, the year, our life. That's where the circle comes from. The four directions are the most basic: East on the right side of the wheel, south at the bottom, west to the left, and north at the top. These straight lines connect the directions and intersect in the center of the circle making it look like a wheel."

"I'm following," I said.

"Okay," he continued. "To use the wheel for the day: East is dawn, south is noon, west is sunset, and north is midnight."

"Makes sense," I said.

"For a year: East is spring, south is summer, west is fall, and north is winter. You always move from the east as a starting point and go clockwise. For a lifetime: East is birth, south is childhood, west is adulthood, and north is old age."

"Okay," I said. "But what does that mean to me?"

"Don't know. What do you want from it?" he asked.

At the condo, the wheel had been set up around a fire pit. "What is the intersection in the middle? I guess the hub of the wheel, what's it?"

"Mother Earth, or the Great Creator," he said.

"God," Myra added.

"It's the most spiritual position that everything else circles." Topher picked up his wine, but hesitated before taking a drink. "Why all the interest?"

Was this something I wanted to tell them? They knew Ruby and I had found Aubrey. I pulled my cell phone from my pocket, found the picture I'd snapped and held it so they could see.

"A fire pit?" Topher asked.

"Around it," I pointed at the tiny image.

"I see stones," Myra said, "but what about it?"

"It's a medicine wheel." I checked the photo myself and could tell it was hard to identify the configuration. "That was on the back patio of the condo where we found Aubrey. So, I wondered what the significance was."

They glanced at each other. Topher said "That's not uncommon. Maybe the condo owner had it there all along. A medicine wheel at a murder scene doesn't necessarily mean a Native American was the murderer."

Myra took a long drink from her glass. "If that condo was rented out for vacationers, that could be the reason it's there. You know, a little Southwestern decoration for the tourists."

"Could be," I said. The importance of the medicine wheel might be minimal, but I didn't think so. *Topher and Myra didn't seem that interested, or was it they knew more? Time to let the subject drop.* "Can I get you more wine?"

"No, thanks," Myra stood. "I should get home."

"Yeah, me too... After I hit the bathroom. You want me to put this book back?" he asked with the medicine wheel book in hand.

"Thanks. You can leave it on the dining room table next to the laptop," I instructed him. I finished my cigarette, then Myra and I walked back inside.

She and Topher ambled through the dining room and around the corner to the den to say their good-nights to Ruby. The laptop on the dining room table still displayed the list of files from Aubrey's PC. I had some reading to do. I joined everyone in the den.

"I find it hard to believe Aubrey's gone," Myra said standing at the door. "And how he was killed."

"Our concern is Hawk," Topher said. "After I talk to Kimbo tomorrow, I'll let you both know what happened."

Each hugged me as they left. Odd, I thought, how difficult to know the difference between friend and foe.

✂   ✂   ✂

Before nine o'clock the next morning, Topher called to say that Hawk had not been arrested as the rumor mill reported, but had been picked up for questioning. Kimbo had brought him back to his house to stay for the night. It had been too dark to drive Hawk out to the national forest, where he liked to sleep in a tent, which, of course, was illegal. Before hanging up, Topher asked me to meet him for lunch. I accepted.

Mysterious people. I tapped the cell phone with my fingers. "Ruby, what was the address of the condo on Dry Creek Road?"

She poked her head from the kitchen. "It's on that tablet on the coffee table."

Guide books, magazines, and the newspaper veiled the den's low rough wood table. I scooted them to the side and found her little yellow pad with notes about the real estate she'd seen. I wanted to find the owner of that condo to ask if they kept a medicine wheel around the fire pit to confirm Myra and Topher's belief it was only decorative.

The laptop buzzed as I opened it. *There we go. How I love the Internet.* The local government's website listed the owners of every parcel in Yavapai County. I typed in the address and the page loaded.

I couldn't believe what I read.

CHAPTER SEVEN

I met Topher at the Javelina Cantina overlooking Oak Creek and the Uptown of Sedona. The homely javelina themed the Mexican restaurant. Looking more like a cross between a wild boar and huge rodent, a large javelina led a pack of his family and friends through the rental's neighborhood each morning just before sunrise. The group of wiry-haired creatures consisted of several adults about the size of an ottoman with juveniles and babies. The cute babies with their short legs and over-sized snouts made the pack endearing as they galloped alongside the adults. What a javelina had to do with Mexican cuisine, I wasn't sure, or maybe I didn't want to know, but the restaurant served great Margaritas. The Margarita relaxed me while I sat on the deck with the red rock skyline spread out in front of my table. Chips and salsa threatened to fill me up before lunch, so I pushed the basket out of reach.

"Sorry I'm running late," Topher said and pulled out a chair to sit down at the table.

"That's fine," I said. "Glad to hear Hawk wasn't arrested."

"Yes, he was only questioned, but when people see the police pick up someone, the rumors fly." He ordered iced tea from the waitress, then said to me, "Thanks for meeting me for lunch. I wanted to talk to you about something."

I waited while my mind pinged to topics surrounding Aubrey's murder.

"A few years ago," he began, "I made a pledge to myself not to leap into any relationships."

Oh, this is about us. I had thought he wanted to talk about Aubrey. This could get interesting. I mean, we had almost kissed in the desert behind the real estate office, but other than that nothing more...yet. Was I being too casual? Had we started something I didn't know about? A warning sign flashed in my head that this guy moved quick. I waited to see where he went with the subject.

"When I left North Carolina," he started and leaned forward as if what he told would be confidential, "I also left behind a relationship. Alex would string me along, and I allowed that, at least for awhile. Since being in Sedona, I'm on my own. And I'm getting used to it. Actually, I like it."

"That's great." I said.

The waitress arrived with his drink. He thanked her for his tea, and we ordered our lunch.

"You're a wonderful guy," he continued after the waitress left. "But, I don't want to lead you on. I'm honestly attracted to you, but I still have that vow to myself to learn to be okay alone."

"That's an important part of being a full person." I sipped my Margarita. *Should I comment more?* This seemed to be relevant to him, and he wanted to talk about his past. Besides, curiosity stroked my mind, promising an insight into this rather mysterious man. Stay quiet, my inquisitive side warned, let Topher do the talking and you might just learn something.

His ice blue eyes stayed on me. His past seemed to cloud them a bit as he appeared to review what to reveal. "Sedona draws people," he said. "Some are looking for healing. Years ago, the New Age movement claimed to discover energy vortexes in Sedona that radiate from the land. Some of the rocks are even considered landscape temples or natural energy sources. It can be as simple as that or you can get into the different types of energy: magnetic vs. electric, male vs. female, or components of the chakra system."

My eyes must have glazed over, because he laughed and continued, "Let's just say some people are drawn to Sedona because they feel it's a healing place. That's not exactly why Myra and I came here, but I think we have both healed from our time in Charlotte. That city took life from both of us. Some people thrive in the corporate world, but I wanted more. Money wasn't as important as my peace of mind."

"Money makes its mark here," I said. "Real estate developers are making a killing."

"As Aubrey can attest to," he added.

The murder threatened to derail Topher's thoughts, so I brought us back. "How did Sedona heal you?"

"First off, the art scene encouraged me to start painting again, to find the muse, to experiment. I found inspiration in the beauty of the land," he said and looked out across the restaurant's deck at the horizon of rock formations and clear cobalt sky. "And other people cheered me on. I found the corporate world lacking in support for the ever-popular and frequently said 'thinking outside the box' since that would be too much change. Here, there are no boxes. Of course, getting things done takes forever. People are extremely disorganized, back in my corporate days I would have labeled them unprofessional. Most business owners here could never make it in the corporate world. It's funny how fast businesses here go under, only to resurface as something else. But what they lack in management skills, they make up with determination. So, with my corporate background and willingness to start over, I've done well in this town. I've cultivated a sense of self-worth."

"A bit of the best from both worlds," I added.

He nodded. "That acceptance and encouragement has welcomed me here. Knowing that Kimbo appreciates me more than makes up for the reduced salary from my Charlotte life. I find more satisfaction in life here, more balance."

"What is the balance?" I asked wondering if it included celibacy.

He picked up his tea, took a sip. "Back East, my life consisted of work and trying to find a relationship. So, I spent my days in my cubicle, then at the gym. Creatively, graphic design was my only outlet. I wanted to paint, and did paint for myself. I cluttered my house with canvases, finished and unfinished. Friends would see my work and nod politely or comment about the colors, but no one really thought art was worthwhile unless you did it for a living and only if it brought in big money. Of course, you probably know all about that from your family's company. If you had wanted to build low-income housing in the Gulf Coast after Hurricane Katrina, would the company have cheered for you?"

"No." I had to laugh. "No, they would have asked where the

profit was."

"Exactly. Follow the money. Is it profitable?" He fingered a sugar packet as he talked, then ripped it open and dumped it in his tea. "One of the first things people in Sedona ask about is your art. Doesn't matter if you make a profit, just what type of art?"

"So, you paint. Could I see some of your work?" I asked.

"There you go. You sound like a local."

The waitress delivered our lunch, grilled shrimp tacos for Topher, a black bean burrito for me. We ate and talked, and I wondered if my life had developed fully. Work was important to me. I had no creative outlet. My on and off relationship with Daniel didn't offer any stability, and hell, I was closing in on thirty fast. The Harris family business would never be mine. My cousins had been anointed to run that. Aunt Ruby and my sister were the only family I really cared about. The family clouded my thinking. Maybe that was what Topher meant. The ability to know myself had been lost when I moved to Charlotte; I was colored by the views of the family. For me, corporate life wasn't the culprit; it was the smothering effects of a blanketing family. *Who was I really?*

After lunch, we took Topher's Jeep up a hill to a large art gallery that represented his work. A hefty building by Sedona standards, it stretched near the road with massive polished bronze sculptures gleaming in the sunlight. We parked at the side and walked up to the glass doors that opened to a dizzying array of art: oil paintings, sculpture, photography. Everything seemed big, bold, and brassy. Sales people hovered around tourists browsing the gallery, and glass enclosed offices anchored the corners of the interior. I watched as a pretty young woman, wearing a cocktail dress, led a customer to one of the glass offices where a thin, smiling man, in a dark suit jacket over black bibbed overalls, greeted the potential customer. *What's with the Farmer John overalls and suit coat?*

Topher must have noticed my attention on the strange man. "That's Ty. He's the owner of the gallery. He likes to meet every collector when they make a purchase."

We followed a corridor toward a series of alcoves, each with different forms of art, until we came to one with Sedona landscapes in bright, brilliant colors. The crimson spires and buttes of the land and the azure sky were heightened to blazing reds and shocking blues in broad, loose brushstrokes. An abstract but bold interpretation of Sedona, the paintings seemed to radiate energy, and the artist's enthusiasm bounded across the canvas with a delight that hooked the viewer.

"Wow," was all I could say.

One corner of his mouth curved up into a mischievous, lopsided smile, as he arched an eyebrow.

In the bottom right of the painting was a simple block-lettered signature: Topher.

The next painting represented Oak Creek Canyon with sweeping cerulean water cascading over pearly boulders and sycamores with patchy, sepia trunks highlighted with yellow, lime, and mauve. "You're a colorist."

"Yes, thank you." He pointed to another painting, one of ramshackle buildings and a curving road that clung to the side of a hill. Brilliant hues and loose strokes colored the townscape and the hillcrest in the background. "That's a plein air I did up in Jerome. We can go up there one day. It's an old mining town a few miles from here."

His zeal for painting spilled over as he pointed out techniques he had tried and colors he'd mixed with surprising results.

A buxom woman dressed in cowgirl drag paused behind him as he explained his concoction of colors. "Are you the artist?" she asked. She wobbled on high-heeled boots with too-tight black jeans and a silk western shirt in the shades of an Arizona sunset—gold, saffron, fiery-red. Her coppery hair flowed from under the black cowboy hat, and I wondered if all the black and bright colors were too hot when she went outside in the blazing sun of mid-day. She would wilt like an orchid.

Topher shook her manicured hand and confirmed that he was the artist.

"Beautiful," she said. "I'm visiting from Pennsylvania. Here to see my daughter and grandchildren in Phoenix, and I told Marv, my husband, that we should make a trip up to Sedona. Marv wanted to play golf, and I tell you, the Scottsdale courses are too hot this time of year, so I told him, I said, 'Marv, let's go to Sedona. It's cooler than Scottsdale. You can golf and I can shop.' That's what I said. And that's what happened." She took a breath. "And now I walk into this lovely gallery and meet a real artist." She took Topher's arm and walked him over to a painting he'd done of Cathedral Rock. "I love that swirl there." She pointed to a faint paint eddy in the sky above the rock formation. "Is that a vortex?"

He shot me a quick glance then placed his hand on her shoulder. She leaned in toward him. "I painted what I *felt* there," he said in a low voice. "Currents in the atmosphere *do* cause energy, and I encountered that one at Cathedral Rock. Some call it a vortex, but I call it the life all around us."

That didn't make a shit bit of sense to me, but the woman seemed to be eating it up. Not only was Topher an artist, he was a salesman bull-shitter too. A sales person lingered in the background as Topher talked to the woman and appeared to wait for the right moment to step in and seal a deal.

Topher must have noticed because he motioned to her and introduced her to the Pennsylvania cowgirl. "Courtney, this lovely lady is interested in the Cathedral Rock painting."

"Well, I really love it," the woman said. "And to talk with the artist makes it so special."

"When you have a connection," Courtney, the young sales person, began her pitch, "the piece speaks to you. Topher is too modest to say, but he's won several awards and is collected by several high-profile celebrities."

The cowgirl swung to look at Topher. "Really? Who?"

His smile lit up the entire gallery. "Now, we don't like to name drop."

"Oh, tell me, please." She took his arm.

I wondered if it was a sign of going in for the sale when Courtney hooked her shoulder-length blonde hair behind her ears and glanced over her shoulder, as if she was ready to share a confidential confession.

"Let's just say a well-known talk show host who has a home here bought a couple of Topher's paintings for her house in L.A. and one for her studio dressing room."

The cowgirl's eyes clocked back and forth as she tried to connect the clues.

Courtney waited.

But the woman seemed to have a difficult time guessing the mystery celebrity.

"Would this person have hosted the Oscars, and does she like to dance around her coffee table?" I asked.

The cowgirl's face brightened. "Really? I love her."

"Your tastes are in good company." Courtney nodded.

The woman nodded too.

"Let's go write this up," Courtney said. She led the woman toward one of the glass offices.

"Oh, Topher," the cowgirl called back. "Would you please sign the back of the painting: 'To Margie and Marv, my good friends and collectors.'"

"I'd be happy to," he said.

With a quick glance at the wall tag, I calculated how much Topher had just made on that little encounter. "Not bad for an artist not concerned about big money."

A blush colored his cheeks. "Margie really liked the painting, and Courtney just gave her a reason to go ahead and buy it."

"Did she need a reason?"

"Funny thing about art," he said, "it's not a necessity, and people feel a bit guilty about buying it. But if you find a connection to a piece, a real love for it, then you just want someone to give you permission to acquire it. To have another person say it's all right to buy something that makes you feel good, that you want."

"Being an artist is more than painting well," I said.

"Like most things, there're a lot of sides to it. I want people to enjoy the work, but I know it is part of a business. There's a balance between—"

Before he could finish, a blonde nicely dressed woman in her late fifties, but with an extremely tight face, wrapped her arms around Topher and gave him a Hollywood kiss to both sides of his cheeks without actually touching him or messing up her makeup.

"Topher," she gushed. "Why didn't you have someone tell me you were in the gallery? And I heard through the grapevine that you assisted in selling one of your paintings."

"Assisted, hell," I said. "He sold it."

She spun around on her stiletto heels to regard me, and the pulled-tight skin of her face tugged as she forced a smile. She wore bangs. I didn't know many women over fifty-five who wore straight-cut bangs. Leveled across her eyebrows and down the sides of her face, her blonde, almost platinum, hair framed her face in strict lines. The style might have looked cute on a junior-high cheerleader, but for this woman, it just drew attention. A modern-day Cleopatra fighting the aging process with the best surgery money could buy. "You are?" she asked.

"Derek Mason." I extended my hand, and she lightly shook it. "You must be from Southern California," I said

"Oh?" She tilted her head. "Why's that?"

"No accent, your shoes are fabulous, and your make-up is perfect." I knew I laid it on thick, but this woman needed it. "My guess would be former model or actress."

Her eyes shifted to Topher then back to me. Her smile remained fixed. I wasn't charming her, even with some of my best compliments.

"You," she said, "are a Southern gentleman. You have an accent. Slight, but detectable, although not as pronounced as Topher's. You live in a city since your shoes are polished, but now they're covered with Sedona's red dirt, and it bothers you that your oxfords are dusty. You are visiting Sedona, from Atlanta, I'd guess."

"You are a little Nancy Drew," I cooed. "Good deduction, but a little off. Charlotte, North Carolina, and the dust doesn't bother me."

"You are darling," she said, and turned back to Topher. "I knew that the series of Sedona landscapes would sell. Ty has some ideas for you. Although your landscapes are moving well, we are thinking we could use some petroglyphs and shaman paintings. Your figurative oils are nice, but to put an ancient Southwest spin on them could be a real boost." She stopped and looked at me. "Now, all this is extremely confidential. Other galleries are always trying to scoop us on the next sales trend."

Shifting his stance, Topher seemed uncomfortable about the suggestion for a new direction. Apparently, artistic freedom isn't always free.

"Alison, I thought the trend had moved away from shamans and petroglyphs. I mean," he said, running his fingers through his hair, "I've seen those images on posters. Hell, by the time a trend hits the poster market, it's over."

"Let's talk about this in my office." She took his arm and attempted to lead him away from me. His feet planted firm, Topher refused to move, and that caused Alison to quiver on her heels.

"Nothing to discuss. I appreciate your feedback and will give it consideration."

She squared her shoulders, adjusted her tight jaw, and hooked her straight blonde hair behind her ears. "Yes, you do that. And please see me or Ty when you come into the gallery. We want to know when an artist is here." She nodded to me and returned to the sales desk.

"Controlling, isn't she?" I asked.

"Bizarre," Topher turned his back to the main part of the gallery. "Ty and Alison are quite the team. See these sales people? I bet not one of them has been here for over six months. That's the owners' way. Paranoia runs wild through their minds. They make their employees sign non-compete agreements. And most of them do because they're new to town and think this is the only game around."

I had seen the same thing in Silicon Valley in the high times. Trade secrets were well guarded, and employees had to sign their life away. They couldn't work for a competitor for years after leaving. "But," I said, "are the galleries really in competition? All art is different. It's not a commodity."

"Ty and Alison think everyone is out to get them. Half the town has worked here and left. A few businesses have the reputation of snaring the newcomers before they talk to people to get the facts. I'm ready to find another gallery, but haven't had the time to take my portfolio around."

The mood had shifted, and I felt bad that Topher had conflicts with the gallery. "Have you ever thought of opening your own gallery?"

"No way. As an artist, it's too much of a business. So I'm certainly not going into retail too." A quick wink and he laughed. "You know, I really pushed back when she suggested I produce a different style. Am I being stubborn? They *are* the business side. Ty and Alison know how to sell."

"Don't ask me about being stubborn. That's my downfall."

"What bothers me," he said, "is that they know business, but not art. I mean, who tells an artist what to paint? That would be like suggesting a chef change his style."

The debate continued in his questions. Questions that were more for himself than me, so I just stayed quiet and let him talk it out.

We left the gallery through a side entrance and spotted the saleswoman Courtney, sheltered by a juniper at the corner of the building, smoking a cigarette. With a quick twist of the toe of her pump, she ground out the butt and blew smoke away.

"Don't stop on our account," I said and pulled out my pack of Marlboros. I offered one to her and to Topher, then lit them all. There we stood: a trio of smoking fiends.

"Ty makes me so tense," Courtney said.

"They piss me off." Topher huffed out a cloud of smoke.

"I feel fine," I said.

"Ty yelled at me in his office. He said I should have made contact with that stupid woman before she talked to you. Now, how can I get to every tourist that walks through those doors? Most are here just to look." She sighed. "My sales aren't as high as Ty thinks they should be. I had a couple interested in a painting, and do you know that Alison came over and took them away from me? When she wrote up the sale, she put it in her name. The bitch." Courtney shook her head. "How do I make my numbers when the owner takes away my sale?"

"She told me to paint shaman. Who the fuck wants a shaman over their mantel?" he asked no one in particular.

"What is a shaman?" I asked, since I might have one and not know it.

They both looked at me, then at each other. Courtney grinned, and Topher wrinkled his forehead in thought.

"A shaman, Mr. Mason, is a medicine man of the tribe," he explained in a curator's tone. "Usually, you see them in the paintings and petroglyphs in ancient ruins. They are popular symbols of the Southwest, simply drawn, almost like stick figures with some adornment. And," his voice began to rise, "because of that, *why* would an artist want to paint ancient stick figures?"

"Speaking of stick figures." Courtney took a drag on the cigarette. "Skinny Carmen got fired. Ty said she had talked to another gallery about a job, and he wouldn't have disloyal workers. Workers? Not associates or even employees. Makes us sound like illegal day laborers."

I could tell this bitch session was getting deeper, so I asked Topher if we could go. Courtney thanked me for the cigarette and waved good-bye to Topher as she popped a breath mint in her mouth.

"I really liked your paintings," I told Topher as he dropped me back at my car. "Don't let the shaman suggestion get you too upset. She was just being a businesswoman, a clumsy, tight-faced, tight-assed businesswoman."

"Thanks for lunch. Listen," he said. "Myra has a date tonight with this guy she's been seeing for a few months. I had planned to meet up with them, but I always feel like a third wheel."

"Do you want me to come too?" I asked thinking he intended to round up the number.

"I had a better idea. Do you want to watch the sunset? I know of a great place off a Jeep road."

A tingle stirred in my nether regions. "It's a date," I said.
Without hesitating, he corrected me. "It's a *friend* date."
The tingle dissipated.

"Okay, but you can't stop me from bringing a bottle of wine," I said. "Then, we'll go back to the house and see what Aunt Ruby has cooked for dinner. You still need to help me decipher those files from Aubrey's computer." The owner of the condo still hung in my mind, and I wondered if Topher knew what I had already discovered.

He drove off, and I leaned against the warm metal of the Explorer watching the clouds build over the distant mesa.

CHAPTER EIGHT

My cell phone rang just as I drove onto the street of our rental house. Mark's name flashed on the screen. Technically, he was my work associate, my cousin, my ex-lover. Which role was he today? I decided not to answer.

Not because I needed to avoid Mark for any of the twisted relationships we found ourselves in, but because he usually found a way to mix up my mind. The fact that we grew up together, and he was now an executive at Harris Construction proved to make a professional manner difficult when we interacted. It's hard to make a presentation to the board of directors when you've had one of them bent over the office couch. Nevertheless, he was the project lead for this little adventure into the Wild West, so I would call him back once I had time.

Inside the house, Ruby was napping, so I stood on the deck and watched the Gambel's Quail scurry through the brush with their fuzzy, walnut-sized babies following. The birds seemed to have a better family structure than most humans. An adult quail would navigate the way with the offspring lined up behind them while, another adult rallied the end of the train, keeping stragglers on course. I had seen them hurry across the road in front of my car before, one male stopping in the middle of the pavement to glare at me until all the birds made it across safely, before darting off the road like a hyper crossing guard. With Ruby alone and moving two thousand miles from North Carolina, I felt like it was my turn to guide her after all the years she had taken care of me. Maybe this newly emerging sense of responsibility was amplified by the confusion about my relationship with Daniel, or the tension I still felt with Mark, or the hurt that lingered with my mother and the rest of the family. We were no quails. Our family was emotionally scattered in all directions, with no one trying to keep us together.

The cell rang again. This time I answered.

Mark made small talk at first, the Southern tradition, then he steered into the reason he had called. "With Aubrey passed," he said with his voice low in reverence, "the Apache Trails project is in limbo. When you get a chance, go confirm the status. According to the funding, grading and utilities are in. Actually, paving on the main road should be complete."

"No one here likes the project," I said.

"No shit." He sighed, slipping into the Mark I knew.

"Do you remember a group from here, the Sedona Gentry, coming to Charlotte to ask you to stop Apache Trails?"

"Oh, yeah. That group of small business owners. Not a unified thought among them. Why? Are they trying to step into the project?"

"No," I said and considered voicing my suspicions about the group's possible ties to Aubrey's murder. "Is Apache Trails still going forward?"

"That's what we need to determine. Get a current physical status. I'm worried about the bookkeeping. Aubrey was the only on-site contact. With you and Ruby going to Sedona, I had hoped to get you working with him…" His voice trailed off. "I might need to come out there. I already mentioned it to Kathleen that I would be gone for a few weeks."

No, I thought, no, the last person I wanted to deal with—alone— was Mark. Away from his wife, away from the prying eyes of the family, and me feeling lonely. That was a trap I didn't want to get close to again. "I can handle the status, thanks. In fact, I met Myra Greer. She's Aubrey's loan officer."

"Stop right there." He seemed unusually short. "Don't discuss what you're doing with her. Keep this to yourself."

Taken aback by his tone, I started to make a joke about the secrecy of my mission, but thought better of it when he continued.

"Her bank is financing part of the project," he said. "Several checks have been cashed, but I don't have a good feeling about our portion."

"You lost me." I walked inside and to my laptop on the table.

"Harris Construction is a major investor in Apache Trails. The bank has loaned Aubrey money to bridge the gap between investor money and the total cost of the project. To mitigate investment risk, we all contribute our portions as the project goes along."

"So, it's not like he uses all the Harris money first, then taps the bank loan?" I tried to get the process right in my head.

"Right, we all chip in as the project continues. So, we've paid out quite a bit already, mostly based on the bank advancing their portion on the loan."

"Wait a minute." I booted up the computer. "You're telling me you doled out money based on what the bank said the project's status was?" This was not the Mark I knew; he would stop to pick up a dime from the sidewalk. He didn't throw money at a project based on third-hand reports. "That's why you encouraged me to come out here with Ruby?"

"Listen, I needed an eye-witness status of the project. I still do. Aubrey sent Gantt charts and work breakdown structures along with receipts to support his progress. The bank had an inspector approve progress for them, but I want you to be my eyes. Something doesn't feel right."

"No, Aubrey was murdered, it sure as shit doesn't feel right," I said. "If the bank's inspector said things were progressing, why do you doubt it?" I opened my e-mail knowing that he would send me documents as he talked.

"Our portion is a hell of a lot more than the bank is putting in." He clicked his keyboard as he talked. "I don't like to say things like this, but you're family, and I can be frank. I worry that Myra Greer and Aubrey might have been embezzling from the project and using the bank loan disbursements as the proof to pull money from us."

Myra? I felt I was a good judge of character—well, outside the romantic realm at least—and Myra seemed solid and true. "Have you ever met her?" I asked him knowing that anyone acquainted with her wouldn't suspect her of misdeeds.

"Not yet," he said. "You know, not all criminals have handlebar mustaches and shifty eyes."

Implying I was naïve didn't sit well. "You've got that right.

Remember, I'm the one who fingered the frauds in our family." I let that statement hang in the cell phone hiss.

His long sigh broke the silence. "I don't want to keep repaying for past sins. That is all history."

Was I wrong to harbor ill feelings? Could I dismiss the past? *No.* Not just no, but *hell no.* "You need to keep your ass in Charlotte with your wife. I can handle this. Send me the latest status, and I'll document the progress Aubrey had made. As far as Myra goes, the documentation I collect will be completely independent of anything her bank has used; that way we have two separate sources." I clicked open a newly-arrived e-mail from him and saved the attachments in my work directory. An e-mail from Daniel had also arrived, and I would have rather read it. "How's Kathleen?" I asked.

"She's doing fine."

"How could you think of coming out here? Bet she pitched a hissy fit when you suggested leaving for a couple of weeks."

"She knows I have work responsibilities."

"Just the same, a woman in her condition isn't always rational," I talked as if I knew what the hell a pregnant woman was like.

Kathleen had finally made Mark prove his heterosexuality by knocking her up, and now the little heir to the Harris Empire waited to be squeezed out of Kathleen in two more months. When I saw her last, she seemed excited to finally have some curves. Kathleen had always been boyishly trim, but now she had cleavage and a belly. Actually, Mark had added a few "sympathy" pounds as well. His belly had almost outgrown Kathleen's. Catty? Yes, but people still saw him as a prince. I was the only one who knew Mark's true fabric. Well, maybe Kathleen knew too. And damn, did she know how to play him. A child would seal his commitment and tie him to her forever. Their marriage hadn't been passionate, with Mark finding men as alluring as women and particularly me, his long-time playmate, arriving back in Charlotte to rip the seams of his carefully tailored life. But now, with his wife bearing a child and the extended family excited for a new son to carry the Harris name, Mark secured his standing in the Charlotte elite: young, handsome, successful, and reproductive.

The magnetism he had over me had faded. I still loved him, I had to admit. How can years of affection, passion, and desire stop cold? But the more I knew him as a man, an adult, not the college athlete and swaggering cousin he had been in our youth, the less I respected him. For me, respect reigned over any physical attraction. Could I be maturing? Thank God.

"She could get along without me for a few weeks," he said.

"No. You need to be with her." I did not want him in Sedona. "Besides, Harris Construction has other projects going that require your attention."

Voices in the background of his call took his interest for a moment. "Call me back if you have questions on the information I e-mailed. By the way, what time is it out there?"

I checked my watch. "Almost four o'clock. Arizona's Pacific Time during the summer. Shouldn't you be home by now?"

"Actually, we're heading to the gym."

"We?"

"A buddy and me." His voice sounded tight.

"Mark, keep your dick to yourself."

A stiff chuckle wafted over the cell towers. "You do the same."

I snapped the phone shut just as Ruby walked into the room. Her scarlet hair, sprayed and teased, formed a perfect frame for her rouged cheeks and smoky shadowed eyes. Her make-up and hair told me she planned to go somewhere.

"You sure are dolled up," I said.

"Did you forget?"

Apparently, I had. My mind searched for something I had promised to do with Ruby, but I couldn't place it. "I'm sorry," I said. "I did forget. What are we doing?"

She cocked her head to the side like a brash cardinal that had outwitted a blue jay. "We," she said, "aren't going anywhere. I am having dinner with my Palm Springs friends, girls' night out."

"A bit early for dinner," I said.

"Drinks first, then supper. You know how us senior citizens like to have supper by six."

The older she became, the more she lived by daylight. Up with the first rays of dawn, then heading for bed as the sun set. She complained of not being able to sleep all the way through the night, but who could when she went to bed so early? The emptiness from the loss of Walterene still clouded her days and nights. After several years, I had hoped that void would have been absorbed by something, or someone else, but she was different when she was with Walterene. They were a team. Ruby had grown more independent without Walt, but she was less the flirt, the bubbly good-time girl. Oh, she still had her moments, but the responsibility that Walterene shouldered had fallen to Ruby, and that had taken away some of her carefree attitude.

"Is it just the three of you?" I asked.

"No, Zandra invited a friend of theirs to come along." She seemed to avoid my eyes.

A date? Did Ruby have a date lined up? The possibility brought a smile to my face, but I didn't kid her about it. She needed companionship. "The four of you have a wonderful time," I said and adjusted a curl of her claret-colored hair. "So, it's Zandra, Mavis, you, and what's the other lady's name?" I felt like a father mining details from a teenager.

"Their friend Alice," she said. "Now, I won't be late. Should I bring you something back from the restaurant?"

"No, I'm meeting Topher to watch the sunset."

"Woo woo woo," she teased. "That sounds romantic. I didn't know you two were an item. He's a cute boy. When did this happen?"

"Nothing has happened. We're just friends, and he's taking me on a Jeep ride."

She plopped her handbag on the dining room table and dug through it. Without looking up she said, "Don't have to explain to me. I say 'live and let live.' That's my motto. Now, where's my house key? I can't find the dang thing. I should have put it on a key ring"

I went around the bookcase to the den to check the coffee table for her keys. Through the front window, I saw an ivory Cadillac sedan roll into the driveway. "They're here," I said.

"Well, I just can't go without a key," Ruby said, flustering about.

"Hold on." I headed into the bedroom and grabbed the single key off the dresser. "Here," I said, returning to the den, "take mine. You'll be home before me."

"Mine is around here somewhere." She glanced around the table again. "Maybe you'll find it before you leave."

I didn't worry like she did over little things. "Okay, I will look. Go," I said and led her toward the door. "The girls are waiting."

She placed the key in her pocketbook and kissed me on the cheek. Cheerful and at ease, she greeted the women as she climbed into the back of the car. I stood on the front porch steps and waved while they backed out of the driveway and headed down the road.

When I had checked my e-mail for Mark's message, I'd noticed one from Daniel. An odd thrill rumbled in the background of my mind as I thought about contact from him, like the anticipation of opening a Christmas present or having a new date waiting in the back of a Cadillac. He was a good guy. The reasons we drifted in and out of a relationship were hard to quantify or analyze, but I missed him more than anyone else back in Charlotte.

His e-mail talked about his work, some mutual friends, and he mentioned Aubrey's death and the lack of information on it. In his research, the only data he could find was the obituary from the Sedona newspaper, which was brief and sketchy. "Do they have reporters?" he asked. The local newspaper, which was published on Wednesdays and Fridays, reported that Aubrey had been found dead, but didn't give any details on the murder itself or on Aubrey. Maybe they assumed everyone knew Aubrey and had already heard the details. One columnist had written his commentary on the murder, but with the spin of the outside world invading the quiet, idyllic setting of Sedona and the urgency to combat that from happening. *Well, yeah, doesn't everyone want to live in a place free from crime?*

With Daniel in his bulldog mode pondering Aubrey's death, I wondered if I should have him check out the Sedona Gentry. Then the accusations of Mark came to mind. *Should I investigate Myra?* I snapped the laptop shut. First things first: I would get Mark his visual inspection of the development site, then deal with Aubrey's death. *Was there a connection?*

Cabernet Sauvignon snuggled into my backpack, along with two wine glasses wrapped in cloth napkins. A wedge of cheese might be good too, I thought, a little bread and that should be enough. I considered water. The Arizona climate was so dry, I constantly drank water and I didn't know if this sunset watching adventure would include a bit of hiking, so I added a couple of bottles of water. Just as I zipped up my backpack, I heard Topher's Jeep pull into the driveway.

I opened the door to a grinning Topher. He wore shorts, a t-shirt, and hiking boots. "Ready to see the beauty of Arizona?" he asked.

"You mean there's something more than you?" I said.

He blushed, which I found so endearing. I had made this talented, handsome, striking man blush.

With a dismissive smirk, he tried to change the subject. "The sunset should be awesome, and I don't mean that as 1980s slang. It is amazing; it will take your breath away."

"Are we doing any hiking?" I asked and looked down at my tennis shoes.

"Not much, but I do want to walk up to a top of a hill. If you have boots, you might want to wear them—the rocky soil tends to cause turned ankles."

"Have a seat. I'll change." I went to my bedroom and quickly pulled off my shoes, jeans, and shirt, then replaced them with shorts, t-shirt, and boots like Topher had on. I patted my pockets as I emerged to ensure I had my wallet and key ring.

"Sunglasses and hat," Topher reminded me, and I grabbed them from the side table.

"I'm ready for anything." I winked and hooked the backpack over my shoulder.

We drove through neighborhoods, the back way to Dry Creek Road, and intersected with the street north of the condo where Aubrey had been murdered. Just being in the vicinity gave me a chill. Topher steered the Jeep away from town and toward the open desert. The late afternoon sun cast long shadows on the rocks that highlighted the texture and shapes on the cliff sides. Warm wind swirled around me in the open Jeep, a cozy embrace that felt safe. Topher pointed out and identified the distinctive western flora like the clumpy juniper, prickly pear cactus, spiky yucca, and slender ocotillo that lined the road and added shades of green to the red dirt and rusty rocks.

The vastness of the landscape seemed to open my thoughts to all the possibilities I had in my life, the experiences that had shaped me in one way or another, for good and for bad. No wonder the desert drew people looking for inspiration and enlightenment. The pure air and sunshine changed my outlook.

My cousin Mark wasn't a complete asshole. Daniel was a driven, hard-working journalist, and damn sexy. And here I sat next to Topher, a handsome artist who intrigued me. He had the mysteriousness of a man with a hidden past.

"Most people go up to the Airport Mesa for the sunset," Topher said. "It's easy getting there and has a great view, but extremely crowded."

"So, where are we going?" I asked.

"Out near Bear Mountain, on the way to Honanki and Palatki." He said it as if I should know what that meant. We took a left fork and drove past a sign that had the odd names and arrows pointing in our direction.

A Blue Jeep, heavy with tourists, approached. The driver sported a long, dark ponytail under his cowboy hat. His sunglasses reflected the road ahead, as he motioned toward a red rock ridge. The tourists snapped their digital cameras, then checked their LCD screens, and snapped some more. As the Blue Jeep passed us, the driver nodded and tipped his hat to Topher.

"There's Hawk," Topher said.

"Looks no worse for the wear of police questioning."

"Yeah, already back at work. I wonder if he's staying at Kimbo's place or if he's back out here."

"Here?"

"Hawk lives out here in the national forest. He has a tent, camps. Says he'd rather sleep under the stars than in a house."

"Doesn't that make him homeless?" I asked. "I mean, where does he get his mail?"

"The post office, like a lot of people."

"Where does he shower? Go to the bathroom?"

"He says he has a device hung up in a tree for a shower, and the bathroom, well, I guess he goes like most people when they camp."

I considered the difficulties of living without conveniences. "I couldn't do it. I'm no Nelly Girl, but I have to have a working bathroom, hot water, and a soft bed." If Hawk lived in the wilderness, who would be his alibi when he was away from work? No one would know what he did or where he was. "Why do you think the police picked up Hawk for questioning?"

He bit his lower lip as if in thought as he pulled up to a Stop sign. "Hawk is well-known around town. He's had dealings with Aubrey." Topher leaned on the steering wheel. "He sold his tour company to Clarity and worked for her before working for us."

I itched to tell him what I had discovered at the county's website, but held back. A sign in front of us pointed to the right for a resort and to the left for Honanki and Palatki. "We're going to the resort?" I asked.

"No, Nelly." Topher winked. "Out this road toward the ruins, but not that far out. Actually, we're going to Apache Trails, or what was supposed to be Apache Trails."

Aubrey's development. I guessed I would get Mark's assessment completed sooner than I thought. The anticipation mounted as we drove west. The pavement ended and Topher bounced the Jeep along a dirt road. Dust plumed behind us as we carefully crawled over rocks and rolled through washes. I hadn't had the time to review the latest supposed status of the project, but according to Mark, paving of the main road should have been completed.

"One thing the Jeep tours don't like about the Apache Trails development is the plan to pave this road," Topher said. "We take people this way to see the ruins, and it makes the ride more of an adventure if they spend thirty minutes on a bumpy dirt road to get there."

I saw the connection. "Jeep tours hate pavement. I mean, as a tourist, why would I shell out money for a Jeep ride, when the road is paved and I could have easily driven my rental car instead?"

"Exactly." He hit a rock, and the Jeep shifted to the right. "Isn't this more fun than driving on an asphalt road?"

"Yeah." I had to agree it was more of an adventure. "So, no paving has been done at Apache Trails?"

"Last time I was there," he said, "a few stakes had been driven. Not much else."

The Jeep bounced and rolled along the road, and I worried about the wine glasses in my backpack. We might end up drinking out of the bottle. "Is this national forest or private land?"

"Mostly national forest, but a few old ranches still remain. Aubrey snatched up the old McMurtry ranch for Apache Trails. It's surrounded by national forest, so the residents will have their own private island of estates encircled by forest land."

He guided the Jeep onto a newly graded road around the base of a mesa and up a sloping hill. "This is Apache Trails."

I had to admit, it would be a wonderful place to have a house. The dirt road curved over hills and dips revealing spectacular views in all directions, unspoiled by other development. Twisty juniper and gangly manzanita covered the hillside. I had the feeling I was hundreds of miles from civilization, yet we had driven only about three miles from the city limits. Topher parked the Jeep at the end of the road.

"I think this will be the summit estate lot. If the builder and owners aren't totally self-absorbed, they'll position the house on the side of the hill. That way it doesn't ruin the ridge for everyone else, but who's to say they would think of anyone but themselves?"

He shrugged. "Let's walk up there and you can see what a great view it is."

Relief—the backpack didn't clank of broken wine glasses when I hung it over my shoulder, and we started up the hill. Loose rocks made the climb a bit slippery, but I soon found my footing and scrambled behind Topher toward the top of the ridge. In the high desert, the mostly evergreen trees rarely grew taller than a house, so that made for unobstructed views, and as we hiked up the slope, the more spectacular the panorama became.

I stood on the crest, with the wind bellowing my shirt. To the south, the rock formation called Cockscomb rose in a jagged ridge. To the west, I could see Mingus Mountain in shadows as the sun lowered behind it. I turned north to see darkening canyons cut into the high line of red rocks, and to the east, chiseled spires, buttes, and cliffs shifted silhouettes with the sun's lowering rays.

The colors awed me. During the bright sun of mid-day, Sedona's rocks tended to look burnt orange, that odd shade of between red and orange. But as the sun waned and began to set, the changing light caused the rusty limestone to change by the minute. I unzipped my backpack and pulled out the wine and the glasses, still fully intact. We sat on a rock and toasted the sunset.

"This is one town where the sunset is even more brilliant in the opposite direction," Topher said. He placed his hand on my shoulder to help focus my attention to the east, but my attention centered on his touch. "Those rocks will ignite in color."

My rocks will ignite if he keeps touching me. I took a deep breath and a gulp of wine. "Rhubarb," I said.

"What?"

"Rhubarb," I explained, "that's a hue of red. When I was little, Aunt Walterene would have me come up with as many names for colors as I could think of. I can't name ten NFL teams, but I can give you ten shades of red."

"A true gay man." He toasted me with his wine. "I, on the other hand, can name ten NFL teams, but not ten shades of red."

"A true lesbian," I toasted him back. "Wait, you're a painter, you should know more about color than anyone."

"I can mix the bitch, but don't ask me to name it." He propped his left hand behind me on the rock then leaned in. "That's Thunder Mountain," he said pointing with his finger extended from his wine glass. "Your house is on the other side of it. Boynton Canyon is back over there. Enchantment Resort sits at the front of the canyon, and there are trails that go back into this beautiful small canyon."

The setting sun changed the landscape to a deeper scarlet. With alternating looks to the west for the sunset and back to the east for the changing colors of the rocks, we witnessed Sedona's magic. Topher stayed close as we watched the shifting colors, his breath warm against my cheek. The backpack sat in front of him, so I leaned across his knee to dig out the bread and cheese. *Nice legs.*

"Now, as the sun sets," he said, "the shade from the mountains around Jerome will start to creep up the rocks."

Darker hues of red—claret, burgundy, and plum—painted the rock formations, and below that, the gray of evening followed the red up the ridge. Darkness threatened to come on fast.

"Perfect, wasn't it?" he asked.

"Yeah." I reached up and turned his head to face me, then leaned in and kissed him. He resisted for a moment, but I felt his body relax and his lips respond. *I love the sensation of light beard stubble, just enough friction.* My left hand held his head close, but my other hand still held that damn wine glass. I wanted to fling it across the rocks and have both hands free. Then my mind went to how dangerous the broken glass would be to the coyotes, javelina, and rabbits. Why did I let my mind wander?

He pulled back. "I smell smoke."

"Oh, yeah. Me too, baby," I cooed.

"No, seriously, I smell smoke."

In the distance to the northwest, a gray plume of smoke rose from the desert, flames flared too large and too wide for a campfire.

"Wildfire," he whispered, part wonder, part fear.

CHAPTER NINE

The twilight shadows allowed the fire to be seen easily from the ridge. I hadn't spotted any other people or cars since we'd passed the Jeep tour leaving the area.

"It's too big for a campfire," Topher said. "But, I don't see it spreading."

"You had mentioned there wasn't a lot of rain this spring," I said. "Isn't there some sort of restriction on fires?"

He dug in his pockets and pulled out his cell phone. "Damn, no reception."

"Hold on." I unzipped the backpack and found my phone. "Two bars, no wait — one bar. Anyway, give it a try." I handed Topher my phone.

He dialed 911 and waited. "I'm calling to report a fire in the Coconino National Forest." He turned to try to get better reception, "No, in Sedona, off Forest Road 152C. That's northwest of Dry Creek Road." He turned again, cocking his head as if trying to hear better. "Can't tell. Sorry? I thought that was your job." He shut the phone. "She said to call the Forest Service."

"You're kidding," I said.

"She said she didn't have the Forest Service number handy." He dialed 411. "I'm going to try to get the number—" He shook the phone as if would help with a connection. "No signal." With the fading light, the fire appeared brighter. "Let's go," Topher said and placed the wine and glasses back in the pack. "If it gets much darker we won't be able to see our way down the hill."

The deepening darkness made finding my footing difficult, plus the prickly pear cactus and spiky yucca seemed invisible in the twilight. The high-topped hiking boots had been a good decision. Once in the Jeep, our headlights led us back out of Apache Trails.

But at the forest road, Topher turned toward the fire. "We need to see exactly what that is. Could be a campfire, or maybe, a bonfire, just as long as it's attended and not out of control."

I agreed, but thought the authorities would be better equipped to investigate, and started to say that to Topher, but then it hit me that there didn't seem to be any authorities nearby. Personal responsibility. That's what Aunt Walterene had taught me. *If it needs done, don't wait around for someone else to do it.*

The fire seemed to be off the road about a quarter mile, but the darkness made placing distance difficult. It could have been farther. A lot of situations went through my mind: drunken teenagers, drug lords holding a conference, illegal aliens making fake IDs, devil worshipers in an orgy of revelations. I was beginning to question the limits of my personal responsibility when Topher parked the Jeep and found a flashlight in the toolbox in the back. I had to admit, I liked his tenacity, but it would have been more attractive during the daylight.

"Looks like the fire is just off this trail," he said. We walked along a narrow path with scurrying sounds from the brush on either side of us. "Rabbits or quail," Topher reassured me, but kept the flashlight's beam straight ahead.

"What do we do when we come upon this fire-starter?" I needed a plan.

He stopped and switched off the flashlight. "Good question. My intent is to make sure it's not a fire out of control, a wildfire. Now go slow," he instructed. "And watch each step to keep from tripping over a rock or exposed root. We can't risk the flashlight."

The light from the flames could be seen up the trail, but we weren't close enough to hear anything or anyone. It was a low glow, something that seemed to be managed. A few steps closer and the pop and snap of burning wood accompanied the scent of cedar and sage.

"Dead wood doesn't smell like that," Topher said, "and it doesn't pop since it has no moisture. That's fresh brush burning."

We moved faster. I worried that we weren't equipped to fight a wildfire—I hadn't even brought the remainder of the wine to pour on the flames. Voices, a chant rose above the crackle of the blaze.

Then, drums that made me think of King Kong Island. *As long as they don't stop, we're okay.*

Topher slowed. "Damn it."

"What?"

"Drumming Circle."

"You lost me."

"It's a type of meditation, you know. The steady pounding of the drums. Several groups will host a drumming circle to coincide with phases of the moon."

The fixed beat continued with a bongo improvising a few jazzy licks in between. Topher kept walking toward the fire and the sound of drumming.

"You sure these people aren't on drugs?" I asked. "Out in the wilderness, huddled around a fire, beating drums and chanting... This town is fucking cracked."

The increasing glow of the fire and thudding drumbeat made my palms sweat. I grabbed Topher's belt to slow him down. "I don't want to seem too girly, but do you think it's safe just to walk up to this group in the dark—unannounced?"

"We'll stay hidden," Topher said. "I need to confirm it's not out of control." The sky beyond us glowed from the flames. A voice rose above the drums, a female voice. Topher stopped to listen.

"Burn, burn! I tie you up, I bind you, I give you over to Gila, who singes, burns, and binds, who lays hold of the sorceresses...."

The voice was full and strong, echoing off canyon walls. I became aware that my breathing synced with the rhythm of the drums. My curiosity drew me closer.

"As this flesh is torn asunder and cast into the fire, and as the blaze devours it..."

Sizzling spit into the air, and I smelled the tangy odor of meat burning. The thought of searing human flesh stopped me. I reached out to feel that Topher was still by my side.

"...So too may the curse, the spell, the pain, the torment, the sickness, the sin, the misdeed, the crime, the suffering that oppress our bodies be torn asunder like this flesh! May the blaze consume them tonight."

Inch by inch, Topher moved closer, staying low to the ground. I followed, hesitating and unsure if we should go farther or just turn and run. He stopped and grabbed the front of my shirt, motioning for me to come to his side and look through the branches of an alligator juniper. A group of about fifteen men and women, all looking to be in their forties and fifties, stood naked around the bonfire. Their faces were blank, as if in a trance, as their hands beat primitive-looking drums. For some reason, the sight of a few of them wearing glasses calmed me. I mean, what kind of cannibal wears designer frames? Clarity Received, dressed in a black robe, had climbed onto a boulder to the side of the flames and tossed the last of what looked like a beef roast into the bonfire. She motioned to the group to intensify their drumming. Some sat down on towels, others began dancing, moving to the quickening rhythm.

Short, tall, fat, thin—all types swayed to the beat. Clarity, perched on the boulder, stretched toward the moon and directed the drumming with broad swings of her arms.

A ring of rocks corralled the bonfire and a stack of brush lay ready for feeding the flames. A balding man, with a firm body and swinging dick, stooped and gathered up branches then placed them with care at the four sides of the fire. The juniper needles sparked and singed, creating yellow flashes. A gray-haired woman with pendulous breasts twirled behind him as the fire flared. The ebb and flow of the drumbeats synced with the rise and fall of the flames.

"What the fuck?" was about all I could say.

Topher seemed to understand my bewilderment. He pulled me back from the juniper. "No, it's not a sex orgy."

"Why would you think I would assume that?" I asked. The smell of burning beef wafted around us. "Just because I saw a large array of vaginas, breasts, cocks, and swinging balls dancing to the rhythm of beating drums… Anyway, just like a nude beach, no one here is anyone I'd want to see nude. It seems very natural, kind of like *National Geographic*."

"Not sure what the nudity is about, but I haven't been to a lot of drumming circles." Topher leaned back against a branch and sucked on his upper lip as if in thought.

"I have to admit to participating in a few circles in my time," I said. "But we didn't use drums and there were no women allowed."

This broke him out of his thoughts, and he glanced back at the people gathered around the bonfire. "I didn't even look at the faces," he said. "There could be someone here I know."

"All that bare flesh distracted you?"

"Yeah." He crawled under the brush and watched. I snuggled up next to him. "These are probably all tourists attending one of Clarity's retreats."

"You mean all these people will have to have breakfast together in the morning?" I asked. "What kind of conversation do you make after a naked night of dancing around a campfire?"

"I don't know, what do you usually say the morning after a naked romp with strangers?"

I bumped his shoulder with mine. "I only romp with guys I know, or at least with guys I've crawled under a bush with to watch Sedona nightlife."

His eyes twitched in the low light and his grin faded. "Let's go. The fire seems to be under control."

His fire was certainly under control, and he was an expert in dampening mine. We backed out from under the juniper and headed back down the trail toward the Jeep. I didn't know what to make of Topher's silence.

"You okay?" I asked.

"Sure."

"I didn't mean to imply that I expect us to spend the night together," I said.

"I know." He stopped and turned to me. "Sorry, I just want to take it slow."

"That's fine. My flirtatious side gets the best of me."

A few steps later, I added, "He must have really put you off—this guy in Charlotte."

"Alex," he answered.

"Do you want to talk about him?"

"Not really."

I let it fall as we continued down the trail. The drumming behind us continued and faded as we arrived at the Jeep.

Topher guided the Jeep onto the road, but left the headlights off until we had some distance from the bonfire. His spirit seemed to lift once we hummed down the dirt road. The cool evening breeze swirled around us and the stars and moon bathed the desert in a silver hue. "So, what types of retreats does Ms. Clarity Received conduct beside the dick swinging one we just saw?" I asked.

A smile snuck onto his face and he cleared his throat, "Well, besides the balls-out-in-the-night-air retreat with the optional weenie-roast, she does some really serious ones. Like a breast cancer survivors retreat, a few New Age primers for people interested in that, and she also enlists local artists to hold painting and sculpture workshops."

"She's a sharer," I said, a little too flippantly.

"Actually, she is," Topher said and turned onto the paved road that led back into Sedona. "That's what was so odd about her and Aubrey. He was a taker. She's a giver."

"Sounds like a good match."

"Maybe, but sooner or later the giver gives out."

I could tell he had switched from Clarity and Aubrey to him and this Alex guy.

The headlights of the Jeep flashed across a sign for the Devil's Bridge trailhead, and the ominous name struck a chord of what Detective Sarras had mentioned. "Devil's Bridge," I read the sign out loud. "That sounds sinister."

"Yep," he answered.

"Ever taken that hike?"

The Jeep slowed a bit, and Topher glanced over at me. "What have you heard?"

The question caught me off guard. Here I was out in the dark desert with a man I hardly knew, asking him about a death that he may have had a hand in. *Was I stupid?* "Just something about Myra's husband having an accident there." Maybe that wasn't too incriminatory.

He didn't say anything.

I pushed on. "Did it happen?"

"Yeah."

Cool wind rushed past us as the Jeep continued up Dry Creek Road toward Sedona. Not sure if I should pursue it further, I leaned back in the seat and watched the stars, letting the subject wane.

He didn't say anything else until we turned at Thunder Mountain Road to go back to the rental house. "You want to grab a bite to eat?"

"Sure," I said, glad that my Devil's Bridge inquiry hadn't dampened the evening. "Let's stop by the house, and I'll drop off my backpack. Do I need to change clothes for dinner?"

"No, we're fine. Few people dress up. Maybe it's being a tourist town, but you see everything from t-shirts and shorts to sports jackets at restaurants. Besides, I thought we'd go to the brewery—there's an actual micro brewery off Coffee Pot Road that's a lot of fun, but it doesn't have much in the way of food. The brewery's restaurant is in Tlaquepaque—good food and great beer."

"Perfect," I said as he pulled into the driveway of the rental house. The lights weren't on inside. Just as I started to reach into my pocket, I remembered that I had given my key to Ruby. "Guess we'll just go on. I loaned Ruby my house key, and she's not back yet."

"Why'd you give her your key?" he asked wrinkling his brow.

"She couldn't find hers and she had dinner plans." Was he disappointed we couldn't get into the house?

He seemed to hold his breath for a few seconds, then let it out slowly. "Hot date?" he asked.

"Could be." *Yes, if he played his cards right it could be a really hot date.* Then I realized he was asking about Ruby. "Oh yeah, probably. She went to dinner with that couple she had met in Palm Springs years ago and a friend of theirs."

"Ruby's a lesbian?"

"As far as I can guess," I said. "We never discuss it."

"Cool," Topher started up the Jeep and backed out of the driveway. "I love lesbians. Honestly, I tend to have more in common with them than gay men."

"You mean like this manly Jeep?"

"Oh, yeah, I was never the little convertible kind of guy."

I reached into my backpack and pulled out my cell phone in case Ruby had called. No messages. I slipped it into my pocket so I could hear it if she did.

After a few minutes, we arrived at Tlaquepaque—a shopping area modeled after a Mexican village complete with cobblestone streets, fountains in plazas, and adobe buildings situated to create private courtyards and meandering alleys.

We settled into a booth at the restaurant and ordered some of the local brew. We had downed several each by the time our food arrived. My pesto chicken penne tasted tangy, sharpening when I bit into a piece of sun-dried tomato sprinkled throughout the dish. The brown ale I downed added to the flavor of the pasta, deepening it, making the meal a sensual experience. *Okay, I was hungry.* Hiking and fire-spotting does that to a guy. The deep, high-backed booth we sat in felt safe and sheltering while the restaurant's granite walls added to the sanctuary experience.

Topher seemed more relaxed as well and opened up a bit about his journey to Sedona with Myra. Her abusive husband and Topher's rocky affair with Alex had spurred them to break free and drive west. He didn't give many details as he nibbled on his veggie burger, but the gist seemed to be that there was very little else they could do. The death at Devil's Bridge didn't enter the conversation, since the story ended when they arrived in Sedona. I wondered if revenge had entered into Myra's husband's demise, although from what I had seen of Topher, he didn't seem the type to allow his emotions to overtake his reason.

"Wonder where they put their clothes?" I asked.

"Who?"

"The drumming circle jerks."

"I'm sure they had them close by," he said. "This town is liberal, but you don't transport a van full of naked people down the highway."

"Would you do it?"

"What? Drive naked people through town?"

"No, shed inhibitions and dance around a bonfire nude?"

He looked up from his burger. "Who says I haven't?"

"You did," I kidded him.

"You got me there." He thought for a moment, and then said, "No. I'm not that open with strangers."

No shit.

"But," he continued, "if you want to try it, I'll be glad to hold your wallet for you."

A peppy tune rattled my pocket. On reflex, I retrieved my cell phone and checked the caller ID—Daniel. *Must be working late again.* I pressed a key to stop the ringing so it would go to voicemail.

"Not Ruby?" he asked.

"No, just a friend from Charlotte."

He sipped his beer. "So, tell me about you. What secrets do you have back in Charlotte?"

Shit, if he only knew. I picked at my pasta, stabbed a piece of chicken. "Not many. Just a goofy technology guy with a crazy family." I plopped the pesto soaked chicken into my mouth and savored the aromatic spice.

"All Southern families are crazy." He lifted his glass to toast the fact. "How's Ruby's house hunt going?"

"After finding Aubrey dead in the last condo we looked at, the hunt can only get better." *Okay, the beer was getting to me too.* "The odd thing is," I said trying to settle my flippant mind, "Aubrey was laid out on the floor, arms spread and feet together. I mean, it wasn't like he had been in a struggle, just like he had been asleep and someone scalped him."

"So, he had been knocked out first?" Topher asked. "Then someone arranged his body and scalped him?"

"Yeah. I wish I watched those television crime shows to know what that meant." My cell beeped to let me know I had a voicemail, so I hit a button to quiet it again.

"Logically," Topher began, "Aubrey would have had to be out cold to be placed there. Secondly, if there was no blood anywhere else in the condo, he didn't receive a wound until *after* he was positioned. You mentioned the medicine wheel outside; did his position correspond to the compass directions?"

"Hell if I know. That bathroom wasn't big enough to accommodate too much placement." With my stomach full, my mind wanted to cap the meal off with nicotine. Also, the smoke would help counteract the beer buzz. "I'm dying for a cigarette," I said. "Can we smoke at the bar?"

"No, but hold on and I'll pay the bill, and we can walk over to the creek."

Outside, the night air felt light and fresh as I lit my cigarette and offered one to Topher. We strolled around the buildings and down one alley to another and came out to a large cobblestone plaza with a fountain. He led me to an art gallery at the creek that had copper wind sculptures twirling in the breeze. Once under the sycamores of El Prado Gallery's sculpture garden, Topher pointed out chairs and tables made of granite slabs, then walked me over to Oak Creek flowing by the gallery's building. We settled into a couple of the stone chairs and watched the silent dance of the copper sculptures in the moonlight. Steel sculptures shaped like seven-foot desert flowers with lighted blooms highlighted the garden with a soft glow. The low murmur of water cascading over rocks drifted up from the creek.

"This is nice," I said and lit another cigarette. Topher waved off my offer of a second one to him. "I can see why you love it here. Seems like the whole town embraces creativity. I don't remember seeing much art in Charlotte."

"Oh, it's there, but you have to search it out. My painting career has taken off here... Something that never would have happened back in North Carolina."

"I loved what I saw at the gallery up on the hill."

"I have quite a few more at home in my studio."

My heart raced. Okay, calm down, I told myself. "Could I see them sometime?"

"Now's as good as ever." He stood and held his hand out to help me from the rock chair.

The damn cell rang again, but this time I resisted looking to see who was trying to squelch this romantic spark.

CHAPTER TEN

My curiosity got the best of me as we walked back to Topher's Jeep, and I checked the cell's missed calls: Daniel and Ruby. "Hold on," I said to Topher.

We stopped at the fountain while I called Ruby's cell phone.

"What's up?" I asked.

"That darn key won't open the door," she said. "When they brought me home, the key wouldn't turn. I'm back at Mavis and Zandra's house."

She gave me the address of the ladies and I repeated it to Topher, and he said he knew where it was. The situation troubled me. *Could Ruby be having problems with something as simple as unlocking a door?* I tried to think if I had let her do anything since our arrival. I drove everywhere. I always unlocked the house's door. The thought that she might be too dependent on me in a new place worried me. What would happen after I left? She had no problems at the house in Charlotte, but then, she had lived there most of her life. Was a new town and home too much for her to handle alone at her age?

Topher's paintings would have to wait.

My mind kept churning Ruby's abilities as Topher drove us to the ladies' home. I knew she couldn't do the same things she had just a few years ago, but she seemed to get along fine. Was it a good idea to have her so far from the rest of the family? Yes, our family was fucked up, but it was still a family that looked after its own. I seemed to have forgotten that in the excitement to move Ruby, the development project, and Aubrey's death.

We arrived at a sprawling slump block house with an iron gate at the front courtyard. The Cadillac sat in the driveway and Topher pulled behind it. The gate creaked as I pulled it open prompting a frantic yap from a small dog inside the house. Zandra greeted us at the door holding the white toy poodle in her arms. She was a handsome woman in her early eighties with quick eyes and a friendly smile.

"Come in," she said. "The girls are in the den."

The walls were checkerboards of paintings, covering most of the available space. Topher turned around twice as he seemed to try and take in all the visuals. "Some of these paintings are yours," he said to Zandra.

"Yes, and some are from friends throughout the years." She stopped to show him something, when I heard Ruby laugh.

"Lord, you are so funny," she said as I turned the corner and spotted her fanning her cheeks and sitting close to a woman wearing jeans and a denim shirt. Of the three women, Ruby was the only one in a dress; the others wore pants and blouses. She would fit in eventually. The object of Ruby's attention, Alice, seemed to be mid-seventies and quite comfortable with her sexuality, what we'd call a "tomboy" back in North Carolina for her mannerisms and dress. Her short, curly chestnut hair had silver highlights that caught the lamp's glow. As I considered it, she reminded me of Walterene. No wonder Ruby enjoyed her company.

Zandra's partner, Mavis, carried a bottle of merlot into the room and asked if I would like a glass of wine.

I declined.

"It's always nice to have the boys over." Mavis nodded to me and Topher, then refilled Ruby's glass. "We don't get to socialize with young men like we used to." She was taller than Zandra and Ruby, but about the same age, and appeared to enjoy the job as host.

Ruby struggled to get up from the couch. My hand and Alice's both extended out to help her, but Ruby took Alice's assistance. "Now, Derek," Ruby turned to me. "That was the wrong key you gave me."

"No ma'am," I said. "That key was on my dresser."

"Your house key is on the rental car keychain." She raised an eyebrow. "I remember you opening the door with it because it rattled so with that big plastic tag clanging around. My missing key was by itself, but that ain't it."

I followed her logic and she was right that my keys for both the car and the house were together. Instinctively, I patted my front pocket and pulled out the keychain. My two keys and the rental car ID tag dangled from the short loop of chain.

The path of keys untangled in my mind as the women stared at me as if waiting for a rationalization of my mental lapse. Topher walked away to look at the painting over the fireplace. *If the single key wasn't Ruby's...* Then I knew.

"Hmm, I'll take that key and figure out what it goes to."

Ruby dug the key out of her purse and placed it in my outreached hand. I had it, and I had had it all along.

"Okay, let's go. I can let you in the house with my key," I said to Ruby. Two things kept my mind occupied: How should I use that odd key and where was the other key to our house?

I pulled Topher away from his discussion with Zandra about the painting over the mantel, and then we said our good-nights to the ladies. Ruby confirmed a lunch appointment with them for the next day. Topher helped Ruby into the passenger side of the Jeep and I climbed into the back. He asked her about their dinner and where they went, becoming quite chatty. All the while, I fingered the single key in my pants pocket as if it burned.

Had enough time passed that I could use that key without being detected?

I don't know what I thought I'd find in the condo where Aubrey was killed, but that key opened the opportunity.

Even with the rush of knowing I had access to the scene of the crime, I was bothered that Ruby's key to our house was missing. No one had access to it—except Myra and Topher. They were the only other people to have been in our house. Unless... A rental house— who knew how many keys to the place floated around town—a house that anyone could have slipped into, maybe even during the night, while we sleep...

Stop it. Maybe Ruby just left it in a pocket of her sweater.

Topher stopped in front of the house and I jumped out to help Ruby from the Jeep and to the porch. I unlocked the door and flipped on the light, then jogged back down to Topher's waiting Jeep. "I need to get Ruby settled in. I had a great time watching the sunset and the drumming circle. Dinner was wonderful." I didn't want him to forget about the private showing of his art. "Can I see your studio tomorrow night?"

"Let me give you a call," he said with a hint of non-commitment.

"Okay," I said and kissed his cheek. I didn't want to rush him, and my mind was partially occupied by the opportunity of the condo's key.

Inside the house, Ruby had gone to her room to remove her girdle and change into her housecoat and slippers. I knew her routine. She would soon emerge with a relieved look on her face. "Did you check all your pockets for your key?" I yelled into her room.

"Yes, sir." She came out dressed as I expected. "That darn key is nowhere to be found."

When we had arrived at the condo the day Aubrey was murdered, the door had been open with the key stuck in the lock. *This key in my pocket.* My intention that day was to return it to Aubrey. Then, I forgot about it. So, that was how I had it, but the second problem was still Ruby's key to the rental house, the place we slept. Who had it?

In the kitchen, Ruby uncorked a bottle of Shiraz, and poured a glass for both of us. "Hand me that bag," she said and settled at the dining room table next to my computer. "I can look again, but it wasn't there before I left for dinner."

The pocketbook rattled as I carried it over to her chair. "What's in here?"

"Just my pills, cosmetics, my billfold. Stuff a woman needs."

A Bottega Veneta patent leather billfold slapped the table as she dug through the scuffed Nine West tote she used. Amber plastic bottles of medicine followed a gold compact case, a hairbrush, and a can of White Rain hairspray.

"Damn, woman, it's a wonder you don't pull your shoulder carrying that stuff around."

"You gave me that billfold for Christmas," she said as if that was the one unnecessary item she hauled around. Three lipstick tubes, one without a cap, clinked across the table along with fluttering scraps of paper she had scribbled notes on. Loose tissues and breath mints tumbled out as she shook the bag over the dining room table. "Well, that's it," she said. "No key."

Just what I was afraid of.

I woke with a jolt, like a nightmare that startles the body into a spasm. But I didn't remember a dream. The waning moon cast its sallow light through the window's blinds. I sat up, eyes searching the dark bedroom. Confusion splotched my consciousness. Was I really awake?

One thing was sure: I had to pee. The bathroom paired with my room was small, but sufficient and full of terra cotta tile, which robbed the warmth from my bare feet. I leaned with one hand on the wall above the toilet and the other aiming in the dark. My eyes fluttered closed as sleep tried to seduce me back to the bed. The splash in the toilet pinged as my mark drifted to the side and I jerked my eyes open to redirect the stream. A high window to my right distracted me when I thought I saw a stir in the manzanita bordering the open land behind the house. The sound of my fading dribble was all I could hear. I stopped myself from flushing and slid open the window to see if any sounds came from the bushes.

Nothing.

I closed the window and decided to walk out onto the deck for a better look. My bedroom had a door directly to the back deck, so I unlocked the door and walked out to the railing that faced the manzanita thicket. The moonlight wasn't enough to get me arrested for public nudity, but it wasn't enough to allow me to see very far into the brush, either. Cool breezes ran chilly fingers across my body—I liked it.

That noise was probably just a coyote hunting in the brush, I thought, while I strained to see into the night.

I had left my cigarettes out on the table between the deck chairs, so I sat down, shook out a smoke and lit it. The lighter flared in front of my face in the dark and a scurry of leaves and branches sounded to my left.

Something was there, something that could see me when I lit the cigarette, something that didn't want to be seen. Javelinas had bad eyesight, coyotes probably wouldn't have noticed, but something or someone knew I was awake and outside. A chill ran down my back and this time it wasn't enjoyable. Two steps led from the deck to the back yard, and I took them slow. Once my bare feet touched the dirt and rocks that served as an Arizona lawn, I knew I couldn't investigate the noise without cutting my feet on the rocks or impaling myself with unseen cactus needles and yucca tips. I waited on the bottom step, listening.

After a few minutes, I heard a car start in the distance and drive away.

❊　❊　❊

Ruby served me a breakfast of scrambled eggs, cheese grits, and sausage. She had searched both grocery stores and a health food store to find a box of grits, but found only the instant type, which she self-consciously dished out onto my plate.

"Eat up, boy," she said. "It's not the best, but it'll do."

I sat there in my boxers rearranging the grits on the plate as I thought about going to the condo to look for—*what?* Having entry to the crime scene seemed to be a perk, but I wasn't sure what I could find. Aubrey had been scalped. No weapon would be there; certainly the police would have taken it if one had been left behind. But what about Topher's observation that the blood hadn't flowed until after Aubrey was laid out on the bathroom floor? I knew I wouldn't get that image out of my head anytime soon—I remembered exactly how he was positioned. Did that arrangement mean anything?

"A woman from the real estate office called," Ruby had sat down across from me and stirred sugar into her coffee. "She said she wants to show me more condos, if I'm still interested."

"Are you still interested?" I asked, since we hadn't talked about her move since Aubrey's death.

Her eyes darted to the right, then she stared at her coffee cup. "Yes," she said in a breath as if it had come from a resolution deep within. "Yes, it's time to find a place of my own."

"Do you want me to call her back and set up some showings?" I intended to help her ease back into the home search.

"Now, I can do that." She nodded at my plate. "You eat that breakfast or you'll be hungry in another hour, and once my skillet is put away, I'm not dragging it out again."

By the time my plate was empty, I had decided to go to the condo with a notebook and sketch out what I remembered and how Aubrey's pose corresponded to other things at the site. Ruby gathered the dishes from the table and I helped her rinse them and load the dishwasher.

"I'm going to check out some things for Mark's project," I told her. "He wants me to confirm the status of Apache Trails."

"What will they do now?" she asked. "Now that Aubrey is gone?"

The other vested parties, which included Myra's bank and Harris Construction, would have to decide if another developer could take it over or if the project would be scrapped. "That's what I need to help Mark decide: Should we pull out or try to keep it going?"

"A good investment," she said to the dishwater. "I think this place has a lot to offer."

I dried the skillet and slid it into a bottom cabinet. "I'm glad you're making friends here," I said and kissed her powdered cheek.

My backpack sat by the front door. I checked to make sure I had my cell phone in it and added a pair of nylon jogging shorts and my running shoes. *I have to find some time to go for a run.* With one strap slung over my shoulder, I adjusted the pack's position and called good-bye to Ruby in the kitchen. "Back soon."

The warm sun greeted me when I opened the front door, but the clink of metal hitting the concrete walkway stopped me. I searched to see what I had inadvertently kicked with my shoe.

Shining in the morning sunlight was a house key.

On reflex, I grabbed my pockets and felt the condo's lone key in my left pocket. I pulled out the key chain from my right pocket and confirmed that both the Explorer's key and our rental house key were still together.

The key I picked up from the sidewalk was warm from being in the sun. I turned and slid it into the doorknob.

The lock clicked.

When I opened the door, Ruby yelled from the kitchen, "You forget something?"

"No, just making sure the door was locked." My mind felt numb, as too many things raced through it, and I couldn't clutch any one idea for more than a moment before something else pushed in and took its place. One thing was certain: I held Ruby's missing key.

During the night, someone had left it on the front step.

The drive to the condo gave me time to sort out details, but nothing fell into place as it should. Was Hawk still a suspect in the eyes of the police? Could Kimbo Blue and the Sedona Gentry be beyond suspicion? What about the ex-wife Tricia or the girlfriend Clarity? Then there was Myra and her dealings with Apache Trails and Aubrey, which had implications for Harris Construction and was Mark's biggest concern. These thoughts still occupied my mind when I parked the Explorer near the condo complex's pool. I wasn't the type to park in front of a crime scene and walk right in.

The approach to the front door revealed little sign of what had happened just a few days before. No police tape marked off the courtyard, no armed officer patrolled the front door, and to my amazement, the window blinds had been left open to allow light in. Just as I steadied the key toward the door knob, I considered that someone might be inside, so I rang the doorbell and composed a story of looking for an address that would be just a street off from this one. No sound came from the other side of the door.

I checked over my shoulder to make sure no one observed me entering and slipped the key into the lock and opened the door.

"Damn," I said. I had some doubt that the key would still work since I thought the locks would have been changed, but no, I stepped into the condo. The last door Aubrey had ever walked through.

The odor of bleach welcomed me as I latched the door closed. The entry hall was chilly from the running air conditioner. Just as it had been on that day, no furniture occupied the great room, the kitchen counters held nothing but a guestbook that the real estate agents sign when they show the property. I checked to see who had been there—Aubrey's signature was the last one. The thought of fingerprints hit me as I closed the book. I hoped that prints had been collected the day of the murder, so mine wouldn't matter. But I wiped the cover with my shirttail just to be smart. Ruby had inspected the kitchen cabinets that day, but I thought I would scan them again just to make sure they were all empty. I pulled off my white polo shirt and wrapped it around my hand so I didn't have to rub off any more potential fingerprints. Each cabinet I checked held nothing, not even dust. Apparently the condo had been scrubbed after the police finished with it.

A quick review of the great room confirmed what I remembered, that nothing sat on the built-in bookcases or on the fireplace mantel. The beehive fireplace housed gas logs, so no ashes littered the lava rocks covering its brick bottom or the stucco hearth. Down the hall, I opened and closed the linen closet doors, then the laundry room's and verified that the second bathroom as empty. Another door in the hallway seemed to be a closet, but its door was locked. I pulled out the front door key, but it didn't fit, so I moved on. The front bedroom looked blank and the closet doors stood open exposing an empty rod and shelf.

I knew I avoided the master bedroom and bath, but I had ventured into the condo to see it again. So, I braced myself and walked in.

The bedroom's beige carpet had vacuum tracks on it. The opening to the bathroom yawned open in the shadows. I reached in and felt the wall for the light switch. The light clicked on to reveal the murder scene. The flutter of the fluorescent brought back flashes of the vision burned into my mind. Aubrey's body had been positioned longways in front of the vanity. He was fully clothed in a white dress shirt, jeans, and cowboy boots. The shirt had a splattering of blood – tiny droplets like gnats spread across the collar and shoulders. I closed my eyes to remember. Nothing was in his hands, they were both palm up and empty. His face seemed calm, as if asleep. His eyes were closed. Spots of blood clung to his bristly, blond goatee. The blond hair—wait. Sandy blond hair, thinning, I could see it in my mind around his ears, but the top...

The scalp was missing.

He had been scalped—yes I knew. But for some reason, I thought the actual scalp was there, peeled back, and maybe still attached. But, no, the skin from the head wasn't there. It had been taken.

I opened my eyes and the room seemed too small, too tight. I steadied myself by grabbing onto the sink. My head hurt, specifically, my scalp. My chest was damp from perspiration and my lungs labored to get oxygen. The strong odor of bleach lingered. The tile floor was spotless—no signs of the blood I saw in my mind. I slung my shirt on my shoulder and pulled the tablet and pen out of my back pocket. With quick sketches, I drew a simple stick figure and the relationship it had to the sink, doorway, tub, and toilet. The sunlight slanted through the bedroom's window and I guessed that it lined up with his head, due east. Then that meant, his legs were west, and each extended arm was north and south.

The four directions again: the medicine wheel.

A quick note on my sketch turned the stick figure into a compass.

The back patio's fire pit had the stones around it that I assumed formed a medicine wheel. I switched off the bathroom light and tried to scuff my footprints from the tidy carpet as I backed out of the room. With each step, I tried to erase my presence.

Down the hall and into the great room, I stopped and listened. Paranoia wrapped around me. The front door was locked, yes. No fingerprints, no footprints, I crossed the tile floor to the sliding glass door to the patio. I unlocked it with my shirt wrapped around my hand and pulled back the door slowly and carefully. I left the door open so I could hear if anyone opened the front door. The back patio was tucked away from the adjoining condos by privacy walls on each side, and the eastern side hosted a low wall and a hedge of nandina. Above the hedge, the view opened to a panoramic of Thunder Mountain and the Mogollon Rim. Good privacy, especially since a deep arroyo ran beyond the hedge, and the condos opposite were at a lower elevation. I wouldn't be seen here.

The fire pit still contained ashes in it. Flaky and fluffy, the ash had spread around the stone patio from the wind. Wedged between charred wood, dark flakes of paper crumbled when I touched them, except for one that had a bit of a fold in it. The wrinkle had been too much for the fire and it hadn't been consumed. I worked it out from between bits of wood without tearing it. When I unfolded the piece, I saw the words: Apache Trails.

CHAPTER ELEVEN

Blue lettering spelled out the name of the project on the scrap of paper. Other surviving markings looked to be survey lines of the site. I had come this far and the idea was gruesome, but I knew I needed to stick my hands into the ashes to see if the scalp had burned with the Apache Trails site survey.

I tossed my shirt over a nearby garden hose reel. Scattered ashes clung to my arms and sweating chest as I dug my hands in. The sulfur smell had faded, but still flared up when I burrowed deep. Bits of charred wood quickened my heartbeat when my fingers ran over them: unseen fragments that refused consumption by the flames. I remember hearing that with cremation, not all the body is incinerated by the fire. Even with the extreme temperature, pieces of bone and teeth remain, so I wondered if a small fire could reduce skin to ashes.

"Cinder Fella," a male voice said from behind me.

Stepping over the low wall and through the hedge, Kimbo Blue dripped a trail of water from his lemon swim trunks. His eyes stayed on me. The startling interruption had felt threatening, but he smiled as he walked toward me in his baggy trunks and Birkenstock sandals with a beach towel thrown over his shoulder.

I withdrew my arms and hands from the pit. "Kimbo," I tried to sound nonchalant. "Swimming?"

"Yeah, I own a condo across the arroyo and sometimes use the pool." His chest was well-defined with a scattering of trimmed dark hair specked with highlights of gray that fanned across his pectoral muscles, funneled down his flat stomach and circled his naval before disappearing into his swim trunks. He nodded toward the fire pit. "You lost something?"

"My innocence," was the first thing that popped in my head and when I said it, Kimbo laughed. "Uh, no, really." I searched for a cover. "Wow, you're in great shape." Which was true and I had learned when you get caught doing something you don't want to explain, just toss out a compliment.

His chest puffed out a bit and he stood straight. "I'm rebuilding the pool at my place, so I thought I'd do my laps here." He picked up my shirt and I reached for it, but instead of handing it to me, he laid it across the hedge and unrolled the garden hose. "You're covered with ash," he said and gripped the hose with both hands like a firefighter.

My hands brushed at the gray smudges on my arms and stomach, which only smeared it more.

"Take off your shoes and jeans. I'll rinse you off."

Things were getting a little too homoerotic for someone I had only met once and accused of murder. *Did he hold a grudge?* And his request seemed odd for a man who was supposedly straight. He wasn't forcing the issue of what I was doing there, so I thought why not humor him and let him see the "Masonic Rod," as a former boyfriend called it. I sat on the edge of the fire pit and pulled off my shoes and my jeans, and then placed them next to the door to the condo. With eyes on Kimbo, I dropped my boxers.

His gaze followed my shorts as they fell to the patio. I knew I had him, but wasn't sure what I needed him for.

He twisted the spigot handle and the water flowed.

I backed into a corner of the patio. He followed. I could feel his breath as he guided the water over my shoulders and chest. His right hand channeled the stream across my pecs and down the hairline trail of my stomach, but just as I was sure he was heading for the rod, he moved the garden hose around my shoulder and let it wash down my back. He didn't move around me, he just reached so that his chest was brushing against mine, his swimming trunks grazing my crotch. The cold brass nozzle of the hose raked across my spine and Kimbo's hand rubbed up to my shoulder, then back and forth down to the small of my back. His chin rested on my left shoulder and his chest hair intertwined with mine while he continued to trace his hand and the hose across my back.

I kept my arms and hands to my side, allowing him to do what he thought was necessary. His aging pixie looks still had charm, but I didn't find him sexual. I looked down to see if the Masonic Rod responded, and it hadn't—and neither had Kimbo's. The water washed over the front of his trunks and nothing stirred.

Should I have been insulted? Although, I had to admit the water was cold.

His head moved back as he focused his attention to my arms and washed each one. His right hand stroked down from my armpit, with his thumb scraping my nipple, and came to rest at my waist. The sound of his breathing reminded me of the drumming circle: slow, deep, rhythmic.

"There," he said and stepped back to check his work. "Clean as a virgin again." He winked and handed me his beach towel. "Dry off."

"Thanks," I said and wiped the beaded water from my skin while he watched. Maybe he was a voyeur, or maybe it was a power play. Either way, it ended as I pulled on my jeans and retrieved my shirt.

"Isn't this the place where Aubrey was found?" he asked and looked at the open sliding glass door to the condo.

"Yes, that was tragic." I didn't want to get into why I was there.

"I better get home and shower," he said, then added, "Call the office sometime and we'll get together for dinner."

"Yeah, maybe Tricia can join us."

He smirked. "She's busy a lot. Anyway, I could tell you a thing or two about Aubrey and his dirty dealings."

Dirty dealings seemed to soak the town, and the man in front of me dripped with his own secrets, and I bet, the secrets of a lot of people.

✖   ✖   ✖

The drive to Apache Trails seemed quick, as I replayed the Kimbo incident in my mind. But as I followed Topher's route from the night before, I discovered a slow procession over the dirt road. Blue

Jeeps transported tourists, a rental Chevy Aveo scrapped a driveshaft over the rocks but kept going, rival Jeep touring companies lined up vehicles in different color hues carrying their own *turistas*, while they all coated each other in rusty dust kicked up by tires crawling over the red rocks.

The turnoff to Apache Trails came into my view when I rounded a curve, as did the reason for the desert traffic jam. Two bulldozers and a backhoe obstructed the entrance to the site and partially blocked the Jeep road, requiring vehicles bound for the Indian ruins to squeeze between a dozer's blade and a steep, rocky dry creek bed. A woman leaned against a moss green Subaru Outback parked next to the backhoe and I recognized her right away: Myra.

Her body language displayed frustration, and I wondered if she had tried to move the construction equipment. No construction guys seemed to be around, just Myra. As I inched closer, I pulled off next to her car.

"Derek?" She seemed surprised to see me there.

"You doing some excavating?" I motioned at the dozers and backhoe, and got out to see if I could help, or at least find out what had happened.

She ran her fingers through her dark hair and looked up the hill toward Apache Trails. "I came out here to check on some things," she said. "When I pulled in I saw this mess. I called the company, but the receptionist said everyone's in Camp Verde at another site."

"How long before they get here?" I asked.

A shake of her head told me it wasn't a big priority for the construction crew, and I could understand that they didn't want to send a driver away from another project to move the equipment. "If the state police show up, I'm the one to be held responsible. Aubrey's gone. The other principles in the development are out of state, so my bank is the only one left in Sedona with skin in the game."

"Are there keys in the ignitions?" I asked and climbed up the tread to the bulldozer blocking the most traffic.

"Be careful," she said. "Do you know anything about it?"

"I've handled bigger equipment," I said and winked at her. The dozer started up with a turn of the key. "Go stop cars from pushing by and I'll get this mother out of the way."

She halted the traffic with a forceful hand, while I tried to find the lever to lift the blade so I could turn the thing around. The blade lifted up a few feet and I jerked a handle to swing to the left, and then rolled out of the Jeep road to the graded road of the development entrance, barely missing Myra's car. I never said I was good at driving a dozer.

That opened the road and loosened the traffic snarl. I jumped down and climbed into the backhoe, but there was no key that I could find. Luckily, it wasn't hampering the flow, just creating a surprise as people rounded the corner. Within a few minutes, the backup of Jeeps and cars had gone through, and the road reverted back a lonely, dusty trail.

"Thanks," Myra said. "I don't know how this happened." She looked around again. "I'm in deep shit."

"Why?"

"This," she motioned at the graded road up the hill. "It should be further along."

"With Aubrey's death, not much is going to happen."

"He lied about the status." She leaned against her car again. "That son-of-a-bitch told me that the roads here were paved and that electricity was in."

I had Mark's report in the Explorer, but I knew it must echo what Myra had found. Aubrey had deceived both Myra's bank and Harris Construction. We both must have doled out funds that were tied to phases never completed.

"This is the first time you've been here?" I found that hard to believe. Since she lived in town, what would it have taken to drive out and check on the project?

"No, but," she started with a sigh. "The bank has a construction lead, and he reported that Aubrey had made more progress than he did."

The prospect that Myra was part of a scam lessened in my mind. She hadn't authorized the transfer of funds on her own, someone else at the bank had. "So, you aren't in deep shit, this guy is."

"No, I am. It's my responsibility." She paced back and forth, kicking at rocks. "I called Conley this morning and his phone was disconnected."

"Conley works for the bank?"

"He's not part of the bank. He's an independent contractor, and now, he's AWOL."

"Not to sound negative," I said, "but why would you allow someone else to give you updates? I mean, you could have driven out here at anytime."

"Conley had been our guy for a couple of years; I thought I could trust his reports." She stopped, eyes wide. "Reports that he did for Aubrey's loans. Damn." She kicked the tread of the back hoe. "He started doing this for us when Aubrey took out his very first loan for his development company."

That fell into place. "So, they were in this together?" I asked. "One took out the developer's loan and the other verified that construction progressed to keep the funds flowing."

The pacing began again. "I have to get our attorneys to seize Aubrey's books so the money can be tracked. His line of credit was frozen when I found out about his death." She seemed to be talking herself through it. "Sorry, you don't want to hear about this. I need to get back to the bank." She turned to her car.

"Wait," I said. "How did the equipment get out here in the road? It wasn't like this last night."

"What? You were here last night?"

"Yeah, Topher and I rode out here to watch the sunset."

The loss of expression on her face told me that she wasn't happy about that. Was she trying to keep Topher as her own little gay poodle? I had seen this before when a straight woman couldn't accept that her gay best friend might have a life away from her.

"The equipment," I continued, "was parked down here, but not blocking anything. So, someone moved it into the road last night."

She started to open the door to her car, but stopped. "Do you still have Aubrey's files on your computer?"

"Yeah. Why?"

"I need to see if he had another set of books. What he gave me was fraudulent. I wrote out checks from his Bank Control Account to subcontractors for work never completed."

Harris Construction's 1.5 million was part of that Bank Control Account. "So, had you begun to fund him from his loan?"

"We had planned to close it on the day he was killed, so no, but I was really close."

I reached through the window of the Explorer and pulled out Mark's status report from the passenger seat. "So, all the money Aubrey and Conley used came from the investors and not the bank?"

"Right, the bank only funds the loan once the investor money is used." Her stare rested on the papers in my hand. "Who are you?"

The connection was made, so I knew I should own up to it. Although I had told Topher about my job, I hadn't mentioned it around Myra. I guess he didn't share everything with her. "I work for my family's business: Harris Construction."

"Fuck." Her car keys slipped out of her hands and hit the red dirt in a clang. "Honestly, I had no idea what they were doing. Loan officers have so many projects going that we can't baby-sit each one."

"I wonder why you wrote checks from the account, an account funded by my company's 1.5 million, and didn't verify the authenticity of the invoices. Were the subcontractors well known?"

"I need to go." She scooped up the keys and slid into her car. "Thanks for moving the bulldozer." With a sure grip, she backed out and steered the car onto the road leaving me wondering what liability she faced.

Before I left too, I drove up to the spot where Topher and I had sat the night before. The mid-morning sky held no clouds, just pure azure from horizon to horizon. The red rock spires and cliffs cut into the blue with sharp distinction that made the world seem precise and exact. Sedona answered a call from people searching for a place of clarity. The pure air and simple life beckoned tourists to stay, but I guessed any place would do the same when there wasn't the concern of day-to-day living. But as Aubrey found out, adding complexity to such an idyllic location could be deadly.

The more I discovered about the town and its inhabitants, the less it seemed like a desert Mayberry and the more it turned into a Peyton Place.

I sat on a rock and read through the status reports, making notes as to what was actually completed and what had been paid without physical evidence. Myra's thought that Aubrey could have another set of books prompted me to head back to the house and check the laptop's files. I walked by the bulldozers and backhoe and wondered who had moved them. Even with Aubrey gone and the project close to collapse, someone still worked to kill it.

Just as I drove into the city limits, my cell phone beeped and alerted me I had a voicemail. Topher's voice was rushed and explained that he would be working late with Kimbo to get a full page ad ready for a visitor's guide that was due the next day. So, getting together that night was out. He promised to call the next day.

A second message was from Daniel. I returned his call. "What's up?" I asked.

"Heading to interview one of the county commissioners," he said. "I wanted to make sure you and Ruby were okay."

Sweet guy, I thought.

"Oh," he continued, "you had mentioned the police found an eagle feather at the crime scene."

"Yeah, that's what they said during my questioning, but I don't remember seeing one," I said.

"A few years ago I did a story on the Eagle Feather Law. All parts of an eagle are federally protected, including his feathers. No one can possess an eagle feather unless you're a member of a federally recognized Native American tribe, and then it should be used for ceremonial purposes."

"No shit?" No wonder the police hopped on Hawk so quick.

"You said it, but just because possession is a misdemeanor doesn't mean a killer would worry about it. That's the least of his crimes."

Feather, medicine wheel, and a patio that Kimbo knew how to access. "Say, what can you find out about Kimbo Blue—not the usual child actor stuff, but personal life, business interests."

I gave him the details of Kimbo's acting career, as best as I could remember, his Blue Jeep ownership, and Sedona Gentry involvement.

"Why the curiosity?" he asked.

"Not sure. Maybe he's tied to Aubrey's death, either directly or by way of the ex-wife. I just know that Kimbo has some quirks—more so than most people. I know you don't like the gossipy stuff, so I'll research that, where can I find out who he sleeps with?"

"Ask him," Daniel said. *That's my boy. Go the direct route.*

"No," I said with more whine in my voice than I cared to hear. "I want the secret stuff, liaisons he hides, the things he buries."

"The things only a lover would know," he said in a low, rumbling voice.

My heart rate doubled. How did Daniel do that to me? Even with us in friend-mode and me getting jazzed by Topher, Daniel could say something in that bedroom voice that curled my toes. "Okay," I said. "I... I know what you're saying. Talk to the people close to him." I tried to center my thoughts. "Tricia, Aubrey's ex-wife and Kimbo's current girlfriend. I need to talk to her."

❋ ❋ ❋

When I arrived back at the rental house, Ruby said she'd set an appointment for the next day to tour more condos. The lure of Sedona pulled her closer even with the frightening death of Aubrey. She was tougher than I realized. Just as I opened my laptop to check Aubrey's files for a second set of books, the ladies from the night before stopped by to take Ruby to lunch.

"I'll see you a little later," she said and kissed me on the top of my head.

"What restaurant are you going to?" I asked.

"They want to take me to one in Oak Creek Canyon. Can I bring you something back?"

"No thanks." A file I had opened distracted me. "I'm good."

Happy greetings spilled in as she opened the door and said hello to her new friends. I heard the car doors close and the car back out of the driveway.

Aubrey had a spreadsheet listing expenses and that was his alimony to Tricia. "Fifteen hundred a month? That will put a crimp into her clothing budget now that he's gone."

Other figures listed various costs of being Aubrey. His entertainment numbers overshadowed all the other expenses. No subcategories offered any description of what went into that, but another large sum fell into his gasoline bill. "So, he drove a lot." I tapped my fingers on the dining room table as I considered it. "Trips to Nogales and the Mexican border," I said and opened my connection to the Internet. After a few minutes of searching, I found that many men took sex trips to Nogales. Bars and clubs catered to American men with cheap lap dances that allowed all the fondling the man desired, then private dances permitted the prostitute to take a man into a room for a few minutes. Would Aubrey drive five to six hours for a few nights of easy sex? The only thing that bothered me about that idea was that he seemed to be more profit-minded than sex-minded. Maybe he had a stable of girls who worked for him.

My cell phone rang and I checked the display to see that it was Mark.

I flipped the phone open. "Howdy."

"Hey, buddy. How are you and Ruby getting along?" Mark seemed to be in a good mood. We talked for a few minutes about Ruby's new friends and her wanting to look at more condos. The conversation weaved around to Apache Trails and I told Mark about the discrepancy between the status reports and the actual progress. He wanted to know why Myra had written checks from the Bank Control Account to subcontractors when no work had been completed. The tone of his voice indicated his rising stress level, and he mentioned sending out the company's attorneys.

"Now, hold on," I said. "I think there is more here than misappropriation. Give me a chance to unknot this mess because I think Myra is clean."

"Why?" he asked. "Why do you think she had nothing to do with this?"

Good question, I thought. Could my hunch on her character ease Mark's suspicions? I doubted it, but didn't want the attorneys here threatening lawsuits. This was going to be Ruby's new hometown, and the last thing she needed was to be connected to a lawsuit with a local bank. "Just give me some more time."

Grumbling signaled his reluctant agreement to hold off. Then his mood changed, "Check out my page on DiscoverDick.com."

"What?"

"I have a profile set on a site called DiscoverDick.com. It's a place to hook up."

"You *have* to be kidding me. Mark, don't you think people in Charlotte will recognize your face?" I typed the address into the browser and saw images of cartoon dicks waving back and forth. The only way to browse the different cities was to sign in.

"My face isn't pictured," he said.

I made up a name and password and clicked all the warning and legalities to get in. Then waited for it to send me an e-mail so I could browse. "But, your face is your best asset." The laptop beeped that a new e-mail had arrived which I opened and confirmed my existence. "Okay, I'm in. How do I find closeted married men? Oh, wait—the low-self-esteem link?"

"Go to North Carolina, and click on Charlotte," he said and clicked in the background as he instructed me.

"Damn." I couldn't believe the number of profiles listed with explicit pictures. None seemed to display faces. "Okay, if memory serves me, you are the one with the teenie weenie."

"Shit, you know better than that. Search for 'Hardhat Stud' and you'll find me."

The profile opened to a full, nude body shot my cousin had taken of himself in a mirror, but with his head cropped off. "You know, I recognize your office bathroom. The executive furnishings don't really play into the fantasy of a construction worker. You should have taken the picture on a job site."

"Enough critiquing my photography skills," he said. "Nice body for my mid-thirties, everything still stands at attention."

"Late-thirties," I corrected him. "Yeah, you're hot. So, how many men have you met through DiscoverDick?"

"Really? None." He sounded a little disappointed. "I've exchanged instant messages with a few, but I tend to chicken out when it comes time to meet."

His mind would never make sense to me. If he didn't intend to hook up, then why did he go to the trouble of posting pictures and messaging these guys? Was it just to prove he was still attractive to other men? "That's good because you don't need to be cruising men."

"Hell, Derek, it's just fun to flirt a little."

"Okay, at least if I get lonely, I know where to find a picture of a handsome nude man to warm me up." Yes, he needed to feel desirable.

"I have more pictures if you want me to e-mail them to you."

"You do realize that I designed the architecture of our e-mail system? Which means that I know every message sent through the system is scanned for inappropriate material and a log is sent to the administrator each Monday. So, don't send anything from work you don't want your employees to know about."

Silence filled the line.

"You didn't, did you?"

"No," he said in a slow breath. "Just trying to remember. No, I didn't, since it has my name and company as the address. I use a Web account for that."

"Smart choice. It's already lunchtime here, and I have things to discover, besides your dick."

I snapped the phone closed and tossed it into my backpack. Just as I started to shut down the browser, I wondered...

I navigated to the Arizona portion of DiscoverDick and clicked on the Sedona link. Several pages of profiles appeared. "Now, who in their right mind would post themselves on this site when the town is so small? Everybody would know even without face shots." Curiosity pushed me forward and I started opening each profile and checking the pictures and reading the guy's statistics. Most seemed to be young guys traveling through town, so I started checking the older men. I didn't expect to find Topher, but sometimes I tend not to see the obvious. He didn't want a relationship, but these were not relationship-oriented sites. Not DiscoverMinds or DiscoverFriends, but this was DiscoverDick and that said it all.

The site wouldn't allow me to sort the listings by age, so I scanned down the page and checked anyone who claimed to be in their thirties. A profile opened to a familiar torso sitting balls-out nude on one of Sedona's red rocks. Yep, it was the right build, the age was a bit lower than it should have been, and his list of preferences seemed to line up with what little I knew or assumed about him. His ID was BlueBoy and I knew that was the same man who had hosed me off just a few hours earlier. Kimbo Blue had listed himself on DiscoverDick.com.

CHAPTER TWELVE

As tempting as the prospect of sending him an anonymous note was, I refrained. Kimbo Blue dated Aubrey's ex-wife, Tricia, and he posted nude pictures of himself on a gay hook-up site. Not exactly the kind of man he portrayed as a pillar of the Sedona community and one of the leaders of the Sedona Gentry. Then again, my cousin Mark did the exact same thing in Charlotte. He was married with a child on the way, the president of Harris Construction, a member of several prominent Boards of Directors for large corporations and nonprofits. I guessed I was naïve.

Several more pages of men could hold other surprises and I hoped that Topher wasn't one of them. I wanted him to be what I thought he was, who he seemed to be: a nice guy, no secrets, no kink, no hidden agenda. But, is anyone ever that? The jaded side of me wanted to kick my ass and make me realize that people are complicated with ropes of hidden desires that tie them to a dark place concealed from their public persona. I knew that. I had played those games before.

"Come on, Topher," I said, "don't be here." Stopping at profiles where the ages seemed to be around Topher's, I opened a few more. Some actually had face shots and I tried to remember if I had seen them around town. "That's the guy from the grocery store," I said when I opened a page with a face shot. "Knew it all along."

The list ended and I hadn't seen any profiles that remotely looked like Topher. My faith in his good guy character stood firm, but I had to admit, I was a little shaken by Mark's decision to post himself on DiscoverDick.com. I thought I knew him better than that, but I had accused him before of one-night-stands on his business trips, and he never denied it. Let Kathleen worry with Mark's covert sex life. I was over it.

Although, the bizarre exposure of Kimbo Blue bothered me too, and I wasn't sure why.

The kitchen chair creaked as I rocked back onto its two hind legs and scratched my stomach. Hunger threatened to snatch my focus, so I grabbed my backpack with my cell phone in it and headed out the door in search of lunch and a couple of Cosmopolitans.

By the time I turned onto Highway 89A, I knew where to go: Plaisir de Sedona. Tricia, the self-appointed queen of Sedona, owned a French restaurant on the main strip of highway. I had seen ads and commercials, on the local tourist channel, of Tricia spewing French phrases while slinging custard and caramelizing prickly pear fruit.

The restaurant's façade yearned to be French-inspired chic, but the flat roof produced a blocky building with extravagant faux painting attempting to convey old-world limestone. Before I entered the canopied, arched, fortress-style doors, a quick rub of the wall confirmed my suspicions that the building was cinderblock. What she wasn't able to accomplish on the outside, Tricia achieved a *coup d'état* with the interior. A deep lapis lazuli blue, complete with veins of emerald green and eggplant, covered the low dividing walls separating the waiting area and bar from the main dining room. Cappuccino-colored wide-plank floors echoed the footsteps of the wait staff, while the cornflower blue walls peeked from behind sage green fabric draped from columns and above the paned windows. Stands of dried lavender topped ivory vases positioned around the entrance and French countryside oil paintings intermingled with antique, white-washed shutters along the walls. Sturdy wooden chairs encircled the rustic dining tables that hosted quite a few customers. I passed the russet plaid upholstered arm chairs grouped together in the lounge and headed straight for the bar.

"Stoli Cosmo, please," I said to the cute bartender. His starched white shirt accented his tan skin and curly blond hair crowned his handsome square face. His nametag read, Gavin.

"On vacation?" he asked.

"Not really. Some work, some sightseeing," I said as he placed a cocktail napkin in front of me. "Is Tricia in today?"

The mention of her name captured his full attention. "She should be here anytime. Are you a friend of hers?"

"Sure, I met her and Kimbo a few nights ago. Cute couple. Tragic what happened to her ex-husband."

The clanging ice cubes in the cocktail mixer caused Gavin to speak louder, "Yes, they were still friends. That's a hard thing to get over, but Tricia is doing well."

"Glad to hear it."

He poured my drink and asked, "Want to start a tab?"

"You bet." I held the glass up to him. "Cheers." Smooth and sweet, the drink felt like an old friend.

No one else sat at the bar, so Gavin hung around. "What kind of business brings you to Sedona?"

"Construction." I sipped the martini.

"Let me guess, Texas?"

"My accent?" I was a bit offended that anyone would think I was a Texan. "No, North Carolina and San Francisco."

"Wow, those are two very different places."

Was my gaydar picking up? "You don't look like you're from Arizona. California? Let me guess. LA or San Diego?"

A perfect-teeth smile answered. "LaLa Land. I had to get out for a while."

I leaned across the bar, and he leaned in too. "What's the gay life like in this town?"

He laughed. "What gay life? We're assimilated into everything. People here don't really care one way or another."

"So, where do you meet eligible men?"

"I don't really know. My partner and I have been here for over a year, so I'm not in tune with the dating scene."

He must have thought I was trying to hook up with him. "I was just thinking that Kimbo was really handsome, for an older guy. Do you know if he swings both ways?"

"That," he said, picking up a glass to polish it, "is something you have to ask him."

"Not that I would assume anything, but he was such a cute child actor and he's still hot."

"Can I get you a lunch menu?"

"Sure." I thought, as Gavin walked to the other end of the bar, that I had become too pushy on the subject.

He returned with a leather bound menu. "If you're interested, there's a group of guys that get together for drinks once a week. Just a nice social thing. I know they would welcome you to."

"Thanks, man." I perused the menu while Gavin busied himself with bar tasks. "Hey," I called to him. "Can I smoke in here?"

"Just outside," he said. "There's an ash can to the right of the door."

"Let me order the calamari and another Cosmo. I'll be right back." I headed for the door, and the bright sunlight blinded me for a second, before I found the smoking area. I stood with a cigarette and looked around. I hated smoking in the parking lot like some transient nicotine fiend. Voices drifted in from the rear of the building, so I roamed back to see what was going on.

At the kitchen door, two Mexican guys in aprons swapped a joke as one headed back into the restaurant. The remaining guy seemed young. His large brown eyes twinkled as he puffed a cigarette, and his raven black hair shined in the midday sun. I tossed my cigarette in the parking lot and pulled out another, while walking up to him.

"Got a light?"

He smiled and pulled out a lighter and flicked up a flame for me.

"Thanks," I said and exhaled smoke. "How's the food here?"

"Aw, the best in town, *Señor*."

What a cutie he was. He looked like a miniature Ricky Martin since he couldn't have been much over five feet tall. Tricia certainly hired handsome employees. "Sedona's a beautiful place. Does your family live here?"

"No, they are in Mexico." He didn't elaborate, but just squinted into the sun. I wondered if he thought I was Immigration.

"I'm here working too. My family is in North Carolina." I tried to keep my words basic since I didn't know how much English he understood, although he seemed to grasp everything I said. "How long have you lived here?"

He finished his cigarette. "Three years." He ground it out in a bucket of sand by the kitchen door.

"Do you know anyone working in construction?" I asked.

"*Sí*, lots of us Mexicans do. Too hot for me."

"Apache Trails. Out the Jeep road. You ever heard of that one?"

"Bad blood there. Men say it will never be complete. Some won't go there to work. Glad *Señorita* Tricia picked me to work here. She liked my," he struggled for the word, "assets." He nodded to me as he headed in the kitchen door. "Come in and have a meal. You will like it."

Yeah, I liked his little assets too. I thanked him, dropped my cigarette into the bucket, and walked around the building and into the restaurant. Gavin set another Cosmo at my barstool and placed a plate of calamari in front of me.

"I'm here on a construction project," I said to Gavin before he walked away again. "Where could I find some day laborers?"

"Just down the road." He nodded to the west. "A mobile home park houses a lot of Mexican workers. They gather by the road each morning looking for work."

"What kind of work can they do?"

"Just about anything: carpentry, landscaping, masonry, roofing, busing tables— whatever needs to be done."

The wrench of a high-pitched laugh caused me to turn toward the dining area. Tricia, dressed in a short black dress, greeted guests of her restaurant. The queen had arrived. I focused on my lunch and martini, just waiting for her to make her rounds to the bar customers, of which I was the only one.

Dust had settled on the tops of my shoes, so I rubbed them against my jeans to clean them up a bit. A swish of martini helped freshen my cigarette breath, and I was ready for her majesty's greeting. The click of her high heels heralded her approach.

"Oh," she cooed before I turned around, "calamari. One of my favorites." Her hand lingered on my shoulder, the same shoulder that just a few hours before, her boyfriend had rested his chin on as he hosed ash off my naked body.

I turned to her and smiled.

Her voice cooled. "Mr. Mason. I didn't recognize you from

behind. So nice of you to stop by my restaurant."

"I heard it's the best in town." I pulled out the barstool next to me. "Do you have time to join me?"

She rubbed her bare arms and searched around the bar for something, probably a way to leave gracefully. But apparently not finding one, she slid onto the stool and crossed her legs away from me. "I can't linger long," she said. "I just arrived and need to attend to a few things in the office."

"First off, Tricia, you can call me Derek. Secondly, I wanted to apologize for offending you and Kimbo at Aubrey's wake. I realize you were in a horrible state, and I was too. Ever since I walked into that condo and found him, I just haven't been as cordial as my mama raised me." I thought I'd play up the Southern gentleman role, since she didn't know me. "Of course, a martini helps take the edge off." I raised the glass to her.

"Gavin," she called, "please bring Derek another martini." She turned and her coffee-brown eyes, a bit dilated, scanned me as if assessing my sincerity. "I still can't fathom he's gone," she said.

"He'll be missed." I sipped the martini. "Did you ever meet a Mr. Conley, his business associate?"

She only rubbed her arms and looked over her shoulder as if she had something better to do.

"A Mr. Conley?" I asked again.

"Who?" Her attention came back to me.

"There was a Mr. Conley who worked with Aubrey on some development projects. Did you know him?"

"Never heard of the man." She blinked more than a normal person, and I wondered if she had been to the optometrist since her pupils crowded her irises into just a rim of brown, making her eyes seem deep and dark. She caught me staring into her eyes. "Please accept your lunch and drinks on me, Derek. I'm glad we straightened up the confusion from the other night." And with that, she slid off the barstool and headed into the kitchen.

Gavin set down the other martini Tricia had ordered for me. I had to admit, I was starting to like the woman.

A little more than lightheaded, I dug in my pockets for the car keys. To the west, a pewter plume of smoke rose into the clear blue sky and sirens howled in the distance. The smoke looked like it came from the other side of the high school property, just outside the city limits. A road called Lower Red Rock Loop gave access to several Jeep trails and old ranches where movies had been filmed in the height of the Western genre. Just like Apache Trails, new housing developments sprouted from old ranches and abandoned Hollywood sets.

"Just like Apache Trails..." I said as I started the engine. Since Ruby had gone to lunch with her girlfriends, I had some time on my hands and decided to see what the commotion was about. The newspaper had listed several fires at new construction sites, and my hunch was that this was another one. No fire trucks passed me on the highway to the turnoff for the Loop Road. But after a couple of miles, I saw plenty of them and several police cars. The police had blocked a road going into a gated development. Smoke bellowed from beyond a hill to the south. Only a scattering of houses were visible from the road, but I could tell by the red dirt tracks leading in and out of the blocked road, that a lot of construction progressed inside.

Several people had gathered by the entrance, probably neighbors, tourists, and even one Blue Jeep tour had stopped. I parked the Explorer and walked over to the group.

"Arson," one woman whispered to another.

"I don't feel safe leaving the house anymore," her friend said back to her.

An older man with wispy gray hair lifting and dropping with the breeze nodded to me as I stood beside him.

"House fire?" I asked.

"Yep," he said. "One of the new houses being built went up in flames." He shook his head back and forth. "Just like a bunch others. These damn environmentalists don't see nothing wrong with destroying a man's property to save scrub brush and coyote trails."

"You think it was arson?"

"Hell, yes." His face contorted in disgust. "The police need to get off their asses and find this son-of-a-bitch. He's burning new houses left and right."

The Blue Jeep's engine started up, and I turned in time to see Hawk driving off with a load of tourists.

So did Detective Sarras, who walked up to the small crowd of gawkers. His badge clipped to his shirt pocket added authority to his strut. He watched Hawk drive away, then turned his focus on me. "Mr. Mason," he said with a nod. "What brings you out here?"

"Smoke."

The wispy-haired old man wandered away from us.

"You like following fire trucks?" he asked.

"Depends on how handsome the firemen are."

He smirked. "Fire is a dangerous weapon in the desert."

"Yes, sir. I hear this isn't the first fire at a construction site. Who do you think did this?"

"You know I can't answer that," he said. "But let me ask you— who you think is doing it?"

"I'd say someone with a grudge against developers. Of course, this isn't as bad as killing one."

"These arson cases aren't related to Garner's death." He seemed sure of himself with that statement.

"Aubrey Garner planned to develop a large parcel of wilderness, and then he's murdered. You have a city with new construction going up in flames. As a matter of fact," I said as it occurred to me, "the morning Aubrey died, I remember seeing smoke rising out in the desert—another fire. I would call that a major grudge on development." I considered his certainty about Aubrey. "You think his murder was over something besides his business practices?"

"Not saying that." He adjusted his *Sedona Police Investigations* cap to keep the sun from his eyes. He turned to address the crowd. "I need all of you to clear the area so the fire department and sheriff's office can control this fire."

"They can't control shit," a voice within the crowd yelled. I knew it was my wispy-haired little old man heckling Sarras, but he didn't show his face.

Sarras took a more authoritative tone. "Let's go. Move on out of here."

"This is outside the city limits," I said. "Why is the Sedona Police Department here?"

"That means you too. Move on." He extended an arm as if to direct me to my car.

"My company has an interest in what's happening here," I said. "Our money is gone and there's nothing to show for it."

His eyes cut back to me. "Is that a motive?"

"For murder?" I knew he couldn't be serious. "No, it's just a pissed off construction company that lost money from some crooked developer in a pretentious, petty Peyton Place." I should have chosen my terms better because I ended up spitting the last words. The Cosmos hadn't helped my pronunciation.

"Get going," he said. "And be careful driving back." He patted me on the shoulder, turned and walked away.

I wanted to clear my head, and aside from the last smoldering smoke of the dowsed construction site, the sky stretched wide and deep blue with a scattering of stark white cumulus clouds floating over the Mogollon Rim. A left onto Dry Creek Road led me back toward Apache Trails, but I pulled off at the Jeep road going to the Devil's Bridge trailhead. The Explorer bounced a bit as I traveled up the dirt road, but it took the route well without engaging four-wheel-drive. The trailhead emerged on the right, and I pulled in next to a couple of other SUVs, a Jeep, and a Honda Civic. I decided to take my cell phone from my backpack and carry it with me. The backpack also contained a pair of shorts and sneakers. The shoes I had on would never make the hike, so I changed clothes and shoes in the car and stuck the cell phone in the pocket of my shorts.

The trail followed an abandoned Jeep road that had large boulders and downed tree trunks stopping any Jeep from driving on it, but the hiking was easy. The trail eventually started to climb up a canyon wall. A young man and woman passed me on their way back down and I asked them how far the bridge was.

"Just about ten more minutes," he said.

"There's a nice overlook around the next turn," the woman said. "You can see to the west. It's beautiful except for some asshole that is grading the land for a housing development."

"The bastard," I said. "Thanks, I'll stop and take a look."

Stands of sage sweetened the air and bees swarmed the creamy flowers of a sugar bush. The contrast of the pale greens of those plants with the rusty dirt stole my attention, until I happened to see a pile of rocks marking the trail's bend and the overlook to my right. More hikers congregated near the edge of the cliff taking in the view. The group of four seemed to be two older couples. The men drank water, while the ladies snapped pictures.

I nodded to them but kept walking. Something about the sweeping vistas of Sedona begged to be observed in solitude. A steep climb revealed itself in the form of red rock steps into a tight crevice and I couldn't see where the path reemerged. To my left, and I had to look twice, I saw the natural bridge. Part of the cliff had sheared off and left a sandstone arch. Since this wasn't the end of the trail, I decided to go forward and see if I could get a better view. The natural rock steps led into a gap between rocks and up about twenty feet. The climb wasn't difficult and I had lost my buzz after I started the hike, so I had no trouble getting to the top. The trail twisted around and soon revealed the bridge as an outcropping that hugged a precipitous opening to the canyon floor. The bridge itself looked to be about five feet wide and arched over to a sandstone spire, close to, but not reconnecting to the cliff. It was a bridge to nowhere, not that I wanted to walk across it.

A glint of silver flashed in the sunlight. A hiker sat at the far end of the bridge and the sun had caught his watch. I knew before I approached that it was Topher.

CHAPTER THIRTEEN

He saw me as I approached, fidgeting on the low rock ledge he sat on as if he had been caught somewhere he shouldn't be. No other hikers explored the bridge at the moment, so it was just the two of us.

"I didn't expect to see you here," I said.

He looked up at me with his hand shielding the sun from his eyes. "Me either."

I didn't want to intrude because I felt he wanted to be alone, but Sarras's original questions about Topher and Myra and her late-husband still lingered. Hundreds of hiking trails crisscrossed Sedona with plenty of places to find solitude, so why had he come here? "I saw Myra today."

The edge of Devil's Bridge stole his attention, and I glanced in the direction too, but saw only a rock ledge that dropped off to the canyon floor. I wondered what he saw.

"I'm sorry," I said. "You must want to be alone."

"No, that's okay. I was just getting ready to leave." He stood and stretched as if he had been there for awhile.

"Did you and Kimbo finish the ad that's due today?"

He sighed with the air escaping in a tense breath. "Kimbo came in for a short time this morning, then had a few appointments. I gave him a draft, but I can't do anything until he comes back to the office later this afternoon. Seems like it's going to be another late night to meet the deadline."

The thought of Topher having to restructure his day around Kimbo's swim and other personal activities didn't sit well with me, especially since I knew exactly what Kimbo had been doing that morning. "He's a closet case isn't he?"

"Gay?" he asked as if it had never entered his mind.

"Duh, yes."

"I don't think so."

"Okay," I said. "Then he's bisexual. I mean if he and Tricia are having sex."

"It's really none of my business, his sexual life." Topher took the high road. But I still found other people's hidden sexual secrets extremely interesting. Maybe it was that they didn't talk about them or that they tried to hide it from the world. Just the fundamental act of sex fascinated me because it was so basic, animalistic, and if it was done well, the most controlled people would let themselves go in unimaginable ways. Topher tried to control his life with all the avoidance of relationships, his protection of Myra, his devotion to Kimbo, and especially his reluctance to discuss what happened at the place where we stood.

"Yeah. Big, fucking deal who anyone sleeps with." I played up being bored with the subject myself. "What brought you up here today?"

"I wanted to get outside and think. You know, get out of the office, let some ideas flow."

Don't try to convince me, I thought. I knew he had come here because of the accident involving Myra's husband.

"So this is the place?"

"To think?" he asked.

I didn't answer him because we both knew that wasn't what I was getting at. The silence stretched out until he turned and walked toward the arch.

"Have you been here before?" he asked.

"No."

"This natural bridge is popular with hikers." He stepped over some rocks and stood at the one end of the outcropping that was attached to the cliff. "They like to have their pictures taken while they stand on it." Without looking down he paced out to the middle where the arch seemed the thinnest. "You see," he said, raising his voice so I could hear him across the large chasm that I tried not to glance down into, "the bridge is not scary once you are on it, but from where you are, it looks dangerous and the pictures they take make the hiker look like an adventurer. It's all in the perspective."

"What's your viewpoint of this place?" I asked.

The wind lashed around him fluttering his shirt. "It's an end… And a beginning. The Alpha and Omega." His thoughts seemed to take him away then he looked back into my eyes. "Did you know that I was a good Episcopalian? Back in Charlotte, I went to Saint Peter's every Sunday. It was there that I made the decision to leave the city. I say I made that decision, I believe it was made for me." The breeze swirled around him then gusted into a howl. "One thing we Episcopalians believe is that Evil is real. I saw pure Evil on this spot."

He was lost in his thoughts, although he stared at me as he talked, I didn't think it was me he addressed.

"All I wanted to do was save her. He would have killed her. He would have killed me."

The only thing I could do was nod. The memory had taken him, and I worried about his state of mind, especially since he stood alone on that treacherous span of sandstone suspended over the canyon.

My palms began to sweat because I knew I had to walk out there to bring him back to safety.

Slow, measured, sure steps took me around the gap between the cliff and the bridge while I focused on the solid ground under my feet and not the drop-offs on either side. Faced with the bridge and Topher in front of me, my courage increased, since I could see that the arch wasn't nearly as narrow as it looked from the end of the trail.

He hadn't moved except to turn and peer off the side to the canyon floor.

My hands reached out and touched his arm, and then I pulled him to me in an embrace. "You did what you had to," I whispered into his ear.

His weight leaned on me and his arms hugged my shoulders.

"Let's go back," I said.

We didn't say anything until we had traveled about ten minutes down the trail and he stopped at the overlook that had a view of the Apache Trails site.

"Sorry about that," he said. "I'm just stressed from work and other stuff." We sat down on a red rock ledge facing the vista. He picked up a manzanita twig and snapped it while staring into the horizon where the sun had fallen lower in the sky, our faces in its warm grip.

My hand rubbed his shoulders as we sat there. He leaned back, stuck out his chin and stretched his neck. Then to my surprise, he turned and tilted his face toward me and brushed his lips against mine, hesitating for an instant, then over again just grazing my mouth, but sending shivers through my body. The softness of his hair stroked my cheek as he bowed his head as if he couldn't look into my eyes after surrendering to such a bare display of tenderness. He lifted his face to me and fixed his eyes on mine, his passion raw enough that it seemed to overcome any tentativeness and, with a bit more pressure, his lips caressed mine. His breath intermingled with my breathing and the soft, slow kisses that we exchanged. The stubble of his afternoon beard raked my lip and I pressed into it for more friction. Hands caressed backs. Tongues explored, unsure at first, then with more daring.

The crunch and scatter of small rocks from the trail caught my ear and I pulled away from Topher just as a group of four older ladies huffed, gasped, and panted up the section of steep trail leading to the overlook. The shorts I had put on from my backpack were loose running shorts which could not and would not constrain the steel-rod erection I had, and the women headed straight for us.

Topher stood and adjusted his khakis and made sure his un-tucked shirt covered his own crotch. Then he looked at me and blushed the color of the rusty rocks. "Put that away," he whispered.

The short ledge I sat on didn't give me a lot of options for crossing my legs, so I just pulled my knees in as close as possible to conceal my excitement. The women greeted us as they walked past and scoured the horizon for photo opportunities.

I kept one hand over my crotch, stood, and followed Topher down the trail. Time helped deflate the situation, but it also lowered the intimacy level we had reached, since Topher didn't mention the kissing. We had kissed before, but I remember initiating it and he had just seemed to not resist. This time he ventured into an intimate moment. He had been vulnerable and exposed. I didn't push him. Topher had decided. As we hiked back down, I wondered if I made too big a deal of it. He wasn't saying much of anything.

"That was nice," I said.

He walked on without glancing over at me.

"The kissing, I mean. It felt connected, sensual." I searched for the words. "More emotional than sexual. Do you know what I mean?"

"Yeah, thanks." He stopped and took my hand. "Sometimes I feel isolated here. I have some great friends, but everyone is so concerned with themselves. Sales-oriented artists, grandiose gallery owners, flamboyant performance poets, retiree ranchers, Jeep cowboys, big-dealing real estate agents—every fucking body as an angle to get attention. And, honestly, I just don't have the energy for most of the shit that happens here. Everybody's a star and there's no audience for them, so they end up performing for each other."

"Sounds like life in a circus."

"Exactly." He squeezed my hand. "That's it. We're Big-Top Sedona. You have to turn it on and spin gold out of shit." He released my hand and walked on. "What happened to: Go to work, come home and relax?"

The stress had grabbed him again. "So, in this state of mind, you're heading back to the office?" I asked.

"Yep, Kimbo should be back soon, and I have to get this ad finished. He's a good guy, but the Hollywood side of him still lingers. I think that's one of the reasons Tricia left Aubrey for him: glamour."

"Wait a minute. Kimbo started a relationship with Tricia while she was still married to Aubrey?"

He shrugged. "From what I heard, Tricia and Aubrey didn't have much of a marriage. Again, it was two stars together, each trying to burn brighter than the other. Tricia wanted to bump up her fame and Kimbo has connections to Hollywood."

"Still? I mean he was a child actor from thirty or forty years ago."

"Sure. He still has contact with industry people, and when they come to visit, he will wine and dine them."

"At Tricia's restaurant?"

"You got it."

That must cause Tricia to wet herself, I thought. But I didn't see a connection to Aubrey's murder. Could he have been causing problems for her and the restaurant? I doubted it since he seemed to have moved on with his life and was dating Clarity.

We arrived back at the trailhead where the cars were parked. I wanted to suggest I bring dinner over to his place, but I knew that would just add more stress to finishing his work. "If you need anything that I can help with, say the word."

"Thanks, but I'm heading back to the office. I have a star to cater to."

❈   ❈   ❈

Aunt Ruby washed the dinner dishes and I dried. She told me about her lunch with the girls and their trip up into Oak Creek Canyon. "Oh, the road twists and turns up to the top," she said and passed a pan to me with her soapy hands. "Then, there's a place to park and look out over the entire canyon. The Indians have tables set up to sell their wares. I bought these earrings from a nice old Hopi woman." She shook her head to jiggle them.

I examined the turquoise and silver earrings in the shape of a humpbacked flute player that seemed to be dancing. "Nice," I said.

"She called it a Koko-pelli," Ruby sounded it out.

"Did she tell you the Kokopelli is a fertility symbol?"

"Lord, no." She reached up to her right ear lobe. "She said it was a symbol of joy."

"Sexual joy," I said. "Topher had said the Kokopelli has been toned down from what the original rock drawings had: A little stoop-shouldered flute player with a large phallus. Now, he's just a good-natured guy that brings joy. Can you feel his sexual energy when you wear those?" I extended my arms and wobbled toward her as if being drawn by an invisible force. "Just this close and I'm getting all tingly in my drawers."

"Stop that," she said and slapped me in the stomach with her wet sponge.

"What else did they have to sell?" I wiped at the wet place on my shirt with the dish towel.

She set the sponge into the dish water so she could talk with both hands. "Vases, lots of jewelry, some baskets, arrowheads, things to hang on the wall like dream catchers, some paintings and photographs, nice blankets. Zandra said that most of the stuff is handmade and she would rather pay the Indians directly for it than some store."

The retail concept escaped Ruby, so I didn't mention that a store helped ensure things were original and of good quality. She was pleased with her purchase, so I was too.

"Aubrey had said he had some Indian artifacts that would go well in my new place," she said and turned her attention back to the remaining dishes. "Guess I won't ever get to see them."

I knew she didn't understand real crafts and tribal artifacts versus mass produced souvenirs, and I didn't know that much either, but I did know that Aubrey would not be in possession of an artifact. Those tended to be sacred to the tribes and not on the market. "Aubrey was trying to sell you something made in China." I thought about his Nogales trips. "Or in Mexico."

"No, no," she said. "He said he had a valuable piece from the Yavapai-Apache and wanted me to see it."

That bothered me. Yes, I thought that Aubrey was trying to sell something to Ruby because he knew she had money, but the possibility that he had a tribal artifact didn't seem legitimate. "Did he ever show you this piece?"

"No. He never got a chance. But he had a picture of it." She rinsed the last bowl and passed it to me. "That new real estate woman wants to show me some places in the morning. Can you be ready by nine?"

Nine o'clock came early and we arrived at the same building where Aubrey's office was. The receptionist pointed us down a corridor past Aubrey's door to the office of Doris Weintraub. The lights were unlit in Aubrey's office, but the door was wide open, and I glanced in. His computer glowed in the dark with a rolling text screen saver that marched "Aubrey Garner Watches Out for You" across his monitor.

Three doors down, Doris greeted us as we entered her office. An attractive woman in her late-fifties who seemed to be aging appropriately, her face had the lines of a happy woman who smiled, laughed, ate, and drank with gusto, and her graying hair still held onto streaks of black. She hugged us both. "I'm so sorry about you going through all this with Aubrey's death. That's usually not how we work around here. I'll do my best to stay upright until we find you a condo." She didn't crack a smile, but her eyes twinkled as she studied us as if to make sure we knew she was joking.

"Good," I said and pulled out a chair for Ruby to sit. "Let's all go into the condos together."

"You got it," Doris said. "Now from what you told me on the phone, Ms. Harris—"

"Call me Ruby," she corrected Doris.

"Thanks, Ruby. I have several places to show you."

While they continued to talk, my attention waned, and I examined things on the desk and walls. Doris had a family photo showing a husband and a grown daughter at the seashore. Some southwest landscape prints hung on the wall, but what interested me the most was a photograph of Doris, Kimbo, and Topher standing in front of the Blue Jeep building. This framed picture hung on the wall to Ruby's left, so I could stare at it and appear to be looking at Ruby. Maybe it was a grand opening photo. I couldn't tell for sure. It looked like Doris was handing a certificate to Kimbo.

Several sheets of listings spread across the desk in front of Ruby, and she pushed one toward me. "What about that one?" she asked.

Still distracted, I picked it up and tried to focus on it. "Where did you say this one is?" I asked Doris.

"Uptown." She stood and grabbed a map from her filing cabinet and spread it out in front of us and marked the location.

"I was hoping to get Ruby in a place closer to the grocery stores and medical center," I said. "The condo Aubrey was going to show us had a good location, and it was one story. Are there any more in that complex?"

"Hold on." She typed at her computer. "Three others are on the market right now. One is under contract and the other two are larger, three bedrooms."

"Would you mind living there?" I asked Ruby.

She shrugged. "I liked what I saw. I don't want to buy that one, but another one would be okay."

The printer cranked up and two pages printed. Doris phoned someone and checked on the availability of showing the condos. While she talked, I got up and took a closer look at the photograph.

"We can view those any time. They're both unoccupied and we have the keys here," she said.

"How does that work?" I asked. "Does the owner leave all their keys with you?"

"No, just one or two."

"So, if we wanted to see that condo that Aubrey was going to show us, you'd have the key?"

"I'm not sure…" Ruby said.

"That's okay," I reassured Ruby. "I just wanted to see it again to compare the size with the others we'll look at."

Doris picked up the phone again, and after a few seconds of conversation, turned back to me and said, "It seems we don't have keys. We gave the one we had to the police."

"So, Hawk doesn't have an extra one?"

"Excuse me?" Doris seemed stunned.

"Yes, Hawk, who works for Kimbo Blue," I said, pointing at the photograph, "owns that condo. It's in the county records. Odd, that he camps out in the national forest, but owns an expensive condo in town."

CHAPTER FOURTEEN

Doris Weintraub leaned back in her chair and regarded me as if I were her adversary. "I really don't know that much about the owner."

"But doesn't this agency represent Hawk in the sale of the place?" I asked. "Your sign is in front of it."

"Yes, we do."

"Do you think you could get a key from him? I'd really like to see it again." Someone wanted that key from me and they took the wrong one from our rental house. Only Topher and Myra had been inside. Had Hawk broken in while we were gone? Why didn't he have a key to his own place? How did he get Ruby's key instead of the condo's? Or did Myra nab it while she was there the night of the wake? Or did other people have access to the rental house?

The phone was in Doris's hand again. A commission motivates most people into action. She called Blue Jeep's office. "Hi, Barbara, this is Doris Weintraub. Is Hawk around today?"

She waited a few seconds before continuing with a few pleasantries, apparently with Hawk, and asking him for a key. "Really? That's right. Okay, then. We can wait for the police to return it. Thanks." She set the phone back in its cradle.

"Well?" I asked and sat beside Ruby.

"He doesn't have another key. The condo is a crime scene. The police took his key. Says he gave us the other two keys he had." Her mind seemed to wander but recovered to her agent tactic. "As soon as the police release the key, I'll let you know and we can take a look at the property."

Three keys: the police had two, and I had the other. Mine came from Aubrey who had left it in the condo's lock that day. Apparently, that was all there were and someone wanted my key bad enough to attempt to steal it, but they took the wrong one. My mind ran over what I had seen in the condo, or for that matter, what I hadn't seen. What was inside that justified stealing a key to get in? Hell, the place was empty and cleaned. I stuck my hand in my pocket and stroked the precious key. If the killer wanted in, then why didn't he just break through a window? A burglary wasn't much after you'd committed murder. The image of a courtroom sprang to mind: "You know if you just hadn't smashed in the window," the judge would say, "I could ignore the murder. But, damn it, man, that was an Andersen window. Those things are expensive to replace."

"Shall we ride over and view these properties?" Doris asked Ruby.

"Yes," Ruby said, nudging my knee.

"Yes, I'd love to look around the complex again," I said and helped Ruby up from her chair.

I excused myself as Doris walked Ruby through a condo a block from the one I wanted to see again. "I think I'll check out the pool."

"Now, don't go far," Ruby said. "I want your opinion on these."

When I turned the corner, I saw a van parked in front of Hawk's condo, a nondescript van—white, no markings on the side of the vehicle. The front door stood open. The gate to the courtyard swung back and forth in the breeze since the van's driver hadn't bothered to latch it back. I walked through and up to the door. "Hello?" I called in my most casual voice.

"Yeah?" a husky male voice answered as if annoyed by the intrusion.

"Are you the owner?" I asked and walked inside.

A lumbering, bearded man in jeans and a t-shirt emerged from the hallway. "No, I'm with a maintenance company. What do you need?" He rubbed his graying beard.

"We're looking at some places for sale, and I thought this one was."

"Don't know." He didn't offer anything more.

"Do you mind if I look around?"

"Suit yourself, but I can't tell you anything about the place." He yelled back down the hall, "Miguel, got that window unboxed?"

"Window?" I asked, but knew already.

"Smashed window in the bedroom," he said. "Who the fuck breaks into an empty house?"

Down the hallway behind him, I saw splintered molding around a closet door. "They do that too?"

"Yeah, the only locked closet in the place and the punks bust it out of the framing. Idiots could have taken the hinge pins out and lifted the door off."

"When did this happen?" I had just been there 24 hours earlier.

"Don't know. I got the call this morning. It must have been teenagers. Ain't hardly any crime around here, well, except..." he trailed off.

"Is this the place that real estate agent was killed?" I asked.

"Yeah," he said. "The guy was scalped. Not too nice, was it?"

Hearing the words echo in the empty place sent chills through my body. "Who would do that?"

"Million dollar question," he said and turned back toward the bedroom. "Miguel? You jackin' off in there?"

A low laugh came from the bedroom. "*Si,*" Miguel answered, "I spank it." He appeared around the corner smiling, an older, short, pudgy Mexican man with a large mustache and mocha skin. His eyes widened when he saw me as if he was embarrassed for joking around. He nodded in my direction, and said, "*Buenos días.*"

"Hi," I said and held out my hand to shake. "I'm Derek."

"Miguel," he answered.

"Oh, and I'm Russ," said the bearded man. "This guy's looking at places to buy." He told Miguel.

The thought of the cute Mexican from Tricia's restaurant came to mind. He had said something about Tricia liked his "assets," and I wondered exactly what he meant. "Do you know the restaurant Plaisir de Sedona? The French place on Highway 89A? I heard it's a good place to eat."

"Can't afford that," Russ said.

I looked to Miguel.

"No, I cannot afford it," he said.

"I met the owner," I said. "A woman named Tricia. She seems nice."

Miguel's mustache twitched into a half smile. "*Si*, she is *mucho* friendly to the boys."

"You mean she likes those little brown weenies, huh?" Russ sniped.

"She like sniffing off tight bellies, little belly buttons," Miguel said and reached over and poked my stomach. "Mine too fat." He prodded his own gut.

That, I needed to think about. "Sniffing?" I asked.

He inhaled long and hard sweeping his head from left to right.

"Meth," Russ said. "He's saying the bitch likes to snort Meth out of young Mexican boys' navels. Probably before she goes down on them. Right, Miguel?" He elbowed Miguel in a teasing manner.

"Maybe I shouldn't eat there," I said. "No telling what ends up in the food."

"Just don't order a cream sauce," Russ said with a laugh.

The guys went back to installing the replacement window, and I told them I'd just look around at the layout of the place. They didn't seem to care what I did, so I went out to the back patio where Kimbo had hosed the ash off me. To my surprise, or maybe I shouldn't have been surprised, the fire pit sprawled open and clean. All the ash and debris had been removed along with the stones placed around the tiled edge. With that emptied and the closet busted open, any clues to the murder had been eliminated. But, had it been the police or the murderer who cleared the place? From the work the guys did, I had to guess the murderer had returned.

A car door slammed in front of the condo and I peeked through the patio doors to the front entrance and saw Detective Sarras pushing through the open door while tapping the screen of his tablet PC. I couldn't go back past him, so I pushed my way through the patio's hedge to avoid discovery.

I arrived back at the first condo where Ruby and Doris stood in the kitchen discussing the area. I joined them. "This location is convenient for locals," Doris said. "I live on this side of town too. And you can see Jerome up on the hill at night."

"Jerome who?" I asked.

"It's not a who, but a what," she said. "Jerome is the old mining town on the side of the Mingus Mountain. You should visit the place. It's a lot of fun and has some interesting shops. Plus the town has a wild history." She picked through her leather satchel and adjusted her reading glasses, which had slipped down her nose. "Ruby, do you want to take a look at the other place?"

"Sure," she said. "Derek, this one is nice. It has two extra bedrooms, so one could be yours when you come to visit and the other can be a sewing room."

"Oh," Doris looked up from the search through her bag. "Do you sew? I used to love it, but I became so busy I can't get time anymore."

Ruby stood a little taller. "Yes, I made this blouse."

Over her glasses, Doris inspected the sleeve of Ruby's emerald satin top and fingered the cuff. "Nice work. I tell you, it is so hard to find someone to alter clothes anymore. I had a woman that did work for me, but she died a couple of years ago, so now I just have to go off-the-rack."

Death seemed to take a lot of people from Sedona. A community full of retirees often had lots of funerals, and I wondered if this would be Ruby's last place. I wanted her to be happy and content, but worried that being so far away from the rest of the family she would be lonely. The Harris clan caused plenty of friction among its members, and there was always a feud to some degree brewing, but we were family and no one else could or would care for us like we did. Walterene's death had spurred Ruby to make a change, and I didn't want her to regret her decision once she moved and I was back in North Carolina. Topher had made the same choice, and Topher's recent state of mind didn't reinforce my thinking that it had been the Utopia he had expected. *Was a geographical amputation too extreme to rid yourself of difficult memories?*

Doris loaded us up in her Toyota Camry Hybrid and drove us around the complex to another condo. Its orientation flipped from the previous one so that the morning sun came into the front courtyard and the back patio faced the west. "I don't think you would want the afternoon sun on your back porch," I said and pointed to the motorized canvas awning that shaded the patio. "It looks like the owners have an issue with the sun's heat, and you wouldn't get the views of the rocks back here."

"Good point," Doris said. "The summer can get quite warm, and you don't want to have to fight the glare of the sun in your living area. I think the other one would suit you much better, plus it will use less electricity for cooling. Would you like to make an offer on that one?"

Ruby looked to me as if she wasn't sure.

"Let's keep looking," I said. "That one we just saw is on our list."

"I just don't want Ruby to lose one she really likes." Doris clicked a pen and made a note on her listing. "The market is picking up again and condos like these are going fast. It's still a buyer's market, but I'm not sure how long before it switches over again."

I didn't like a hard sale. For all Aubrey was, he never tried to pressure Ruby into making a quick decision. "Doris, we can afford to wait and find the perfect place. I think we've seen enough for this morning."

The drive back to the real estate office took us along Highway 89A and the trailer park where the day laborers waited along the road for work. A pickup truck driver loaded several Mexican men into the truck's bed while the remaining men returned to their seats on buckets and lawn chairs under a few scraggly trees that offered sparse shade. I wondered if Tricia stopped there to pick out her young Mexicans or if she had someone else make the selection for her. Methamphetamine use was foreign to me, but I thought it wouldn't be something that a person of Tricia's self-perceived stature would partake in. Not that I was an expert on drug use, but I thought

Tricia would choose something more glamorous and expensive like cocaine. Discovering that she used meth was like finding out Prince Charles liked poppers—interesting, but a bit shocking.

"The village," Doris said. "The Village of Oak Creek was a bedroom community for Sedona at one time, but now it has amenities like Sedona without as much tourist traffic. There's a grocery store, post office, medical offices—"

"Did we drive through there when we first came into town?" I asked. "It had all the round-abouts?" The traffic circles at almost every intersection had made me and Ruby a bit queasy.

"Yes, that's it," Doris said. "Nice views of the red rocks and world-class golf courses and restaurants."

"That could be a possibility," I said and glanced at Ruby.

In her usual way of not wanting to offend someone she didn't know that well, Ruby told Doris, "The village is nice, but I have friends here. Could we just keep looking in Sedona?"

"Of course, dear," Doris said. "Really, Sedona is a better investment than the village. But I thought I'd give you the opportunity."

I remembered the photo of Doris with Kimbo and Topher. "Do you know Kimbo Blue well?"

Her eyes locked on me from her rearview mirror. "A bit. Why do you ask?"

"He's a celebrity. Do you think he and Tricia will get married?"

Ruby turned and arched an eyebrow at me as if she didn't know what I was talking about. And she probably didn't. In fact, I didn't know where that came from, but I wanted to get Doris talking about Kimbo and Tricia's relationship and maybe I could find out a little more about them.

"He's just another person," she said. "No more a celebrity than you or I."

"But he starred in movies and on television."

"You'll see that here in Sedona. That and five dollars will get you a cup of coffee at Starbucks."

"So, you don't think his being a former child star has helped his tour business?"

"Not really," she said. "He might have gotten a few doors opened, but his basic business sense has helped him the most. He's a smart and savvy man. Do you know that when the Forest Service closed the Jeep trails during the last drought that he had already negotiated Jeep rights across private land?"

"Yeah, I heard something about that. Didn't that block out the other tour companies from using those trails?" Topher had mentioned that before.

"That caused a big uproar around here," she said. "But it just shows his business acumen. He gets what he wants."

"Do I know this man you're talking about?" Ruby asked.

"He's Topher's boss," I said.

She shrugged her shoulders and flipped down the sun visor to check her lipstick in its mirror.

"Did his crossing rights include the McMurtry Ranch?"

"Probably did." Doris steered into the real estate office's parking lot.

Apache Trails had bulldozed the McMurtry Ranch, or more specifically, Aubrey Garner and Harris Construction had razed the ranch. That had put an end to one of Kimbo's alternate trails for his company.

We followed Doris back into her office where she checked her schedule to show us more homes. She and Ruby discussed a few things while my mind chewed up the hearsay that Tricia was a meth whore.

Ruby wanted to rest after we returned to the rental house, so I told her I would pick up some lunch for us. Plaisir de Sedona would make a great place for take-out.

After parking in the lot, I walked around the building to see if the guys were smoking at the back door. He was there, the young Mexican I'd talked to before, and he was alone.

"*Buenos días*," I said.

"You come back," he said, then placed his cigarette between his lips, letting it dangle as he grinned at me.

"Yes, the food is very good here."

He nodded and his dark eyes focused on my crotch while his hand slipped into the pocket of his jeans and he began to rub himself.

Hell, I was being cruised by Tricia's boy toy. My palms began to sweat. A little flirting does well to set the tone and pave a way to my animal desire, but such directness tended to unnerve me. Blatant come-ons put me on edge. My hands shook as I pulled out a cigarette. Before I could flick my lighter, his pocketed hand produced his Bic and he held the flame in front of my face. I thanked him, and he leaned against the building with one foot propped back on the wall like a cowboy from an old Western.

"You visiting from North Carolina," he said, apparently remembering me from the last visit. "You get lonely?" He pointed his chin at me and his dark eyes closed slightly as if he sensed we both knew where this was going and he only needed to recite the script.

"Ah, not really," I said.

"I get lonely sometimes. Not for friends, but for *especial* friends."

The guy was not only a cook, he was an expert hustler. His assumption was that I was there for him. That would help me in what I really wanted: information on Tricia's personal life. My guess was that this young man knew Tricia's innate desires, and he had probably participated in them. "What time do you get off from work?" I asked. For the right price, I knew he would tell me everything I wanted to know about Tricia.

A wisp of smoke twisted from his smile, and he ran his fingers through his gleaming black hair. "Don't want *mi amigos* to know. I can meet you over there." He pointed to an office building behind the restaurant.

"When?" It would be a negotiation, just like any business deal. I was a fool for love, and I could lose my cool in the steam of lust, but I knew trade when I saw it.

"Now? Or if you need more time, tonight."

He had business smarts; I was being up-sold for more of his company. "Tonight," I said, "and I'll pick you up over there."

His foot slid off the wall and ground out his cigarette. When he picked up the butt to drop it in the bucket of sand, he let his hand graze the front of my jeans. "Selestino," he said and slipped his hand into mine. "Your name?"

"Derek."

"*Si*, Derek. Tonight, ten o'clock."

I had a date with a Mexican hustler that, if rumors where true, was Tricia's plaything—hopefully she wasn't the jealous type.

CHAPTER FIFTEEN

Selestino stood in the shadows of the office building behind the restaurant and I only saw him when the tip of his cigarette flared in the darkness. Ten o'clock at night and Sedona seemed to be a ghost town. A few restaurants still had lights on, but for the most part, the town had gone to bed.

The passenger side door opened and he climbed in. His jeans hung low on his hips and his unbuttoned, plaid, cotton shirt blew behind him in the night breeze exposing his trim, taunt torso and the infamous navel. "I know a place to go," he said. "Out in the desert. It's quiet, nobody there."

"Okay," I said.

He shut the door and buckled himself in. *A kid, that's really what he seems like.* Selestino couldn't have been older than 22 and no more than five foot three, 125 pounds at most. Before I left the house, I made sure Ruby had gone to bed, but just to be on the safe side, I left a note on the kitchen countertop explaining I had gone to meet "Selestino" who worked at Tricia's restaurant to ask him a few questions about Aubrey and Tricia. Now that I sat next to him, I knew I wouldn't have to worry about my safety. I outweighed him by sixty pounds and stood ten inches taller.

"Which way?" I asked as we pulled onto the highway.

"West. Toward Cottonwood."

As the Explorer rolled down the highway and neared the day-workers' hangout, Selestino scrunched down in the seat even though there wasn't anyone in sight. My thoughts stirred as I glanced at him, the wind from his open window blew through his black hair and his shirt hanging open. I couldn't remember the last time I had had sex. *Was it with Daniel?* Mark had tried, several times, but he was off-limits for more reasons than him being my boss and my cousin and married and a soon-to-be-father. Now, I drove a young, cute man to the desert who expected sex. Topher was the one I wanted, but he had placed himself outside the possibility—at least for awhile.

Once we drove past the city limits, I knew that it was open lonely desert for about 30 miles before the first buildings of Cottonwood, so I wanted to get my intentions straight with him, but first I had to level my own thoughts. My imaginary devil sat on one shoulder and hissed, "Fuck him, then talk." While the angel on the other shoulder warned, "Sex without commitment is the slippery slope to whoredom." I planned on paying him, so that was a type of commitment on my part. The decision needed to resolve itself soon, because Selestino placed his hand behind my head and began to massage my neck. His other hand reached across and started to unbutton my jeans.

"Wait a second," I said.

"Pull off at next dirt road," Selestino said and removed his hand from my pants to point ahead on the right.

Highway 89A revealed no headlights in the distance nor behind us, we were the only car in sight and now we turned off the highway to a rutted road that disappeared into the dark desert. The tires of the Explorer jerked into the furrows, and I strained to see the path. The waning moon gave little light, but the headlights caught a dusty coyote galloping across the trail in front of us.

Selestino leaned forward to stare out the windshield. "Up there." He pointed. "Turn and park behind the bushes."

"There's really no reason," I began. "I just want to ask you a few questions." I parked and turned off the headlights. We instantly fell into complete darkness, but my eyes adjusted quickly. Selestino had started shedding his clothes. "No, put your pants back on. I just want to talk."

"Talk, talk," he said. "Talk is cheap, but not me." He continued to shuck his clothes and threw his shirt, pants, and boxers in the back seat, then opened the car door and got out into the darkness with nothing on put his sneakers.

"Selly." I decided to give him a nickname since Selestino was too hard to yell. "Get your ass back in this car." I slammed the door behind me and walked around the back of the SUV. He had propped himself up on the hood of the Explorer like a calendar girl. He didn't seem to be acting himself, not that I knew him well enough to tell if this was his unusual behavior. But his resolve to get naked in the desert was more than good customer service. He was intent on servicing me if I wanted it or not. And this customer didn't want it.

"You not mad at Selestino?" he asked and leaned back on the hood.

"No," I said and stepped up on the bumper to sit next to him. He must have been on some sort of drug, maybe meth. My social circles don't involve amphetamine discussions, so I felt it was a blind guess. But since I heard about Tricia, it only made sense that he would do meth too. The speed had put his mind on a path to be my midnight concubine, so I thought I'd use it to my advantage. "Selly?"

He lay back on the hood with his arms behind his head, gazing at the stars spread across the sky. "*Si*, Derek."

"You know what makes me hot?"

"*Si*, I make you hot."

"Besides you?"

"No."

"Imagining you with Tricia."

"No, really?" He propped himself up on one arm to look at me.

"Yeah, I like to think about her using your hot little body. Can you describe it to me?"

He laughed and slipped a hand under my shirt, without thinking I leaned back on the hood next to him. "I tell you a sexy story." He began to stroke my chest as he talked. "Tricia like to control. She ask me to lie on bed, naked. She stays dressed. Her tongue lick up my leg, along my hip." His hand trailed up my side. "To my shoulder, then she lick over and bite my nipple." He tweaked my nipple.

"Ouch."

"Her lips caress and her tongue finds the good spots. I get hard. She don't touch my *pito*." His hand traced down to my waistband,

and his fingers circled my navel.

"Then what?" I asked.

He took his hand away and held it near his mouth as if holding a pipe. "I hit." He inhaled from the imaginary pipe and he put it to me and said, "She hit."

"Meth?"

"*Si*, but I didn't bring any."

"That's okay. Then what?"

Leaning toward me, he pulled up my shirt and bent his head over my waist, his nose pressed against my navel, a finger holding one of his nostrils shut, and snorted. His laughter bent him over so that he was on top of me. "She sniff out my belly button." He screwed his finger in his navel. He readjusted his position so that he straddled my waist and began to buck his hips over my jeans. "She like that. Then she take my *pito* in her mouth." He bounced and laughed, "*Chingar, chingar*, and *chingar* for hours."

He was young, but "for hours" seemed too boastful.

"You like it too," he said.

A cute, young, naked guy straddled me on the hood of my rental SUV, bucking his hips in the warm desert night. *Yes, I'm healthy.* I couldn't stop the Masonic Rod from saluting. And, Selly focused on it, rubbing back and forth, causing the whole car to shake.

My devil and angel fought each other. I was fully clothed, but that wasn't a bond to chastity. Selly's *pito* slapped his stomach as he thrust, so I knew he enjoyed himself. I could just let it happen, but one thing kept winning the point for the angel: I wanted Topher, not Selly. I closed my eyes and saw Topher while my hands gripped Selly's driving and bucking hips. He took my hands and moved them to his *pito*, but I resisted by gripping his hips again. He intensified his humping. My eyes opened to see his angelic face haloed by stars. His head rolled forward and he braced himself over me with his hands at either side of my head, his face tightened into a devilish grin. The shocks of the Explorer squeaked like field mice, and I thought that would attract every hungry coyote west of town. I easily lifted him off me and rolled him onto his back. I straddled him, mostly to keep him still, but partly to show my dominance.

"Where does Tricia get her meth?"

His hips still kicked under me and his hands gripped my waist. "She keep it in a tin can."

"No, I mean who does she get it from?"

"Husband." He bucked. "Her husband get it for her. Not anymore. Dead."

So, Aubrey was her supplier.

"Let me show you what Tricia do to me." He started to unzip my jeans.

"No." I swung off him and away from his grasp then sat there on the hood watching the stars as he finished himself off. The guy had an on-switch that was easy to trip, but off only happened when he ran out of juice.

Selly sat up, panting and kicked off a shoe to use his sock to clean his chest. "Good for you?" he asked.

The information I wanted, I got. Although I fell somewhere between the devil and angel, I had my need fulfilled, and Selly seemed to have a good time with himself. "Yes, good." I said.

"Me too." He slid off the hood and opened the back door of the SUV and came back with his cigarettes, not bothering to dress yet. He offered me one, but I declined.

Tricia wouldn't have killed Aubrey, since he paid her alimony and supplied her with drugs. "Did the husband ever join you and Tricia?"

"No, not the husband."

"Then who?"

"Other boys."

"What about Tricia's boyfriend, the older man?"

"*Si*, he there sometimes." Selly seemed so casual about it. Was Kimbo in on these meth-fueled trysts?

"What did he do?"

"He watch," Selly said.

Headlights pierced the night sky, not from the direction of the highway, but from the north, the deeper part of the desert road, and then leveled out as the vehicle topped a hill just a few hundred yards from us. A Jeep rolled up behind the Explorer as Selestino jerked his pants on.

A figure climbed out of the Jeep, and I worried that a park ranger might have found us. But as he approached I saw it was Hawk ambling over to us. When I had first met Hawk, when he dropped Topher off at the wake, I hadn't really remembered that much about him. Now, the night shadowed his features. The man stood a bit taller than me, probably six foot two and outweighed me by thirty pounds, but his size wasn't menacing because his manner was so calm, as if he had just walked up to us at a cocktail party. Okay, in Selly's mind we probably *were* at a cocktail party.

"Hawk? Right?" I asked and extended my handshake, keeping the party mindset.

"Yes, we met before," he said shaking my hand. His gaze went to shirtless Selestino and back to me.

My eyes had adjusted enough that I could see his brow wrinkle under the brim of his cap.

"You're Topher's friend aren't you?" he asked.

"Yeah, I'm Derek and this is Selestino."

Selly wiped his hand on his jeans and shook Hawk's hand too, without saying a word.

"Late to be out here," Hawk said.

I had to agree, but didn't see it as his business, so I changed the subject. "Selestino was just telling me about Aubrey, Tricia, and Kimbo."

When he looked down, Hawk's cap shaded his expression from any illumination by the starry sky, but I could see his shoulders stiffen in a slight movement of his body. Other than that, he stood still as the night.

I didn't offer anything more, and he didn't either. The silence seemed to get to Selly because he started to hum a low, slow tune. Hawk turned to him then back to me.

"I saw the car," Hawk began, "and wondered if you needed any help."

A laugh jumped from Selly. "Few minutes ago would have been fun, but too late now."

"No, we're just heading back to town," I said and opened the passenger door for Selly. He climbed in, reached behind the seat, and retrieved his shirt and boxers, which he folded in his lap. I shut the door and the interior light went off again, leaving Hawk and me in darkness. I walked around the back of the Explorer toward the Jeep and stopped to talk to Hawk. "Selestino works for Tricia," I said. "And apparently knows her quite well." I wasn't sure why I felt I needed to explain the situation. It really wasn't any of his business. Then again, maybe it was. He had been the one the police took in for questioning; it was his condo where Aubrey had been murdered. "You see, I know Aubrey wasn't liked, but he had a few people who loved him: Tricia, Clarity, and I'm sure there were others. I don't think you had anything to do with his death, I know Topher believes you are innocent."

"I am," he said, slow and steady.

"And I'm trying to find out who did it."

"The little Mexican knows who did it?" he asked and nodded toward the Explorer.

I almost said that the big Indian probably knew, but restrained myself. "No, but he isn't very discreet about his liaisons, and that sheds more light on this tangle of lies and people surrounding Aubrey."

He only stood there and stared at me.

"Can we talk sometime?" I asked hoping to get his take on Aubrey's dealings and find out why Aubrey was killed in his condo.

"Can I keep my clothes on?"

Ha, the Indian had a sense of humor even though he didn't crack a smile when he said it.

CHAPTER SIXTEEN

After dropping Selestino at the restaurant with a hundred dollar bill, I drove home. The deserted streets showed no signs of life except a small herd of javelina trotting across the road in front of the rental house. Nearly midnight and I was keyed up. My note still lay on the countertop, so I knew that Ruby hadn't stirred. After pouring myself a Stoli White Russian, I went out to the deck for a cigarette.

Hawk had agreed to meet me for coffee the next morning, and I tried to analyze why I felt I could trust him. The personalities that made Sedona unique all had their own stories and agendas—schemes and plans that collided and smashed one another. Topher, I trusted, but I couldn't say why. Myra, I didn't trust much. Kimbo and Tricia were opponents in my game book. Clarity seemed to be a New Age simpleton. Doris Weintraub had inherited Aubrey's real estate contacts, but in the current market that didn't seem a reason for murder. And the Sedona Gentry didn't care for Aubrey, but would they have had him killed? Aubrey's Nogales trips explained how he supplied Tricia with her meth. Could it have been a drug war killing? Who would be Tricia's source now? The Stoli didn't help me sort out the questions, but it did relax me.

A hot shower called me toward the bathroom, then I'd get to bed. Warm water sprayed across my face, and I could feel the desert dust washing off my skin. Selestino wasn't a bad guy; not my type, but he would grow up some and learn that his body wasn't the only way to make money. Drugs, now that was something people didn't outgrow. I wondered if Aubrey had been a meth addict. His autopsy would have said if drugs had been in his system. *How could I get a copy of that autopsy?*

I cut off the shower and dried in a hurry, so I could check something that struck me. After pulling on my boxers, I rushed to the dining room and opened up the laptop. Aubrey's second set of books offered an answer as I scanned the spreadsheets. "Yes, but wait," I said and studied the figures more. TM was a code he had used that reoccurred at regular intervals and the amounts were expenses. "Tricia's Meth" I said. So, if he gave her alimony and meth, she should have been very happy with the arrangement. I checked his incoming funds and couldn't see anything that corresponded to the regularity of the TM expenses. Did she pay him with sex? Food? The restaurant seemed a better tradeoff since Aubrey entertained clients with dinners.

Clients that would have included some of the Sedona Gentry. What had been his relationship with Kimbo? Not that I believed I could raise a man's interest better than Viagra, but I couldn't remember once that I had encountered someone rubbing their hands over me and then displaying such penile unresponsiveness as Kimbo had. If he had issues with his sexual performance, why would he have a profile on DiscoverDick.com? He liked to watch, that was Selly's comment. A position of power, authority. Was that what Kimbo needed? Did Aubrey take that away from him?

The laptop chimed to signal an e-mail had arrived. An automated message from DiscoverDick.com reminded me that I hadn't set up my profile, and that I would be jacking off alone for the rest of my life if I didn't. "Damn, I should have taken Selly's photo with my cell phone and used it on the profile." I noticed another unread e-mail below DiscoverDick. It was from Topher@BlueJeepSedona. com. He apologized for his spacey behavior at Devil's Bridge and wanted to take me to dinner the following night. Since Ruby had wanted to see the ghost town of Jerome, we had plans to drive up in the afternoon. I knew better than to call Topher after midnight, so I e-mailed him back and asked him to join us at a restaurant in Jerome after he got off work.

❅　❅　❅

I woke from a dream, oddly calm since it had been a dream of my death.

In the house I grew up in, I had waited along with two other people—friends from elementary school, now grown. My mother paced the front yard, checking the road for someone, stopping to tell me I didn't need to do it. The sway of the thin branches of an elm ushered in a breeze and with it a scent of summer rain. Nervous glances to each other, the two people waiting with me began to walk toward the road, then ran as they reached the pavement.

"It will do no good," my mother said.

I knew they were scared, and running would be their way of fighting back. Futile or not, it was something for them to do.

We stood in my childhood bedroom then, and I picked through the suits I own today. Holding out the black one I had worn to Walterene's funeral, I said, "This will do. But I doubt I'll have an open casket, so I guess it really doesn't matter."

"They may be able to do something with the collar," my mother said.

"Waiting is the hardest part."

She nodded and lowered her thin body to the bed.

The sheers underneath the heavy drapes blew in the wind, and I wondered if I'd feel the blade. Only for an instant, I thought, since the mind will be separated from the body or more realistically the head will be sliced from the torso. Beheaded.

Decapitated. The thought didn't bother me. I knew he was coming, and when he arrived, I'd die.

And waking up, I did feel calm. As if I had accepted my death and only waited for it without fear or regret. I lay in the bed and stared at the ceiling, focusing on a small water stain near the window. *Had Aubrey felt this calm?*

The night receded as the sun approached the horizon, and I checked the clock: 5:37 a.m. Coffee would taste good, so I headed into the kitchen and started the coffee maker, then went back to pull on my boxers and grab my pack of Marlboros. *Could I leave Ruby two thousand miles from the family?* Charlotte was a direct flight to Phoenix and then it was a two-hour drive to Sedona. In an emergency, I could get to her within six to eight hours. That wasn't what I wanted. But moving was Ruby's decision, and hers alone.

From my chair on the deck, I looked up toward Sugarloaf and spotted someone on top, moving in odd ways, arms stretching toward the brightening sky, legs spread steady on the red rock. I assumed the figure was doing yoga as the day dawned over the Mogollon Rim. I snuffed out the cigarette, the smoldering tip ground into the glass ashtray and the last wisp of smoke dissipating in the fresh air, and returned to my room to put on my running shorts and sneakers. If I was up this early, then I should get some exercise like the person who had hiked to the top of Sugarloaf for yoga. Greet the day with energy was my thought.

The air felt light and cool as I ran along the road, with no sounds but the tap of my shoes, the slap of rubber against asphalt with an occasional crunch of gravel. There was plenty of light to see even though the sun hadn't crested the Rim yet. The route I chose wound through our neighborhood and over to Sanborn Drive, which ran parallel to 89A, but about six blocks north. The road satisfied my need to be far from traffic and close to the rocks that corralled Sedona. Thunder Mountain loomed to my right and I could see the first rays of sun hitting its peak. The stages of Sedona's development as a popular destination had been built along the road. Our rental house was a more moderate sized house than the ones I saw on Rodeo Road—homes with more of a 1950s vacation home style, low and wide ranch homes including the mobile homes of Harmony Hills where many of the immigrant day-workers lived.

Like turning a switch, the next part of the road changed names and income brackets. These were the newest and largest of estate homes—rambling rooflines, chimneys, terraces and courtyards in stucco and glass—where private land had been sold and the developers jumped on it to build Thunder Mountain Ranch. Mansions next to mobile homes.

The thought of this happening to the McMurtry Ranch caused my pace to quicken, and I soon found myself at the intersection of Dry Creek Road, only about two tenths of a mile from the condo where Aubrey was murdered. I stopped to catch my breath. Sweat ran down my chest as my breaths heaved in and out, cooling my skin. The labored panting punishing me for my lack of commitment to cut back on cigarettes.

The development of Sedona had become vicious. National forest circled the town, creating a small island of developable land, and most of it had already been used. A flash in my mind brought in my great-grandfather, Papa Ernest. I had never known the man, but he had started Harris Construction and fathered all of us. Was this what he did, correction, we did to the land? Hell, I thought, I'm part of a construction company that bulldozes acres of land to build skyscrapers, shopping malls, and industrial parks. Why was this land more special? Did a nice view mean this land was worth saving more than hard, red Carolina clay? *That's like saying a pretty girl is more human than an ugly one.* I understood the value of a one-of-a-kind natural wonder: Miles of kudzu-covered Carolina fields could not compare to the Grand Canyon. *But, isn't each acre of nature irreplaceable?* The sudden rush of thoughts made me think I was turning into Clarity Received, or was I receiving clarity?

The chai tea latte steamed sweet in my hands. The *Arizona Republic* newspaper spread before me on the tiny coffee house table reported on drug wars in Mexico and the flow of arms from Arizona gun shows. The article mentioned Nogales as a key entry point for the weapons. I thought about Aubrey's trips to the Mexican border—sex, drugs, arms trafficking—what was his vice? I sipped the latte, my first at the coffee shop after two cups of strong, regular coffee at home, and leaned back in the upholstered arm chair where the shop's window channeled morning sunlight across my face. Just as I reached for my backpack to search for sunglasses, a shadow covered the table, and I glanced up to see a tall Indian blocking the rays.

"Hawk," I said and stood to offer him the chair across the table.

He wore his Blue Jeep t-shirt and jeans and when he removed his cowboy hat, I had my first extended view of the man's face. Not the handsome warrior of romance tales, Hawk looked average, for an Indian. The few extra pounds he carried gave him a soft edge, full cheeks that didn't move much with his expression and dark eyes that didn't stray even when he jerked his head to flick back a long strand of hair that had escaped his black pony tail. The stately set of his jaw seemed regal, yet his narrow nose skewed to the left and added to a slight off-balance feeling I got from him.

"Glad you could meet me," I said after we had settled. "Would you like some coffee or tea?"

"No, thank you," he said. "I don't use caffeine."

Well, something had him up late last night, I thought, and folded the newspaper out of our way. I started with a neutral question. "How long have you lived here?"

"I was born on the reservation next to Clarkdale."

"Is that nearby?"

"At the foot of Cleopatra Hill."

My blank stare must have given away my ignorance.

"Below Jerome, near Cottonwood." His voice stayed level, not like most people who would have made that statement a question by raising their tone at the end as if trying to get me to answer *Yes, yes, I know now*.

"What is it that keeps you here?" I asked.

"Family," he said. Then asked me, "What keeps you away from your home?"

"Family." I winked at him. "Family brought me out here to help my aunt find a home, and family dynamics tend to keep me at a distance from the rest of them."

"And Aubrey?" he asked.

I sipped my chai latte while I considered his question. I could see that he was the type to not use words to concrete the direction of a conversation, but to let it flow from ideas free-associated within the answerer's mind. A cool technique that allowed unsaid thoughts to reveal themselves in the replies to vague questions. Or maybe, he just wasn't much of a conversationalist. "Aubrey probably didn't care for my family either."

"Why?"

"Business. Now, let me ask you something: How did Aubrey end up in your condo?" I didn't want to be analyzed. I wanted answers.

"The place is for sale. He's a real estate agent."

"I'll rephrase that: How did Aubrey end up dead in your condo?" I could see he needed his questions concrete.

"You know the details," he said and tilted his head to the side. "Besides finding him, what is your involvement in the investigation?"

The sun's rays had moved into my eyes, so I scooted my chair away from the beam and closer to Hawk. "He was a human being."

The twitch at the corner of his mouth seemed to threaten a laugh from his stoic face, but he regained control.

"And I see myself in Aubrey," I added.

Hawk's brows creased and he leaned forward. "How's that?"

"He was a driven man, a lusty man, a man who made mistakes, but it's difficult to live a life without error. He didn't have a lot of friends, but I'm sure he must have had a few that he kept close and true. Finding him, scalped and laid out on the floor... Well, it just pissed me off. Not that I play by the rules all the time, but I wouldn't kill someone."

"Even if that person was going to hurt you or someone you cared about?"

"Physical harm, yes. I would defend myself or someone else, but kill someone because he would hurt someone financially. Fuck, no. Get justice. Murder isn't justice."

"Justice means different things to different people," he said

"What does it mean to you?" I asked.

A noticeable shift of his eyes caught my attention when he focused on the folded newspaper for a moment then met my eyes again. "Balance," he said.

"Justice as balance." I considered the thought. "Would a person's death bring balance about?"

"No, Aubrey's death was not justice.   It didn't balance

anything."

"What can I do for you?" I asked. He hadn't agreed to meet me to be drilled by my questions, so I knew he had an agenda too.

The direct query seemed to put him on edge, as much as he could be anxious or tense, but his breathing skipped a beat—just a short intake of air, enough that I noticed while I sipped my latte.

"You're Topher's friend," he said. "I think something is bothering him, wears on his mind, more than obvious stress, but something innate to his nature." He didn't look me in the eyes now, but stared out the window as he continued. "He's discontent."

"He needs a boyfriend." I sat back in the chair and waited for Hawk's response. His discomfort, I guessed, had to do with thinking of Topher's needs.

A full smile made Hawk kind of handsome. "If it were that simple… He is a sexual being, like all of us, but that basic need is not what erodes his joy."

"Last night," I began, but he nodded as if he knew where my explanation headed.

"You used your looks and wisdom to trick the little Mexican into telling you what you wanted to know. I could see he burned with the heat of passion, and you were cool with the solace of knowledge. An exchange had taken place between the two of you, but nothing intimate." He leaned toward me. "I think intimacy is what Topher needs, not sexual, not passionate, but a confidence, a closeness with another."

"He has friends here," I said.

"Not the same," he said.

"Do you have intimacy?"

"Yes."

"But, you live in the desert. Do you have a woman out there?"

The smile came back, so I assumed we were becoming friendly. "I have a woman, when I need, or when she needs me, but I require less social closeness than Topher."

"Myra," I said. "Myra is his friend, they moved here together."

"Sedona does things to people. Sometimes they grow apart. Myra has taken a branch in a different direction."

"Can she be trusted?"

"You ask me as if I'm an intuitive." He stretched out his long legs under the table and leaned back. "I'm an Indian, not a psychic."

"No, I'm asking because I think you have insight into people. You notice more than most."

"Myra is a good woman. She and Topher don't have the same goals anymore."

It clicked for me. "I like you," I said. "I can see why you're one of Topher's friends."

He smiled for the third time. He reached across the table and grasped my wrist with a firm hold.

Tingles raced up my arm from his touch, as if he had infused me with the Noble Indian Brotherhood grip.

He turned my wrist to see my watch, "Already 10:30, my shift starts soon."

So much for the mystical touch of the tribal Brave. I stood as he got up from the table. "Thanks for stopping by, Hawk."

"I thought that was you." A woman's excited voice cut through the general rumble of the caffeinated customers around us. We both looked in her direction to see Clarity Received, in her New Age gypsy garb, weaving through tables to join us, an expression of relief on her face, a face that as I looked at her closely was actually pretty. Some women look better without make-up and Clarity was one. Her eyes had naturally long, dark lashes and her cheeks had a slight flush to them. Her blonde hair held volume and some frizz without the binding of her emerald and gold patterned scarf that had settled around her shoulders, and I wondered how she found enough humidity in the air to kink her hair. She placed a hand on Hawk's arm. "We want to talk to the BLM again. Can you come this afternoon?"

He continued to move toward the exit with her following him. "What time? I'm on shift today."

With my cup in hand, I trailed them as if I headed back to the counter for a refill.

"Two o'clock," she said. "At the Forest Service office on Brewer Road."

I snagged a pencil from the counter and wrote that on the side of my cup.

"I'll check to see if I'm between tours," he said as he left.

A look of disappointment shrouded Clarity's stance, shoulders drooped, arms hanging loose. She turned to find me standing behind her, smiling.

"Remember me?" I asked. "The old soul?"

Unlined, unshadowed eyes scanned me while she took a deep breath, then a smile crept onto her face. "Yes, Derek Mason," she said. "May I join you for a cup of tea?"

We ordered and I dumped my new latte into the old cup, and with the new one, I sheathed my notes on the meeting from her view.

"I didn't realize you knew Hawk," Clarity said and straightened her skirt as she sat in the chair Hawk had occupied.

"He's a nice guy."

"Where'd you meet?" she asked.

"In the desert, some interesting people congregate out there."

She stirred her black tea. "The desert is a sacred place, a site of life, love, and renewal. I take my workshop students there for ceremonies, vision quests, morning meditations, drumming circles."

"I remember reading about Native Americans using a drug for their vision quests."

"You can call them Indians," she said, "since they tend to prefer that inaccurate label over the more politically correct Native American or indigenous peoples. Really, I would venture to say the most accurate term would be to use their tribe, but like the rest of us, we're mixed breeds. Apache, Hopi, Navajo fought each other for centuries but now who can tell whose ancestors are whose?"

"Peyote," I said. "Isn't peyote used in vision quests? Or is that too bitter? Maybe Salvia Divinorum?" I asked since North Carolina had just passed a law against Salvia Divinorum, a species of sage I hadn't heard of before the law, and now the prohibition only made me want to try it. "Is Salvia the new vision quest drug?"

"Sometimes," she answered but didn't bother to look me in the eyes.

My chai latte rested on the folded newspaper. "Aubrey used to go down to Nogales quite often. I see that the Mexican government is trying to crack down on the amount of guns trafficked into their country, the drug lords seem to get plenty of weapons from Arizona. Peyote, or even methamphetamines, roofies, or GHB could be a nice payment for a gun or two."

"Aubrey didn't deal with guns," she said, not denying that he might have supplied her with peyote or other drugs. "He was a peaceful soul, a little lost."

"How was he lost?"

The question changed her mood as if she considered it deeply and thoughtfully, and her stirring slowed and stopped, but she left the wooden stick in her tea. "His priorities didn't align with his true self. That's a dangerous thing."

Her eyelids twitched when she looked back at me.

"I wish I could have saved him from himself."

Even though they hadn't been married, she had been his girlfriend, his confidant, his lover, so I regarded her as a widow. "Aubrey had some fine traits," I said. "One of the things that Ruby and I liked about him was his big-picture view of things, almost a visionary."

"Not a visionary," she said. "His vision was for profit, and that's a false mistress."

"Did he ignore you while he pursued wealth?"

"People don't need other people as much as popular culture believes. I do fine on my own, and our souls are reunited with the Creative Consciousness after this life. We're all taking a path, paths that merge and diverge."

So, I had Hawk saying Topher needed someone to keep him balanced, and Clarity preaching that we should all be independent of each other. One tribal, the other self-reliant. A bit of each was my take.

I excused myself from Clarity when one of her former students invited herself to the table. On the way out, I unsheathed the interior cup with the writing on it: BLM meeting. In a shady corner of the shop's courtyard, I pulled out my cell phone to google BLM.

CHAPTER SEVENTEEN

Bureau of Land Management, that was BLM. The acronym was foreign to me, since the bureau only operated in the western states. *Why did Clarity want Hawk at that meeting?*

Ruby had arranged to view some more homes with Doris. I tagged along. Doris tended to push the limit of what Ruby wanted to spend on a condo, since the ones we viewed cost a bit more than the ones yesterday. "Oh, this it too fancy," Ruby commented as we walked through a place with a bidet in the master bathroom. "I wouldn't know what end to wash with that thing." She had travelled to Europe with Walterene years earlier, so I knew she had seen a bidet before and probably tried it out, but luxuries added to a residence for the sole purpose of jacking up the price didn't sit well with her and this was her gentle way of telling Doris that.

"You're going to Jerome this afternoon?" Doris asked. "You won't see a bidet there, that's for sure."

"Simple, that is what we like," I said.

"Now, at your aunt's price point, you will find more upscale amenities. Things to make life more comfortable."

"Keep the amenities in the kitchen," Ruby said, walking down the hall, "that's where I spend my energy. I can keep my tooty clean in the bathtub like any respectable girl."

A flush of scarlet colored Doris's face. Not to embarrass Doris more by adding my own thoughts, I simply followed Ruby into the kitchen.

"These views," Ruby said, gesturing to the wall of windows framing the eastern horizon, "that's what I'd pay extra for."

"Spectacular. You're right," I said and walked up behind Ruby and draped my arms around her shoulders in a hug. The soft give of her body and the slight scent of her strawberry shampoo propelled me back to my childhood of playing in the backyard with her and

 GREG LILLY

Walterene, the laughter, the hide-and-seek, the bird watching, the endless retelling of tall tales while I sat in her lap. I would miss Ruby. Maybe it wasn't the need to be close to family that I thought her aging required, but my need and my maturing that necessitated the family stay close together. She patted my clasped hands at her shoulder as if she understood my reluctance to let go of her.

"I have another place to show you," Doris said, "that has great views and a gourmet kitchen. When did you plan to drive to Jerome? I want to make sure we have time to tour the other condo."

"Not sure," I said. "I heard there was a BLM meeting in town this afternoon. Do you know what it's about?"

"No, but I'll find out." Doris flipped open her phone and called her office to have her assistant check. She hung up and told me the posted agenda consisted mainly of operational items and an update on the arson fires.

"Why would the Bureau of Land Management address fires set at building sites?" I asked.

"A fire can quickly spread into the national forest," she explained. "Down in the village a few years ago, a contractor grinding a fence post shot sparks into dry grass, and the surrounding land burned for over a week before the fire was brought under control. We're extremely cautious of any fire. The desert can ignite in a second and spread across acres in a just a few minutes. Although whoever is setting these fires seems to know how to keep them under control, no acreage has been lost."

"No," I said, "just development."

Ruby and I found seats in the back of the room at the Forest Service office. We dropped in the metal chairs as if we had walked for miles—miles of tile floors, miles of granite and stainless steel kitchens, miles of marble bathrooms. The prospect of walking around the town of Jerome didn't appeal to me at this point of the day. Ruby dug through her purse and pulled out a compact to powder her forehead and nose.

"Not bad," she said as she tilted her head to the left then right, checking her image in the compact's mirror. "I seem to hold up better out here than in the humidity of North Carolina. You're looking rode hard and put up wet."

Every once in a while she adopted an old saying she might remember from her childhood and used it often, no matter the situation, appropriate or not. This one always made me snicker with the image it produced in my mind. "I ain't been rode or wet lately. I'm tired. The run this morning, then all the coffee and the multiple condos we've seen have worn me out."

"This meeting should give you time to sleep." She glanced around the rustic room, a room that reminded me of a bunkhouse—bare walls, minimalist wooden furnishings—certainly not like the dwellings we had viewed of late.

"Not in these metal chairs," I said.

A few more people wandered in and talked to each other. A man in a khaki uniform walked up to the podium, flanked by several people talking in exaggerated movements before he could take his place. His thick but short hair was combed to the side in a purely functionary style, his short sleeves boasted BLM patches, while thick forearms flexed as he dug in his pants pockets. A ring of keys clattered when he dumped them on the podium, and several people looked up.

The chair next to me scratched across the linoleum as someone pulled it from the back then scooted up next to me. Myra sat down. "Glad to see you here," she said and positioned her briefcase in front of her, smoothed her skirt, and hooked her auburn hair behind her ears. "How did you find out about this? I just got a call about 30 minutes ago."

Clarity breezed into the room, saw me, Myra, and Ruby, then zeroed in on the BLM agent.

Nodding toward Clarity, I answered Myra's question, "Her. I heard Clarity ask Hawk to attend today, and I wondered what the urgency was for them both to be here. So, let me ask you: Why are you here?"

"The word around town is that the Sedona Gentry wants Apache

Trails dissolved and the land bought by the government to be restored to its original condition."

"The Gentry really doesn't have anything to do with it. The land belongs to..." I realized I wasn't sure who owned the land now that Aubrey was gone. Myra's bank had a lien on it, so did Harris Construction and the other investors. "Who is the executor of Aubrey's estate?"

"I am," Myra said.

CHAPTER EIGHTEEN

"No way." I couldn't stop it from coming out. "You and Aubrey were that close?"

"No, I didn't know until I got the call from his lawyer. Why he named me I have no idea, and it pisses me off that he didn't even ask me." She adjusted her jacket, pulling the lapel straight. "I have to go to Cottonwood to the attorney's office to decline it. I barely knew the man, and he saddles me with cleaning up his estate."

At the podium, the BLM agent shooed away the people, including Clarity, and began the meeting. We all stood for the Pledge of Allegiance. I remembered the right hand over my heart, to face the flag, to stand tall, to speak clearly, except I couldn't remember the words. With a voice clear and loud, Ruby recited the pledge like she did it every day. I tried to follow along with her and most it sprang back into my memory. Taking our seats again, I saw Kimbo and several other men slip into the room. It seemed like half of Sedona turned out for the meeting.

The agent noticed too. "Usually, we don't get this kind of a turnout. I'll rearrange the agenda so you all don't have to sit through the boring stuff." He opened the floor for public comments.

Nervous glances poured through the room, people searching the faces of each other to see who would bring up what they had all come here to hear.

Kimbo stood. "I'm Kimbo Blue, owner of Blue Jeep Tours. I have a document here on the old McMurtry Ranch west of town. It was being graded for residential until the tragic death of the developer." He waved a fat, blue binder that looked to be at least one-hundred pages thick.

How did he get his in-depth documentation finished so fast?

"This proposal," he continued, "shows the benefits to the local and state economies of preserving its geographical, archaeological, and historical resources, restoring its recreational opportunities, and safeguarding its open space."

Myra nudged me and whispered in my ear, "So, this is how they'll save the land. The only problem is his heir might want to continue the development."

"Come with me." I grabbed Myra's hand and told Ruby we'd be right back.

Outside the building, I lit a cigarette and leaned against the wooden porch railing. "So, the Sedona Gentry is trying to have the Bureau of Land Management buy Apache Trails."

Myra reached over and took the pack of Marlboros from me, shook one out, and placed it between her lips.

"Tough day?" I asked as I flicked the lighter to the end of her cigarette.

Her eyes closed, she exhaled the smoke in a long breath. "What do you think?" Her lips pursed as if to say something else, but a shake of her head dismissed the gesture. Her eyes stayed shut. The afternoon sun brightened her hair, highlighting streaks of auburn.

"Who inherits this mess?" I asked.

Her brown eyes opened and centered on me, narrowing as she seemed to regain her focus. She blew out gray smoke, extended the cigarette and stared at it instead of me. "Don't know. I haven't seen his will. Like I said, I just found out he wanted me to be the executor."

"Do it," I said.

"I have a fulltime job, no time to sort out his crap." Then she added, "Why would he pick me? We didn't spend time together until this project started a few months ago."

If that statement were true, it might lead to his killer, but I wasn't sure if I trusted Myra. Her hands seemed too deep in this pile for her to smell like roses. Aubrey must have recently changed the will and named Myra as executor. *But why? Why would he want Myra in the middle of it?*

Myra continued talking "...I'm not sure his estate will have enough to pay off the liens, which means the property has to be sold, unless the partners don't want to pull out and the heir wants to continue the development."

"When do we know who the heir is?" I asked. "When will the will be read?"

"Don't know, don't care," she said. "I'm pulling out of it. The bank will probably want to get out too."

"Why's that?"

"Too much opposition, too many arson fires. We'd be crazy to fund a builder with a fire being set at new construction almost every week. At least you can't burn roads and utilities."

"But you can use the equipment to disrupt traffic," I reminded her of the morning I helped her clean up the mess of backhoes and bulldozers in the road. "What did the sheriff say about that?"

"A county deputy came by, but didn't have much to offer. It has to be the same group setting the fires, the anti-development people. The deputy said that the sheriff was talking to Phoenix to get Homeland Security involved—domestic terrorism."

I hadn't considered it before, but setting fires, blocking roads with bulldozers, antagonizing developers to get them to change their operations was terrorism.

The door creaked open, and Ruby sighed as she walked onto the porch. "I'm bored with that meeting. Let's go."

"Where are you two heading?" Myra asked Ruby, flicking ash off the end of the cigarette.

"Up there," Ruby pointed west toward the Mingus Mountains.

"Jerome," Myra said. "You'll enjoy that. Take your sweater if you plan to be up there after dark. It gets cold on the side of that hill. Stop by The Copper Corset, it's a shop that's in an old brothel, or parlor house as they called them. Rumor has it that it's haunted by a working girl called Pearl."

"Great," I said, "that's all we need now is a prostitute poltergeist."

A twisted road, hugging the contours of the mountain, wound us up toward a collection of weathered buildings snagged to the side of Cleopatra Hill. The drive snaked us through the town where we parked along the street across from a bar and grill. Getting out of the Explorer, I felt a bit disoriented, as if the place skewed a few degrees from the rest of the world—the ground sloped, the structures weren't quite plumb, the air, though warm, held a staticky charge that tingled the hair on my arms.

"I need a drink," I told Ruby. The alcohol should relax my nerves, but I wasn't sure if the BLM meeting had rattled me or the knowledge that both the Sedona Gentry and Aubrey seemed to be prepared for his death.

I smiled when I spotted the rectangular rainbow sticker, the Gay Pride flag and a symbol of diversity, in the corner of the front window at the restaurant. "This looks like our kind of place," I said and opened the door for Ruby.

Tourists crowded the tables for late lunches or early suppers, so we weaved our way to the bar. The female bartender's thick black hair cascaded in waves to her shoulders and its dark color made her emerald eyes glow. She was a big girl, curvaceous in a way that other women would appreciate, but straight men would probably dismiss as too rotund. Her smile, genuine and easy, welcomed us to her bar.

"What can I do you for?" she asked and winked at Ruby.

Ruby giggled.

"We need some juice to fuel us for exploring this town," I said. "Ruby, what would you like?"

"Hmm, how about a glass from the vineyards, a Pinot Noir?"

"Good choice," the bartender said. "And you?"

"I think I'll take the juice of the agave," I said. "Tequila. Reposado mixed into your finest Margarita. On the rocks, no salt."

"Perfect," she smiled. "My name is Sid."

I reached my hand across the bar to shake hers. "This is my aunt Ruby, and I'm Derek." We exchanged pleasantries as she brought Ruby her wine and mixed my Margarita.

"After some looking around," I said, "we're meeting a friend here for dinner: Topher Langston."

"Oh, yeah, I know Topher. He comes in here from time to time." She leaned over the bar between me and Ruby. "I tried to fix him up with Doogan over there." She nodded toward a cute waiter serving a table in the corner. He needed a haircut and a shave, but otherwise he wasn't too bad. "But," she continued, "Topher wasn't interested."

"I know what you mean," I said. "He's got a bit of baggage to unpack."

Sid nodded and left to make drinks for one of the waitresses.

"Let's go see that place Myra told us about," Ruby said and batted her mascara coated eyelashes.

"The brothel?" I asked in mock shock.

"The parlor house," she corrected me.

The Margarita, smooth as a sporting girl's silk sheets, disappeared quickly and Sid appeared with another before I drained the first one. "Hey, Sid," I said. "Where's the Brass Brassiere?"

"Uh, you mean The Copper Corset?" she asked.

"Yeah, that's the one."

"Just down the hill." She pointed out the window. "You'll see the sign."

The contents of Ruby's purse spilled across the bar as she searched for something.

"What'd you lose, Lady Chartreuse?" The tequila had smoothed out my mood.

A frown wrinkled Ruby's forehead. "I had a picture in here of that Indian piece Aubrey wanted to show me," she said. "It was pretty, a bowl of some sort, not too flashy, but earthy. I thought if I couldn't get it, then I might find something like it here."

A clue for me, one I picked up on right away: She wanted to shop, and shop for something specific. Ruby's wine had disappeared, and she waved off Sid when she gestured with the wine bottle from the other end of the bar. "You ready to go now?" I asked.

"If you are."

I sucked the last of the Margarita from the remaining ice cubes in my glass, handed Sid two twenties, and told her we'd be back once Ruby scored some Navajo bowls.

"I think it was Yavapai-Apache," Ruby corrected me as we left the bar.

"What?"

"That bowl."

"That's what you said Aubrey was trying to sell you? We can find something authentic, something nicer. Like I said before, I bet all Aubrey had were knock-offs from Mexico."

I smoked a cigarette as we walked down the steep sidewalk to The Copper Corset, avoiding the disapproving stare from Ruby, who had recently decided I was too old to be smoking like some rebellious school boy.

"As you get older," she said, apparently picking up on my avoidance of her gaze, "it's not so cute. I mean, your teeth will get stained yellow, and your hair stinks."

Jesus H. Christ, I thought, this old lady is harping on me—for what? "What's up Ruby? You aren't usually this critical. Did I say something to piss you off?"

"No, no," she said and held onto my arm. "I just feel like I need to look out for you and my time is limited to do it. I mean, when I'm out here, you'll be back in North Carolina, and who's going to watch over you?"

I pulled the cigarette pack out of my shirt pocket. "Here." I held the pack out to her. "Have one, it will calm you down."

"Smart ass," she hissed and slapped my butt. "Give me those, and I'll throw them out."

"No freakin' way, woman. I need these to deal with the moody old ladies in my life." She lost her smile, so I added, "And who stay in my life no matter where they live."

At the building that housed The Copper Corset, I ground out my cigarette into a trash barrel at the corner. Inside, Ruby's attention was snared by a shelf of pottery. I scanned some books about the town's history. Wooden floors creaked as we walked and looked, thick carpets defined different spaces, an old upright piano anchored one corner and an emerald velvet chaise sprawled in front of a brick fireplace. A raven-haired female mannequin stood next to the fireplace, dressed in a late Victorian gown of copper-colored satin, the gown's neckline cut low, a fitted and laced bodice that flared into layers of ruffles and bows gathered in back with a bustle.

Ruby examined the dress. "Isn't it beautiful?"

An older, thin sales woman with an arm load of vintage clothes, mostly 1940s and '50s, laid them across the chaise. "Yes, here feel this fabric." She pulled a ruffle up for Ruby to touch.

Ruby looked at me and smiled. I knew she enjoyed history and loved seeing the fashions of another time.

"Is that the ghost?" I asked nodding at the mannequin.

"No, that's a mannequin," the sales woman said.

Damn, no one gives you a break in this town. "Let me rephrase: Is that what the ghost is supposed to look like?"

"Pearl," the woman said. "This house used to be a parlor house. The best in town, if not in all of Arizona. Pearl was a free spirit and it eventually got the best of her. In her younger days, she was one of the stars of the town because of her beauty and her carefree personality. As she aged," the woman nodded at Ruby since they both seemed to be in the same generation, "her looks didn't get her out of trouble like she had grown accustomed to. She had made some enemies: other prostitutes, wives, even an official at the copper mine. One morning, Pearl was found lying beside the tracks that took mining equipment in and out of the copper mine. Her beautiful dress smudged with dirt, her stockings ripped, a broken wine bottle clutched in her left hand, her head tossed at a severe slant where a rail car had decapitated her."

"God," Ruby said and dropped her hold on the dress.

My hand went to my throat, as the dream of my own impending decapitation flowed back in vivid details. "Why? I mean, what could she have done that she deserved that?"

The sales woman straightened the dress on the mannequin. "Some say it was an accident, while others say murder. She always had her nose in other people's affairs, and when you're in the business of discretion that can be fatal." She scooped up the garments she'd left on the chaise. "I just know that I catch a glimpse of her from time to time around the shop."

"With or without the head?" I asked.

"Oh, she always has her head. What woman would go out in

public without it?""

"Good point." I grabbed Ruby's hand. "We have a lot to see. Have a good day." I almost dragged Ruby out the door. "That was one odd woman. I don't know much about retail, but telling customers about a severed head is no way to sell an Anasazi bowl."

"Yavapai-Apache," Ruby corrected me.

The sun lowered in the sky, setting behind the mountain that Jerome perched on, causing the town to fall into shadow, while blushing the distant red rocks of Sedona ablaze. Ruby couldn't find a shop with the type of pottery she wanted; apparently her heart was set on the one Aubrey had shown her in a photograph. We climbed and crisscrossed the crooked hillside streets and found our way back to the bar where Sid still poured drinks for weary tourists—damn if I didn't feel weary.

"Cactus juice and grape juice," Sid said once we were seated at the bar. "Margarita Reposado, on the rocks, no salt, and a Pinot Noir for the pretty lady."

"You're good," I said.

"Ruby and Derek," she said furthering my admiration of her memory.

"Nice. Hey, we went down to The Copper Corset—that woman working there is odd."

"Yeah, she's a character." Sid placed Ruby's wine in front of her and mixed my Margarita. "You have good timing. I just saw Topher's Jeep drive by."

I twisted to look out the front window that presented Main Street, the parking spaces across the road, and the wide expanse of sky beyond that. No buildings stood opposite the bar, so vistas of the Verde Valley and Sedona to the east were unobstructed.

Topher strode up the sidewalk and through the door looking more relaxed than I had ever seen him. His khaki shirt, jeans, and boots gave him a distinction from the shorts and t-shirted tourists. The top had been down on the Jeep, so he wore a Blue Jeep Tours baseball cap that cast a shade over his eyes. His smile broadened when he spotted us at the bar. "Howdy, kids. What's on tap?" He hugged Ruby then wrapped his arms around me when I slid off the barstool. "Good to see you," he whispered in my ear.

Ruby patted my vacated place next to her. "Here, Topher, you sit next to me."

I scooted down to the next stool so that he was trapped between us. "You seem to be in good humor. Get all your work finished?"

"Oh, yeah. Kimbo and Tricia are headed down to Scottsdale for the weekend. It's Friday," he said with a sigh. "What a week."

"Hey buddy." Sid leaned across the bar and kissed his cheek. "Let me get you a beer."

He checked out what Ruby and I were drinking. "Let me have a 'Rita instead."

Ice cubes clanged as Sid added ingredients to the cocktail mixer. "You got here just in time." She nodded toward the window. The sunset had blazed across the valley igniting the distant rocks in feverish fuchsia, crimson, scarlet, and magenta.

"That's why I love this place," he said. "And Ruby, you will too."

She smiled, but I could tell she wasn't so sure. She dug through her pocketbook, and with a shake of her head, held up a ragged inkjet photograph printout. "Here it is. Stuck to my sunglass case." She slapped the photo on the bar. "That's what I'm looking for."

Topher bent over the picture, then straightened up. "Who gave you that?"

"Aubrey," she said. "He told me it was a real antique from the tribe here."

I leaned toward the snapshot-sized printout in front of Topher, bracing my lean with my hand on his thigh. The image had been shot outside, up against a white stucco wall, with a wooden ruler next to it to show size. A few chunks seemed to be missing from the thin lip of the bowl, and its side also sported a thin crack that ran down to the lopsided bottom. The bowl seemed to have a texture, and with its coloring, looked almost like it was made of copper or bronze instead of clay. "Ruby, this doesn't have any decoration on it, no pattern."

"That's why I liked it," she said. "It wasn't too much. I thought the color would look nice."

Topher leaned back and rested his hand on mine, my hand on his thigh. "I knew he'd try it."

"What?" I asked, afraid he referred to my hand on his leg.

Sid delivered Topher's Margarita, and he took a sip. "Aubrey was always trying to make a buck. That," he said and punched the photograph with his finger, "is what Hawk and I had been searching for. Even in death, Aubrey tried to keep it from Hawk. Hawk actually had to break into his own condo to retrieve it because Aubrey's death made the condo a crime scene and the police confiscated his house keys."

"Hold on," I pulled my hand back and straightened up on the barstool. "Hawk broke into the condo to get that?"

"Yeah. He said he talked to you this morning. Says you're a good man."

I wasn't sure if I needed Hawk's seal of approval, but from the change in Topher's demeanor, it seemed like Topher looked for it.

"Hawk bought that condo a few years ago with the money from the sale of his old tour business. He needs cash now, so he put the condo on the market."

"Why did he have to break in?"

"To get the bowl back and the police had his keys," Topher said. "That bowl belongs to the Yavapai-Apache Nation. It's an artifact that an elder had at his home, but it was lost after he died."

"Aubrey stole it?" Ruby asked.

"I don't think so, he probably bought it on the black market in Mexico," Topher said. "He tried to sell it back to the tribe. They recognized it and asked that he return it."

"So how did Aubrey's bowl end up locked in Hawk's condo?" I asked.

"We put it there," he said.

Topher went on to explain how the tribe tried to deal with Aubrey, but he seemed to think that, since the tribe ran the casino in Camp Verde, there was ample money to pay for the artifact. Hawk had asked Topher to help him negotiate with Aubrey to return the bowl.

"That bowl," Topher explained, "is thought to be from First Woman. The Creation Story is similar to other tribes, in which a girl survives a great flood and is pushed up from a lower world to this one. That bowl was said to have been fashioned by First Woman. It would be like someone trying to sell the Holy Grail to the Catholic Church. No one really owns it, it belongs to the people, to their faith."

"How'd you get possession of it?" I asked.

"Hawk and I took it from Aubrey's house."

"And hid it in the condo?" That wasn't very smart when they knew Aubrey had access to it.

"Yes," he said with a sigh and took a drink of the Margarita. "Hawk wanted to stash it somewhere safe and didn't want me involved anymore than I already was. Since he camped in the desert, he thought the safest place was in that empty condo, in the locked closet where he still kept a few things. We planned to get it the next day and deliver it to the reservation, but when he came by, the police were all over the place."

"Wait a minute," I said. "You and Hawk broke into Aubrey's house the night before he was killed?"

"I didn't say 'break in,' I said we took it. We rang the doorbell and told Aubrey what we were there for and said we wouldn't leave without the bowl."

"A home invasion is what we'd call that in Charlotte," I said.

"Not really. We were invited in, at first. After some discussion, I convinced Aubrey that the Sedona Gentry would appreciate his donation to the indigenous people's cultural heritage. He handed it over, but with a threat that Kimbo would owe him."

"Owe him what?" I asked.

"Who knows? Stature, respect, favors? All I know is the artifact is back where it belongs."

"But, Aubrey is dead," I reminded him.

"Yeah, but it doesn't have a thing to do with Hawk or me or the artifact."

I wasn't so sure.

We found a table and ordered dinner. Topher and I switched to ice water since we had to drive back to Sedona, down Mingus Mountain and its twisting roads, at night. Ruby continued with her wine. The tourists thinned out as the evening came, and the restaurant's atmosphere glowed under the yellow lamp light, soft music played on the sound system, and the sizzling steaks enticed me with their tangy aroma.

"We went to The Copper Corset," I told Topher. "And the woman there relayed the story of Pearl getting beheaded."

"I think it's a fable about 'losing one's head' just like other legends and archetypes."

"I have studied Carl Jung," I said and tried to associate what a beheading could symbolize. "Two things I can come up with, off the top of my head —"

"Aww, bad pun," Topher groaned.

"Okay, okay, here's what I have: Punishment or guilt over something, or the need to use the head less for thinking and go more with emotions."

"Knowing this town," Topher said, "it would be a little of each in the Pearl legend. Jerome is extremely liberal in its political views, using the heart instead of the head, and there seems to be some remorse for the way things happened in the past, like mine strikes and the violence around them, although few of the descendents of those people are still here."

"Pearl being a lady of the night," Ruby remarked, "makes it a morality tale, just like what Mama would tell me about those women that walked the railroad tracks around downtown Charlotte. She would say, 'Ruby, keep your knees together and you'll be a good girl.' And that's what I did."

"That's right. It's that simple," Topher said. "The decapitation adds a gruesome tone to it."

Was I using my head too much? Is that why I had the dream?

Guilt never had much effect on me, but maybe I had looked at Aubrey's death from too many intertwining facts. Logic could be the culprit that tied the truth into knots.

Chapter Nineteen

Rumors had spread across Sedona with wildfire speed. The current tale was that Aubrey's will excluded his ex-wife and current girlfriend and left everything to a charity or an environmental organization. I couldn't pin the grocery store cashier down on specifics, but she assured me that she had heard from another customer that the will left the Apache Trails land to a cult run by Clarity Received. Logic was having a difficult time in Sedona, so I decided to try the emotional aspect. I spent Saturday visiting coffee shops, bookstores, restaurants, galleries, and bars, talking up the rumor—the one rumor I thought would trump all others, the one that would bring out the killer, the one that Hawk would need to neither confirm nor deny.

An idea came to me just as my head hit the pillow, then kept me up most of the night until I called Topher. He came over, and we sat on the deck planning it out until the star-speckled night sky blanched with the first signs of the sunrise. Aubrey's attempt to sell the tribe's artifact played into our plan, as well as the fact that most people knew about it. Evidently, the police knew, since they had picked up Hawk for questioning after the murder. His condo being the scene of the murder, the artifact taken from Aubrey the night before, which a curious neighbor had reported to police, the lack of an alibi and a logical motive all contributed to Hawk falling under the watchful eye of the authorities. After Ruby fixed us breakfast, Topher called Hawk at the Blue Jeep office before his first tour. Hawk agreed to neither confirm nor deny the story.

Topher and I canvassed the town. Logically, it didn't make sense, but I had decided that rational thinking had me chasing my own tail, and the wilder the story the better.

The restaurant bars opened for lunch, and I hit Plaisir de Sedona. The blond bartender, Gavin, worked that day, and the place seemed a little more relaxed without the staccato heels of Tricia tapping across the wooden floor.

"Stoli Cosmo, please," I said. A couple of the waitresses hung around, while Gavin fixed their tables' orders. "Tricia in today?" I asked one of the women.

"No, sir, she won't be in. Is there something our manager might help you with?"

"No, no, I just wondered her opinion on her ex-husband's will."

The waitresses looked at each other. "I don't think she knows anything about that," the one waitress said.

"It's a shocker. I heard about it late yesterday in the city clerk's office." I knew the more reliable the location the better. Never mind that the will had not been read yet, or that Aubrey was probably so far in debt that there would be little estate left to bequeath. It was Saturday, and no one could check any facts until Monday. "A lot of people are going to be upset," I added to reel them in.

Gavin set the Cosmo in front of me. "What? What's in the will?" He leaned on the bar with both elbows, like a high school freshman awaiting the announcement of the homecoming court, a court that he may have a stake in, a stake that could bolster his standing in the social ranks of the gossip tree.

"I really wish Tricia were here so I could confirm this," I said then took a sip of the martini. "It's just so odd, this turn of events, that I'm surprised you haven't already heard."

He leaned in closer.

The two waitresses set their drink trays back on the bar and huddled around me.

"You see," I began, "Aubrey had possession of a Native American artifact that he was trying to sell. It belonged to the Yavapai-Apache. You know, they have the casino down in Camp Verde?"

They all shook their heads in agreement that they knew the tribe.

"Well, I guess he felt bad for trying to make money off something that was sacred to them. He returned it to the tribe."

"In the will?" Gavin asked.

"No, before he died." Then I corrected myself. "I mean before he was murdered."

Another sip of my drink helped to move me on with the story. "Apparently, before that, Aubrey had wanted to be absolved of his past sins against the land and against the people of the land. He changed his will a few months ago before he started that new development Apache Trails out there to the west of town."

"Yeah," said one of the waitresses. "Those houses will be set along the ridge and ruin the sunset views for all of Sedona."

"Exactly," I said. "He knew that and wanted to prevent it. Aubrey loved the scenic beauty of the place too. He was setting restrictions to keep the ridge line natural, and the homes below it. But in case he couldn't finish his project, he changed the will to ensure the stewards of the land would do what was best, what *should* be done."

"What?" Gavin asked, so close I could feel his breath on my cheek.

I swallowed hard to hold my emotions in check. "He willed Apache Trails back to the Yavapai-Apache Nation. That western ridge now belongs to the reservation. For all these years, land was taken from them, their land, and they were pushed to areas that no white man wanted. Now, finally, they have back part of their sacred grounds. The development value of that land is immense with it being on the edge of Sedona. The views are spectacular. The tribe will know what to do with it."

All three of Tricia's employees leaned back as if allowing the information to filter through them. The waitresses gathered their trays and delivered the drinks to their customers. Gavin's eyes flicked back and forth as he thought. He disappeared into the kitchen.

I could imagine his frantic phone call to Tricia.

My own cell phone rang with Topher asking me to meet up with him at the art gallery. "I want to watch Ty and Alison's faces when they hear the news from you; I wouldn't be able to keep a straight face," he said. "Oh, I just got a call from Hawk. Kimbo called him from

Scottsdale, expressing his concern whether the tribe would know what to do with a parcel of land like Apache Trails. He offered his assistance to the Tribal Council."

"Perfect," I said. "When do you think he and Tricia will be back here?"

"It's a two hour drive from Scottsdale," Topher explained, "so I would guess within ninety minutes—Kimbo will be breaking land speed records up Interstate 17."

I drove to the art gallery on the hill and saw Topher's Jeep in the parking lot. He and the saleswoman Courtney each smoked a cigarette at the corner of the lot next to a bushy manzanita.

"This is the only place we can smoke without Ty and Alison seeing us," he said and flicked an ash on the pavement. "They have cameras aimed all over the interior and exterior of the place."

"We know the blind spots," Courtney added. "I don't feel like listening to a lecture from Alison. She's on this 'green' kick: reduce, reuse, recycle. She doesn't have any respect for the environment; it's a way to promote herself to the clients, a way to show how thoughtful and caring she is. Bitch. She drives that huge Cadillac Escalade and then has the audacity to yell at us for coming to work with coffee in a throw-away cup. And smoking 'fouls the pure air of the gallery' she says. I guess instead of smoking, she'd rather I fart."

"I don't know if it's an either/or situation," I said.

"No, but when the bitch dies, all that crap injected into her face and in her tits won't decompose for thousands of years." Courtney wasn't in a very good mood. She apparently thought of something else bad about Alison. "And she's become the new best friend of Doris Weintraub."

That stopped me. "Doris? What about Doris Weintraub?"

"The 'Green Queen' of Northern Arizona," Courtney said. "She's another one that has locked onto environmentalism as a path to fame and fortune."

"Yeah," Topher added. "Doris heads up an organization that helps businesses reduce their carbon footprint. She helped us get Blue Jeeps green-certified."

"I saw a picture in her office of you and Kimbo."

"That was a ceremony her group had for us."

"And that's the kind of publicity Alison wants for the gallery," Courtney added and ground out her cigarette. "Anything to get her mug in the newspaper."

"Come inside with us," Topher told her. "And stand close enough to hear. We have something to buckle the Botox Bimbo."

Along the path to the front door, I noticed the security cameras from each corner of the building, the cables securing the outdoor sculptures to posts, the electric sensor that alerted our approach to the door. A gust of cold air washed over me as the automatic glass doors hissed open. Topher headed straight for one of the offices with the blinds drawn and the door closed. Just as he started to knock, Ty turned the corner, same bibbed overalls topped with a suit jacket, his skinny frame stiff under all the cloth.

"Topher," he said with a smile as frigid as the gallery's air. "What are you doing in today?"

"I was just going to alert Alison that I was in the building. Last time I was here she insisted that she know the moment I walked in."

Although Ty hadn't received an answer to his question as to Topher's appearance, he turned his attention to me. "Mister Mason, of the Harris Construction Company, how nice of you to visit us again," Ty said. "Is there anything in particular you are looking for?"

"I might be. We have a branch of the company that procures art for some of our projects. Topher wanted me to see some of the artists you represent, strictly an unofficial viewing, since that department doesn't report to me."

"Of course, of course," he said and looked over his shoulder to see Courtney. "Call Alison's office and let her know we have a guest," he instructed her. He took hold of my elbow to lead me down a corridor.

I jerked my arm from his grasp. "Please, don't touch me."

He apologized, and began pointing out large paintings and reciting the accomplishments and celebrity collectors of the artist.

"I had wanted to have a monumental sculpture for the entrance to Apache Trails," I began.

"Perfect," he said. "Did you know that Alison and I have already purchased a parcel there to build our new home? And to have one of our artists' works at the entrance... Well, that would be perfect."

"Won't happen," I said. "Now it seems the project will be scrapped. I mean with that heir, who would have guessed it?"

A whiff of sharp perfume heralded Alison's arrival. "Derek," she said and reached for my arm, but Ty caught her just inches from contact and shook his head *no* to her. The surprised wrinkle of her brow under her fringe of blonde bangs told me that I was playing the eccentric, rich art collector better than I thought.

Ty and Alison's method was to befriend a client. Just as a car salesman becomes your best buddy as soon as you walk on the lot, these two worked to win confidence and credibility. But I needed to establish a superior position, one of authority, a man without need, with no position for them to fill. All to make him try harder. Ty had connections throughout the town, and if he could relay our story to other business owners, then the employees we had already talked to would confirm the tale.

"As I was saying," I began again without looking at Alison, "the heir who now controls the future of Apache Trails will probably abandon it." We had stopped in front of a painting of the Grand Canyon. "No, no canyon paintings. Southwest is too regional for our developments. We have buildings all over the country. Show me your diversity." I kept their minds on two different subjects. "The tribe could do anything with that land."

"What land?" Alison asked.

"Apache Trails."

"What tribe?" Ty asked.

I sighed. "The Yavapai-Apache."

Neither one of them moved. Ty's hands stayed in his overall's pockets, and Alison held onto her strand of pearls.

"Seems like. the reservation just expanded to West Sedona," Topher added.

Tricia would believe that she had lost out on any inheritance, as would Clarity. Kimbo and the Sedona Gentry would feel relieved that the development was ditched and the land would be preserved with Kimbo's Blue Jeeps rolling along unsoiled vistas. Myra should think that all her troubles with the project would go away, since the tribe would pay off all liens on the property, including her bank's. The real estate community might be disappointed in losing the commissions, but at least the views of town would be saved. And Doris Weintraub and the environmentalists would be happy that the land would go back to the tribe. So the only people who'd get screwed by our story were Aubrey's women, the two logical candidates for heir to his estate.

Back at the rental house, while Ruby joined her friends for an early supper, Topher and I searched the Internet for information on Doris Weintraub and her green group. Eco-terrorism, I thought, could be the answer to the arson of the new homes under construction. The modus operandi fell into place with what I researched; arson of property seemed to be a popular statement. "The police, Homeland Security, or the FBI should have considered this," I said, while leaning back in the uncomfortable wooden chair, rubbing my eyes.

"I bet they did," Topher said. He handed me a bottle of water and sat on the corner of the dining room table where I had my laptop set up. "Her group isn't militant. It's mostly local people who want to educate and recruit members to help the environment. I think it's a dead end."

"But what would it take for someone to commit murder?" I asked. "To scalp Aubrey?" My mind went to Devil's Bridge and what Topher had said. "Self-defense?"

Topher was quiet.

The sunlight sent a glint of orange off my cell phone lying next to the computer. I picked it up and called Mark.

"What's up?" he answered.

"Sorry to call you on a Saturday afternoon."

"No that's fine," he said. "Kathleen has me up in Hickory looking at furniture for the baby's room. Actually, I'm sitting on a bench while she scours one of the stores. What's up?"

"What is the official name for a guy who inspects construction sites?"

"That could be any number of men. What specifically are you looking for?"

"The bank here, Myra's bank," I said and noticed Topher look up and at me. "The certified inspections of Apache Trails," I began, "the inspection reports that Myra would have received to disburse funds for the project, what certification would that person have?"

"Again, it could be anything, but the most common is a CBO, a Certified Building Official." Mark said. "It really depends on the local and state codes."

"But this person would have access to the buildings, unsupervised access?"

"Sure. You thinking that Conley guy who filed the bogus Apache Trails reports is up to something?"

"Maybe," I said and began searching Aubrey's files we had copied to my laptop. Mark continued to discuss the type of inspectors and specific areas of expertise. I found Conley's full name: Thomas Ray Conley. "Hey, Mark, let me make a phone call to check up on this guy. Talk to you later." Mark had enough to deal with between Kathleen's nursery shopping spree and Harris Construction, so I avoided telling him anything more about the murder.

But I did have a confidant: Daniel. I hadn't returned his calls, but then, he hadn't really asked me to. I excused myself from Topher, so I could call Daniel in private. On the deck, I lit a cigarette and paced from rail to rail. His phone rang several times, and I prepared to leave a message when he suddenly picked up.

"Man, thanks for the timing. One of the city council members had me on the office phone and my ringing cell gave me a good excuse to get out of that conversation. How's it hanging?"

"Dude, swinging low and free," I said 'cause I know he thinks it's funny when I talk all twenty-something. "What are you doing in the office on a Saturday?"

"Journalism never has a day off. You remember that. Seems

like that was part of our problem." His tone didn't make that an accusation, just a statement of fact. Besides, it was his choice to work 24-7.

"You're a hard worker, buddy. Try to get out and have a little fun tonight."

"I would if you were here instead of out there in the Wild West."

God, he was pulling at me. I decided to change the subject. "I need some of your expertise. I have a name of a guy who worked on some shady deals with our ex-real estate agent. He's disappeared. Can you find anything on him? Don't spend a lot of time, just wondering if your sources might uncover something I can't." I gave him Conley's full name and other information I had pieced together from Aubrey's files.

"I'll see what I can do. You can take me to dinner when you come back home."

Daniel felt comfortable and safe, a good feeling, but the sensation from Topher was smoldering and adventurous, something that Daniel and I had lost a long time ago. Just as I began to say my good-byes, Daniel stopped me.

"Hold up. That was easier than we thought." Silence filled the gap; I assumed he was reading what he'd discovered. "Get to your computer," he said.

Inside, Topher leaned over the table with the environmentalists' website up on the screen and was reading their press clippings.

"I think I have a tip," I told Topher. He moved the laptop over to my side of the table, and I told Daniel I was at the computer.

"Google his name and Nogales," Daniel instructed. "I found it on the wire, but I'm sure Google has it by now."

I searched it. "Fuck."

"What?" Topher asked.

"Conley was murdered three days ago on the Mexico side of Nogales."

"Dude, I gotta go," I said into the phone. "Thanks a billion, and I'll settle up with you later."

"I look forward to it," Daniel said. "Sorry that hit a dead end—

uh, bad pun. I'll keep looking and let you know if I find anything more."

I read the article from the Nogales, Arizona newspaper after I hung up with Daniel. Topher leaned over my shoulder reading it too. I had hoped to find out if Conley was certified, and if he worked on any of the buildings that had been burnt down, thinking that he might have had a hand in it, an insurance angle or maybe a he had a beef with developers or...shit, I knew I was grasping. Now, the one person who had been in on Aubrey's scheme to collect funds for work not completed had gone missing, then turned up dead in Mexico.

"They suspect it was a drug deal gone bad," Topher surmised. "Could Aubrey have met the same fate?"

I didn't tell him what I had found out from Selestino about Tricia and her methamphetamine habit that Aubrey fed, so it was possible that Conley had been killed in the drug wars, but I didn't think anyone would have travelled up to Sedona to off Aubrey—that was a long drive. *Hell, gasoline is expensive.*

"Seems like Aubrey had more going on than that," I said and turned to look at him. "In fact, when you first found out, you said you weren't surprised. What's your theory?"

The wooden chair across from me skipped across the tile floor as he pulled it out and slipped into it, his forearms rested on the table in a casual manner, his eyes fixed on me. "Aubrey was an asshole."

I laughed. "No one will debate against that point."

"When we first moved here, he took an interest in Myra. She was dating a bartender I worked with at the Cowboy Club. Aubrey pursued her, but she liked Cal, the bartender. Eventually, Aubrey started dating Clarity. Myra and Cal broke up. Aubrey always made suggestive comments to Myra, but she ignored it, especially as they started working together. I tend to believe that Aubrey went to Myra's bank specifically so he could work with her on this project."

"He's a bit older than her, or *was* older than her," I corrected. "And he was milking the investors and using her to issue the money from the bank control account, dragging her into the fraud." *Revenge for being ignored?*

"What?" Topher blurted out. "He did what?"

I explained the process of the investors' money going to an account that the bank controlled and how the bank would add funds from their loan as needed.

"I knew it. He would do something like that. He would always find a way to mention Devil's Bridge to her, knowing the subject upset her."

"It upsets you too," I said as gently as possible.

"He used it to his advantage. I mean it was no secret what happened, it was an accident, but Aubrey always brought it up when he saw me, just to get to me, to ruffle me."

"Why would he do that?"

"He was an asshole," Topher stated. "No, more than that. He didn't like Kimbo, and I saw that raw side of him when he encountered Kimbo and Tricia together. I'm sure he thought I was the reason Myra rebuffed him."

"He didn't seem the type to let romance alter his course," I said. "I mean he was a lot of things, but a man of romantic passion, I doubt." I twisted the cap off the water bottle, but didn't drink. "Money. That's what he had a passion for. The Sedona Gentry was his ticket to wheeling and dealing with the town's elite. He couldn't get big deals, so he scuttled around in the dirt with black market artifacts, minor drug deals, shady real estate transactions."

The doorbell rang, and we looked at each other as if we couldn't decide if it should be answered.

"You think Aubrey has come back to repute our assessment of him?" Topher asked.

For some reason, that did jolt me. I had been so intent on analyzing him that he was the first person to come to mind when I heard the bell. "Silly," I said, but I checked the peephole.

Detective Sarras smiled when I opened the door. "Mind if I come in?"

With a confident stride, he walked over to the table. His head moved a bit as if scanning the room and its contents, including Topher and the laptop with the article on Conley's death displayed on its screen.

"I see you made the connection to Mr. Conley and discovered the unfortunate news," he said.

"Yes," I said and sat back down at the computer and nodded to a chair at the table for Sarras to take. "It was unfortunate, but not related to Aubrey's death. Right?"

"You know I can't discuss that," he said.

Topher stuck out his hand and introduced himself. I had assumed they knew each other, definitely Detective Sarras knew who Topher was, since he had brought him up during my questioning, but this seemed to be their first in-person introduction.

"If you can't discuss what you know about Aubrey's murder, then why did you drop by?" I checked the clock on the television's cable box. "It's tea time—can I get you a glass of sweet tea?"

He stared at me for a moment, but Topher broke his gawk of confusion with a laugh.

"Sweet tea is just iced tea that had sugar added while it was still hot," he explained. "It dissolves so it's smoother and not gritty. Try it."

While I poured three glasses of tea, Sarras began his explanation of his visit; his academic-mind had been in research mode. The rumor mill had been cranking overtime in the small town, but Sarras knew enough to know that the will had not been released by the attorney, and no one had seen it or read it, except that same attorney who would not have revealed the contents to anyone, not even contents as sensational as what people had conferred confidentially across grocery check-outs, sales desks, and hardware store counters.

"So," he concluded, "I thought, how would a rumor like that get started? Hawk and you, Mr. Langston, secured the Yavapai bowl from Mr. Garner the night before his murder, but I knew the tale needed a kick from someone with a little inside knowledge, maybe someone who had a flare for drama."

"You mean a *gay* man?" I asked. "That's just a stereotype," I added, "like all cops have power issues because of their small dicks."

His demeanor shattered. "No, I mean you have been in the middle of this since you first tracked his blood across the floor. Did you notice that?"

"I stepped in it."

"The blood was pooled around him, but not anywhere else in the house," Sarras said and sipped his tea as if waiting for me connect a few dots.

"Yeah, he was dead before he was placed there..." I thought it through. "If not dead, then unconscious. The scalping didn't kill him. Something else did. But he drove there. His car was in the driveway. He signed the book on the kitchen counter."

"He knew the killer," Topher concluded.

"Someone he trusted and wasn't afraid of," I added. "That clears you and Hawk," I said to Topher.

"Me?" he asked.

I just hunched my shoulders as if to say "everyone's a suspect" and turned my attention to Sarras. His dark eyes stared at the laptop's screen.

"Listen," he said. "We need to watch Hawk. Do you know where his camp is?"

"No," Topher answered. "I've never been to it, and he's never mentioned it at work."

"From the direction the stories are going, Hawk might be a target for some abuse." Sarras didn't elaborate, and my mind backtracked to the night with Selly when Hawk's Jeep came over that hill, his camp had to be nearby.

Topher caught Sarras's statement. "What do you mean by abuse?"

"Just help me find him." Sarras got up and took his empty glass to the kitchen counter. "I'm inclined to think that this rumor has put him in more danger than anyone anticipated."

CHAPTER TWENTY

"His shift ended about fifteen minutes ago," Topher said as he snapped his cell phone closed. He nodded toward the front window and said, "Make sure Sarras is gone. I don't want him following us to find Hawk."

The plain, white sedan had turned the corner and disappeared below the shadow of Sugarloaf Rock. "He's out of sight."

"Let's go then," Topher said. "We can probably catch Hawk at the post office or on his way out Highway 89A."

Topher's Jeep blocked my Explorer in the driveway, so we piled into the Jeep and headed toward the post office. Like any small town, unofficial town centers drew people, and in Sedona it was the post office. At any given time, the post office hosted a full parking lot and residents standing around talking—this was no exception. Topher circled the lot, but didn't see Hawk's Jeep. He decided to stop and ask if Hawk had kept his after work routine of gathering his mail. He spoke to several people when we entered the building and asked a couple if they had seen Hawk. More than one remarked on the good luck of the tribe to inherit Apache Trails.

"Jen," Topher yelled to a woman behind the counter. "Has Hawk been in?"

"Just missed him," she said.

We both turned and stumbled into Clarity, her gypsy skirts swishing, post office box key in her hand.

"Oh this is terrible," she started.

"Sorry, Clare," Topher said. "We need to catch up with someone."

"The casino," she said. "How could Hawk allow that?"

I turned back to her and grabbed Topher's shirttail to stop his exit. "A casino?" I asked.

"Yes, events can't lead to this," she said and swayed back and forth in her sandals. "I heard about Aubrey's will. First I didn't believe it because he never talked of such a thing, but then I was so proud of him. Giving the land back to the rightful guardians, that brings the world into alignment, but I had forgotten how the material world corrupts pure souls."

"Not quite following you," I said.

"Who's corrupted?" Topher asked.

"The tribe. Instead of turning the land back into its natural state, they say it's part of the reservation and a perfect location to build a casino." She twisted her keychain in her hands. "Think about it, a casino built on the ridge just outside the city limits, it would ruin the town and turn this sacred place into a mini-Vegas." Her eyes flashed around the post office as if she searched for someone to explain it all to her, to tell her it was a nightmare. She latched onto Topher's shirt, scrunching the front into her fists and pulling him to her, pleading, "They can't, they just can't do that."

Instead of multi-million dollar estates lining the ridge, blighting the view of the famous Sedona sunsets, the horror of all horrors was a casino. Its flashing lights and traffic spoiling the landscape, and on the Yavapai Nation's land, just out of reach of the state and city's tax collectors. Nothing could be worse for the town. *Why didn't I think of that?* But a rumor has a way of picking up the best details as it rolls across fertile ground.

"Hawk would not let this happen," she reassured Topher, while he tried to loosen her grip on him. "Someone said it was his idea. That he had tired of working for other people and wanted the tribe to increase its financial resources." She glanced down and saw the keys she must have dropped when reaching for Topher. She released him and bent to pick them up. "He said there would be money for a retreat center."

I reached down to help her back up; she seemed broken, muttering about karma.

"Yes, Aubrey's karma—" I started to say, but Topher patted my shoulder in his impatience to find Hawk.

"Clare, don't worry," was all Topher could say before the glass door slammed behind us and we rushed to his Jeep.

The first pass along Highway 89A took us as far as the high school, but we didn't see Hawk on the road, so we turned around and watched the side streets and searched the two grocery store parking lots for his Jeep. Nothing. No sign of Hawk.

Tap, tap, tap, Topher drummed his fingers on the steering wheel while we sat at the far end of the Safeway lot. "We must have just missed him," he said, "and if people think he's responsible for a casino being built, then what happened to Aubrey is nothing compared to what the entire town will want to do to Hawk. As word makes it around... Detective Sarras is right: Hawk needs to be somewhere safe. We have to find him." He looked me up and down, then sighed.

"What? I can help find him. I'm not useless in the desert."

"No, I was just thinking that you need to change into hiking boots, and that we need to get some food, since we might be searching for a few hours." He took my chin in his hand and pulled me close. His lips touched mine, once, then again. "You're very valuable. Never think you're useless."

And never had I or would I, but I let him console me as if I had doubts.

Backpacks with water, apples, sandwiches, and a few beers rode in the back of the Jeep. I had changed into hiking shorts and t-shirt along with boots and left a note for Ruby in case she arrived back home before me. I debated with myself while I changed clothes about telling Topher about Selly and my night adventure in the desert, to help explain why I thought I might have a general idea of Hawk's camp. The Angel and Devil fought across my shoulders: Did it really matter? Did I owe an explanation to Topher? Once in the Jeep, we headed west out of town.

I started the conversation with: "I saw Hawk the other night driving out of the desert." The details started to flow, how I wondered about Tricia and Kimbo, how I met Selly and the information I found out.

The meth snorting surprised Topher the most. "Never would I have thought Tricia would do that. And you heard it from the handymen at Hawk's condo too? This Selly guy confirmed it, had participated in it with Tricia?"

"Yes, he had graphic details," I said and I thought about what Selly had said about Kimbo watching. "Oh," I started, thinking I might as well get it all out, "ever hear of DiscoverDick.com?"

He smiled. "Well, yeah, I'm gay. Most guys know about it."

"I didn't," I said. "Have you ever used it?"

"Browsed through it," he admitted. "Wondered if I knew any of the headless images. Some guys I know get dates out of it, but I couldn't do that. A person's brain and personality attracts me more than the physique."

"A friend asked me to critique his profile, a friend from Charlotte," I explained, but didn't mention he was my cousin or any of the baggage that went with that. "So while I was at the site, I decided to check out the Sedona listing. Ever hear of BlueBoy?"

"Just the painting by Gainsborough. Oh, and there used to be a magazine, not sure if that's still around," he said raising his voice over the wind noise from the highway and the top-down Jeep.

"I'm talking about a Sedona man calling himself BlueBoy on DiscoverDick.com," I said. "I think it's Kimbo."

A quick glance away from the highway, Topher shot me a frown. "I doubt that," he said.

"Why? Why do you think Kimbo is so pure and good?"

"I don't think that. He's different than most people, different in a way that Michael Jackson was, a kid thrust into the business of entertainment, a loss of his childhood. Kimbo, unlike Michael Jackson, developed a business-oriented mind, but like Michael, he seems almost a eunuch."

"Kimbo's *eunuch-ness*," I said to myself and remembered how he had washed the ash off me as if he was washing off a lawn chair.

"Yes, there is uniqueness to him," Topher said apparently mishearing my muttering. "He never discusses Tricia like some men would; you know how straight men talk about women, like we talk about men? It's almost as if their relationship is intimate, but only in a platonic sense."

"Like you and Myra?"

"A little bit, but Myra doesn't fulfill all my needs like Tricia seems to do for Kimbo." He smiled while maneuvering the Jeep off the highway and onto the dirt road I had told him about. "Some I end up taking care of myself." He laughed. "Not that it's my ideal situation, but a man does what he has to do."

"I'm sure there are plenty of guys in Northern Arizona that you could find to scratch your back," I said and reached over and ran my fingernails across his shoulder.

"Stop that or I'll do more to you than that Selly guy did." He mocked a warning that only kept my hand on his shoulder, rubbing, scratching, teasing.

The wheels of the Jeep slipped into a rut, probably the same one I hit with the Explorer that night, and jostled us along the road. We crested the hill that I remembered Hawk driving over, and a wide, flat expanse of land spread out before us. Topher stopped the Jeep on the summit of the hill. The road appeared to continue through junipers, pinyon, manzanita, and cactus, and the scrub brush grew high enough that it hid most of the road from our view. My guess was that two or three miles of forest service land stretched across to the far rock formations that hemmed in this valley. The wind gusted up the hill in a warm, dry blast of air, the faint scent of exhaust twirled around the Jeep.

"I don't see anything that looks like a camp." Topher idled the Jeep and set the brake then stood up in his seat to get a better look. He leaned on the top of the windshield. "Check my backpack for binoculars."

I found them, handed them over, and waited while he scanned the scene.

"Take a look." He offered the binoculars to me, and I searched the horizon while he turned off the engine. "If he's driving along this road, we should see a trail of dust kicked up by his Jeep."

Rusty brown dust had settled on the hood and dashboard, and on me, in just the few minutes that we had driven along the road, and I glanced back to see a cloud of dust blowing off into the blue sky from our ascent up the hill. "He must be at his camp by now. Why don't we drive along and look for a turnoff?"

The Jeep crawled down the hill and over some fairly large boulders that edged a dry creek bed, where I lost sight of the road, but Topher recognized the continuation of it on the other side. The dips and bumps in the road elbowed and shoved us from side to side until I had to ask Topher if we still followed the route, or any route. He assured me he hadn't veered off, and that this was the condition of the Apache Trails road before the development started, and this was what the tourists loved about Blue Jeep's tours. "I'm glad I didn't eat before we left town," I said feeling a bit of motion sickness.

Dry branches scraped against my side of the Jeep with a high screech. "Arizona pinstripes," Topher called the scratch in his door. "It's difficult to keep paint on a vehicle out here."

His smile told me he loved every minute of this drive. "Now tell me why you stopped conducting tours and moved into the marketing office," I said.

"Money," he said and shrugged his shoulders, "and I'm not getting any younger. Now is a great time to drive, but in the winter, in the cold rain... I remember one February night, in the sleet, driving the Jeep to the garage and having to wash it off so it was ready for the next morning. My hands were numb. I was wet, cold, and miserable. That's when I thought I could find a desk job so much more satisfying. The money is good for driving a tour, but for the same amount with regular indoor hours, I couldn't say no when Kimbo offered it. Now, I can drive when the weather suits me."

Branches obstructed my sight, and it felt as if we were at the lowest part of the valley, a fact confirmed by the number of rocks, tree branches, and logs that had been washed through the area in the last storm. The place looked as if it would be under water if a serious rain began. The Jeep bounced and rolled over the boulders and rocks, no dust flared behind us, no trace of our route except for the crack and snap of branches we drove over.

"Look." Topher pointed toward a clearing off the dry creek bed. "There are tire tracks in the dirt by that cypress." He parked the Jeep and jumped out to inspect the tracks.

"What are you looking for?" I asked.

"See how fresh our tracks are?" He nodded toward the back of the Jeep where our tires had left sharp, clear imprints of the tread in the powdery dirt. "Now here." He brought my attention back. "These aren't as defined. The wind has smoothed them a little, ridges are rounded, the valleys aren't as deep."

"So this might be a day or two old?" I asked.

"Probably this morning since the wind's been up today," he said. "Someone pulled out of here and left. Bet there's a camp up that path. Let's go see if it's Hawk's." The backpack slapped his shoulder as he slung it over, and he bent his arms through the straps.

"But," I said thinking this through, "Hawk isn't here. No one has been here since this morning. When he comes back for the evening, he'll park here."

"Maybe, maybe not. I'm sure he can get to his campsite from several different routes. And besides, it will be dark in a few hours so if we don't find him there, we can leave a note about the latest rumor and warn him to be careful. Actually," he stopped and seemed to consider alternatives, "I should ask him to come into town and stay at my place or with Kimbo."

"Kimbo?" I asked.

"Kimbo isn't a killer."

"No, but Tricia may be."

He shook his head in amusement. "She may like tight little Mexican guys and a snort of meth, but she wouldn't kill Aubrey. You said yourself, he was her source for her habit."

I shrugged on my backpack and followed him through the trees along a faint trail. "But, if she found out that he had changed his will to exclude her—"

"Ah," Topher interrupted my theory. "Why would she hurt him then? She would inherit nothing."

"Smart ass," I complained. "We really don't know who is named in the will. Our rumor says it is the tribe, but it could be anyone. Did Myra go to the attorney's office in Cottonwood? She might know."

A rumor had a way of becoming truth when it was repeated often, and my mind kept getting rumor and fact confused. I noticed Topher had his cell phone out and punching keys. He listened, but then shut it closed. "I can't get a good signal. I was going to check with Myra."

Along the trail, he pointed out different plants and a few lizards that we didn't have in the east. He kicked at stands of dead grasses from the wet winter coupled with a long dry spring. Shadows grew long and lean, and my stomach growled for food. Topher continued to talk and hike ahead of me, so I grabbed his belt to stop him and I turned around so my backpack was in his face. "Unzip me."

"Excuse me?"

"Unzip me and stick your hand in there."

He reached around and tugged down the zipper on my fly.

"No," I pulled away from him. "I meant the backpack. Hell, if I had known it was that easy to get you going I would have said that last week."

"Sorry," he said and reached around and zipped my fly back up. "I thought you had become awfully aggressive suddenly. But, I like to comply when I can."

"I wanted an apple from my backpack."

This time he unzipped the backpack and dug around to retrieve an apple and a bottle of water that we shared while we walked.

Ruby's decision to move seemed to be wavering, and I thought it was mainly because she would have no family in Arizona. But the more I watched Topher, hiking, talking, loving this place, I wondered if I should give it a try too. We could rent a place for a year, see if Ruby really liked it, I could find work, get to know Topher a little better. So what if our real estate agent was murdered? That doesn't make the town a bad place to live. What did I have back in Charlotte? Not much.

"Hold up," Topher said. He stopped and searched the surrounding area. "I can't tell where this trail is. I don't think Hawk would stay too far from his Jeep. There's no reason to go that far." He climbed an outcropping of rocks and I followed him. "I want to get up higher to look for a sign of a camp."

The sun had lowered quite a bit from the time we started the hike. My watch claimed it was almost 6:30 in the evening, well past the cocktail hour.

From atop the rocks, we could see over most of the scrub brush, juniper, and pinyon pine.

"There," he said and pointed back toward the east, "I see dust kicked up by a vehicle. It could be Hawk."

"Is it headed this way?"

He jumped down from the rock. "I think so, but the wind is whipping the dust around. I bet that's him coming in from Dry Creek Road."

The steady breeze held a chill as the sun crept down in the sky. "If Kimbo is so eunuch, then why does he have a DiscoverDick profile?"

"You still stuck on that?"

"Yeah," I admitted. "If he has trouble getting it up, why look for dates?"

"They make pills for that," Topher said. "And besides, that's more than I want to know about my boss."

"He has a place in the same complex as Hawk's condo. I saw him there once. Seems like I accidently picked up the key to the crime scene when Ruby and I walked in that day."

"Yeah, I know."

"You know? What do you mean?" Then it hit me that he, not Myra, had taken the key, snatched the wrong one from the table. "Why? Why did you take the key?"

"Clarity asked me to. She said you had Hawk's key, and the Yavapai Bowl needed to be removed from the crime scene. She was afraid that it would implicate Hawk to Aubrey's murder scene."

I sat down next to him on the rock. "Why didn't you ask for it? I didn't know I had it until I couldn't open our door with it. I would have handed it over." Maybe, I thought, maybe not.

"Then I would have had to explain about the bowl and us

retrieving it from Aubrey the night before his murder." He sighed. "Just too much. You didn't need to be more involved." Out of his backpack, he pulled two beers. "Still cold, want one?"

"The bowl wouldn't have implicated him any more than owning the condo and having access to it." I chugged the beer, being thirstier than I realized. Breathing in while I gulped the cold beer, I could almost smell a grill, fired up and ready for a London broil, roasted potatoes, onions, and bell peppers. "A steak would be good tonight," I said and wiped my mouth with the back of my hand. The scent of mesquite made my stomach rumble. "Clarity?"

"Yeah, she told me you had the key." He furrowed his brow as he thought. Then in a slow, measured voice: "She *did* tell me that."

"I didn't know I had it. How did she?" The other events of that morning had been overpowered by the discovery of Aubrey's body and the police questionings, but I remember walking into the condo and pulling the key from the lock. "She must have seen us. She must have seen us walk into the condo."

The sharp odor of burning wood grew stronger. Topher jumped up and scrambled back to the tip of the rock. "Fire!" he yelled. "Wildfire!"

Chapter Twenty-One

The pop and sizzle sounded far away, but when I joined Topher at the top of the rock ledge, I could see smoke moving toward us within a football field's length. I didn't see flames, but the column of rising gray smoke tilted with the wind, arcing over our heads. *Could this be another drumming circle?* But the source of the smoke progressed, fast. Then I saw it—orange-red flames flicked between a few trees, more gray smoke bellowed up. I turned to look in the direction we had come, the direction of the Jeep, and clear skies called us back. "Let's get out of here," I said and grabbed both backpacks, skidding half way down the rock on my butt.

Topher kept trying his cell phone. "No signal," he yelled down. "What about yours?"

My hand searched the side pocket on my shorts and found the phone, but no signal displayed. I tried it anyway. "Nothing," I said. "Come on, let's get back to the Jeep. We can call once we get closer to the highway."

A brief hesitation told me Topher had more on his mind. "A camp," he said after he joined me at the foot of the rock. "I think the fire must have started from a camp. Brush and dry grass don't spontaneously combust, something sparked it and there's no lightning."

The odor of smoke, pungent with sage, and the crack and sputter of limbs breaking and falling warned me that the fire sprinted toward us with the wind. "I don't think we can search for a camp up ahead. The fire has probably already taken it if one was there." I handed him his backpack and started back down the path.

Our pace, urgent at first, turned into a jog as the smoke, thick and gray-black, blocked out the sun, bellowing over our heads, dusting us with the scents of juniper and brittlebush, and singing the screech of steam sizzling out of the pinyon boughs. Dodging exposed roots, clumps of sharp bladed grass, loose rocks, small boulders, and the reaches of prickly pear cactus created a high speed obstacle course as we ran. I led the way, but kept checking to make sure Topher stayed close. Yucca spikes knifed my calves while ocotillo spines stabbed my arms, and just as I rounded a corner, a wall of gray smoke, backed by a furnace of heat halted our retreat.

Topher stopped behind me and twisted around to look for another exit. "There," he said and pointed through a manzanita with branches swaying in the sudden rush of wind that began to swirl around us. "Drop the backpacks, they're slowing us down," he said and slid out of his. I threw off mine and followed him into the tangle of branches, luckily branches without thorns.

Heat assaulted me from two sides, thick smoke shrouding the flames, hiding the fiend that followed us, as if the smoke was the fire's battle shield, its first line of defense that forced our retreat into the dry wash of boulders, decaying tree branches, sticks, and scattered dry leaves—all fuel for the wildfire. Topher coughed. My eyes watered and my lungs felt seared by the flying, flakey ash. An ember landed on Topher's cap, glowing and smoldering. I snatched the hat from his head and beat it against the ground before handing it back to him. He slapped the cap back on his head and his mouth moved as he said "thanks," but I couldn't hear his words. The crack of a tree trunk had usurped his voice. The flaming limb splashed into a stand of dead yucca, spraying sparks across my face and onto our clothes. The flying embers, whipped and blown by the winds, flickered and flashed out. Sweat dripping down my face and soaking my clothes helped to extinguish the kindling spit of the fire as it hissed at us.

Topher stopped, and I ran into the back of him. "There," he said in my ear, his breath ragged and panting, the bill of his cap against my cheek. "It's surrounded us."

Panic melded me to the spot, but as I regained my thoughts, I turned to see smoke and flames in each direction. Scrub brush burned low while the scattering of taller junipers, small oaks, and scrappy maples that lined the dry wash swayed with the advancement of flames from one crown to the next. The blaze seemed to incinerate a tree top as it ignited the next one, skipping across the canopy, raining smoldering ash down.

Charred limbs cracked and fell in front of us, while cinders burned dry leaves behind us.

The struggle to breathe left my nostrils with a singed sensation. I saw soot had collected below Topher's nose as he had inhaled the thick smoke. I wiped my upper lip and saw soot smeared on the back of my hand. Paper napkins and my bandana had been left behind in the backpack, so I pulled the collar of my t-shirt over my mouth and nose, then yelled for Topher to do the same with his shirt.

Panic didn't return. I watched the inferno around me with awe, as if it were a movie, and Topher and I sat safely in a theater. But this theater had torching brush and flames licking the trunks of trees, climbing the loose brittle bark of a sycamore and spreading across its branches to neighboring trees, sprinkling ash and blazing leaves down to the dry ground, and on us.

The scorching heat built its own air currents. The fire leached the oxygen from the air, swirling the winds into a vortex, a whirlwind of sparks, a small tornado of flame and ash formed. The fire devil advanced, swayed, then turned back toward the wall of flames only to re-emerge behind Topher. Blazing tendrils reached out as if to embrace him, but retreated before placing its searing touch to his skin.

I needed my head. Logic had to direct intuition. "We have to find an opening," I said through the collar of my shirt. "We're not completely surrounded. There must be a way out."

He nodded his agreement and pressed his back against mine like he didn't want the wildfire to be able to advance without one of us seeing it. Not a bad idea.

My smoke-stung eyes watered, making the task of focusing on the fire line difficult, and coupled with the fierce heat and blazing red and yellow flames, the scene blurred to the point I resigned myself to only pinpointing the place with the least amount of red. Nothing looked green anymore. A deafening crack smacked the air and blazing twigs and limbs showered around us. Topher grabbed my arm and pulled me several feet until we both stumbled over a large rock at the edge of the dry creek bed and a heavy limb crashed and burst into flames were we had stood.

At first, neither of us moved. The rocky bed of the creek provided some reprieve from the hailstorm of fire. "Topher," I said and pulled him up next to me, "we need to follow the creek bed out."

A quick glance around and he shook his head no. "More trees along the wash, thicker stands, too many trees," he said in jerky breaths. "Away from it, they can't get water. We have to push through. To more barren areas, less fuel for the fire."

"But the Jeep," I said, "the Jeep is along here somewhere."

"We're not driving out of this." He stood and helped me up. "Across the wash, we need to go in that direction." He looked back over his shoulder and said, "We know what's behind us. Pull your shirt up to cover your hair. We have to charge our way through that wall of fire. Don't close your eyes. Watch were you go, but keep moving. Fast." He pulled the shirt down from my nose and mouth and kissed me, hard, urgently. "Now, cover your head and run like hell."

My sweat-soaked shirt helped keep the fire from snaring my clothes and head, but I could feel the hair on my legs and arms singe. The fire wasn't solid. Gaps between flames gave me room to re-navigate, search for breaks, find a passage. At each pause, I confirmed that Topher stayed close, followed my lead. Jump to jump, the decisions on which route became more difficult, my concentration waned, my head ached, my eyes watered. At times, I could feel Topher push me in one direction or another, then I pulled him. Any direction was better than staying still.

The suffocating heat drained my hope. I stumbled. Topher's arm encircled my waist and he pushed me forward. His touch left me, but I continued farther. Through the smoke, I reached around, trying to locate Topher. *Go back, find him.* I couldn't move on without him. The gray air veiled the world. I'd lost him.

Blurs of white embers fell, scorching my arms and legs. My lungs convulsed. My mind numbed. Smoke cloaked my body until I felt...saw...smelled...nothing.

Steamy, that was what I felt. Squeezed and bumped, I was carried. Then the air, cool in my nose and throat, but a hot, wet blanket cocooned my body. Hazy, indistinct images appeared as I opened my eyes.

"Derek," I heard a strange voice say. "I'm leaving you here while I get Topher."

Sharp rocks poked at my back.

A push and pull freed my arms from the blanket, and I rubbed my eyes. The crack, pop, and sputter of the fire continued, but at a distance, while smoke still hovered, but didn't engulf. My vision cleared, and I saw Hawk at the edge of the wildfire, hauling another person wrapped in a blanket. I struggled to stand, to help him, but my arms wouldn't push up, and I tipped back and collapsed to the ground.

Hawk laid Topher next to me. And I thought he looked good, a little sooty and sweaty, but he wasn't burned, he slept.

I woke again as I was nudged and thrust onto a narrow hard stretcher carried by people I didn't recognize. An oxygen mask clamped over my nose and mouth kept me from asking the guys' names. I wanted to thank them for carrying me, since I was so tired I didn't think I could walk back to town.

Chapter Twenty-Two

Ruby held my hand, patting it from time to time, rocking back and forth in the chair next to me as if she had a sad song playing in her thoughts, a lullaby. I squeezed her hand, and she jumped from the chair.

"Lord, oh, Sweet Jesus," she cried, tears tracking her powdered cheeks. "I thought we had lost you."

I started to speak, but my throat wouldn't allow words to emerge, only a racking, razor-edged cough.

Her response was a cup of water held to my lips. Nothing had ever tasted that good—cool liquid, soothing the rough lining of my throat.

"Where's Topher?" I croaked out, not recognizing my own voice.

"Everything's fine," she said and settled next to me again and continued to pat my hand. "The doctor said you had a lot of smoke in your lungs and some burning there too from inhaling the," she seemed to think of the words the doctor had used, "super-heated gases of the fire," she said slow and measured. "You'll be fine, I know it. They want to monitor your breathing." Her lip quivered, and she lost it. "Oh, Derek, I was so afraid you were going to die. It was serious."

"Hawk," I said. "I remember Hawk pulling us out."

"Yes, the police want to talk as soon as you can," she added and rocked her body in the side chair. "They'll come down here when the doctors say it's okay."

"*Down here?* Where?"

"We're in Cottonwood, the regional hospital," she tried to explain as if it made a difference. She stood and glanced out the window. "I like Sedona and this area, but," she said and took a deep breath that made my own lungs hurt just watching her, "I don't think it's the place for me. I can't be away from you. Someone needs to watch out for you. Besides, I miss your sister Valerie and even the cousins. But what's really scary, I miss arguing with Gladys over you. As soon as you're up to it, let's go back home."

I knew what she meant. Family was a pain in the ass, but they were ours. The thought of going back to Charlotte comforted me, but I had unfinished business. Something had happened. Something had bloomed in my mind just before the fire erupted. I needed to talk to Topher to see if he could remember.

Later that morning, Myra walked into my hospital room. Her bloodshot eyes studied me and the defeated droop of her face frightened me. No one would discuss Topher. Although I knew he was in a room nearby, the doctors hadn't allowed me out bed.

"How is he?" I asked, eager she would be the one to offer me a thread of hope.

In the chair by my bed, she rubbed her eyes, as if trying to wipe away the weariness, the fear, the uncertainty.

"Myra?"

"He hasn't regained consciousness," she said. Tears fell onto the white sheet, leaving dime-sized spots of gray. "The fire seems to have seared his lungs, he's in respiratory failure. A breathing machine is pumping in oxygen and trying to pull out the carbon monoxide, but," she stopped and dug in her purse for a tissue. "They—" Her voice cracked, but she started again, "They think the damage is too extensive."

Time passed, but I couldn't comprehend it. Myra cried. I touched a bandage on my arm, aware for the first time of its existence. "Help me," I said to her. "Help me out of bed, I want to see him."

"Derek, I'm not sure you should..." She started to object, but let the protest fall. "Here, take my arm and don't wear yourself out. You aren't breathing that well either."

Well enough not to be on a machine, but I knew I wouldn't be jogging the back roads of Sedona anytime soon. We took a slow walk down the hall to ICU and saw Topher through an observation window, hooked to a breathing apparatus, a few bandages on his arms. His eyes were closed, but it seemed the crystal clear blue from them had seeped to his skin. A doctor and nurse hovered around his bed, so we could only look through the window at him. Apparently, we hadn't endured severe burns, but smoke inhalation had caused the most damage.

"His mother is on her way," Myra said. "They're attempting to keep him..." She inhaled with a shudder. "He's—" She swallowed the words, but tried again. "He won't," she whispered and turned away from the window and me. Sobs shook her whole body. "I'm sorry." She sniffed and blew her nose. "Let me get you back to bed."

I had known him only a short time. She had been his best friend for most of their lives. They were more than friends, more like siblings, parents, and guardians of each other.

Myra wouldn't look up, she couldn't talk, the words stalled in her throat.

I said it so she wouldn't have to. "The pain will be gone. His body can't manage it any more. He can rest." Tears filled my eyes, and I tried to hide it from her, but she hugged me carefully as we both leaned against the beige wall of the corridor and cried.

Someone would pay. As heavy as the grief was, it wallowed in the depths of my soul and blackened to anger.

Before his mother arrived from the Phoenix airport, before Kimbo was able to arrange a connecting flight for her on a friend's private plane, Topher's lungs, even with the assistance of the machines, couldn't deliver enough oxygen or expel enough carbon monoxide. He passed away with Myra, Kimbo, Hawk, Ruby, and me by his side.

CHAPTER TWENTY-THREE

Two bottles of water sat on the table between us, Detective Sarras and me. I had been released from the hospital in Cottonwood, or more specifically, I had left the hospital with the doctor warning me that I needed more observation. What I needed was a cigarette, but Ruby had said she would tie me up and slap me around if she saw me so much as look at a cigarette. Actually, the thought hurt my lungs, so I had taken up sipping water instead. I opened one of the bottles and swished the water around in my mouth before swallowing, then kept the bottle in my hand, loosening and tightening the cap.

"The fire department says it was arson. Started around Hawk's camp, which living in the national forest is a federal crime, and Hawk shouldn't be out there," Sarras stated as if that had been the biggest offence of the past two days. "The wet winter had brought out a lot of grasses that just dried up the past month. That's why it spread so quickly."

"That's not news to me," I said. "I knew someone started the fire. Topher had seen dust kicked up from a vehicle coming toward us."

"Any description?"

"No."

"Ever heard of Salvia Divinorum?" Sarras asked me.

"Yeah, actually, North Carolina just banned it for human consumption. It's legal here, right?"

"Afraid so," he said. "It's become the high of choice for astral projection pilots, not bitter like peyote, and you don't puke your guts out before the trip. It was found in Aubrey Garner's bloodstream." He looked through some file folder he had on the table.

"How do people use it?" I asked. "Smoke?" I leaned forward tapping the water bottle on the table as I waited for him to explain.

"The leaves," he said finally. "You can smoke or chew it like tobacco or brew it into tea. 'The Sage of Diviners' or 'Indian Sage' is what it's called."

"So you still think it has something to do with Hawk?" I couldn't believe he was still following that path.

"I didn't say that," he said, calm as usual. "I hear talk about Salvia use around town. Some pretend Indians try to create a vision quest for the tourists. This is not an illegal drug. People can use it. But Aubrey Garner had a lot of it in his system as if it was his morning smoke and his morning tea."

"Why would he take a hallucinogen just before meeting a client?" My hand stopped tapping the bottle. "It *was*," I said. "It *was* his morning tea, like brewing sweet tea by putting the sugar in while the tea is hot, it dissolves completely. And the dissolved sugar would have masked any odd flavor. How long does it take to kick in?"

"Not long, about fifteen minutes," Sarras said. A quick check of his notes had him flipping pages, slapping sheets off to the side.

"Yeah, Salvia for breakfast would make it hard to concentrate once it kicked in. Fifteen minutes is plenty of time to drive from his house to the condo." I considered it and tried different angles while he re-read his research. "June Cleaver she ain't."

"Clarity Received," he said.

"That's what Topher said, just before the fire: She had seen me pull the key from the lock as we walked into the condo. Clarity, lurking in the bushes like a rattler. Salvia brewed into Aubrey's tea," I said, "then Clarity must have intended to lead him on a spiritual journey once it kicked in—problem was, he had gone to work, to meet us. She must have followed him and waited for the hallucinogens to start."

"A guided trip," Office Sarras said.

"But what killed him?"

"Suffocation," he said.

"She planned out the high, led him on a spiritual crossing to his death, then, apparently, went out to the fire pit and…"

"Fire is cleansing," Sarras said and pushed a photograph across the table for me to see. The image was the fire pit on the back patio, the one I had my hands in when Kimbo discovered me. "A medicine wheel surrounding the fire pit to purify."

"Apache Trails," I added and pulled out my wallet with the folded piece of paper from the fire pit. I flipped over the scrap to show the legend and the Apache Trails title. "This site plan—I found in it."

He took it from me and muttered something about withholding evidence.

With a large amount of argument and a bit of begging, I convinced Sarras to allow me to draw her in. Notice of Topher's death had not been released, and I hoped that word hadn't leaked out of the hospital. The police had instructed the medical staff not to provide any information on Topher to anyone.

The psychics tended to hang out around the New Age shops, giving readings, offering advice, photographing auras, consulting with their fellow intuitives. Clarity's status was above the regular crystal-gazing, tarot card-reading, ancient spirit guide-channeling psychic. Clarity had her own cult. And as Myra informed me off the record, Aubrey's will had named Clarity the lone beneficiary of his life insurance and his sole heir. He had said he wanted her to build the spiritual retreat she had always wanted. I planned to make sure her retreat was to the state penitentiary.

When I entered the shop crowded with pamphlets, books, divining rods, aromatherapy oils, crystals, and goddess clothing, I must have exuded a black aura since the first white-magic woman I walked up to, turned and hurried in the opposite direction. A calming breath and concentration on the Native American flute and drum music wafting from the dusty speakers helped lighten my aura. At the sales counter I asked how to find Clarity Received and was given directions—car-driving directions to my relief instead of spiritual directions—to her office.

A small commercial building housed her place of business, which looked more like a medical office than a spiritual counseling center.

I approached and saw a flutter of eggplant skirts and emerald scarves at the office door as Clarity seemed to struggle with the lock.

"Are you having problems?" I asked in my most relaxed voice. Psychic or not, I didn't want her tuning into my contempt for her.

"Oh," she said when she looked up to see me. "I was just trying to lock the office so I could do some field work."

"Locks can be fussy things," I said and reached for her key ring jammed into the lock. "Some people just give up and leave them in until someone with more patience comes along and can pull them out, like young King Arthur freeing the sword from the stone."

She stepped to the side and allowed me to lock her door, remove the key, and hand back the key ring. "Thank you," she said. "How are the burns on your arms?" she asked nodding at the bandages on each of my forearms.

"Looks worse than it is," I said and tried to smile.

The wind swept waves of blonde hair into her face until she raked it away to say, "I'm going to do a ceremony for Topher's recovery."

I held my breath. After I calmed a bit, I said, "I'd like to participate. He's a good friend of mine, and I want to help."

Suspicion, maybe—that's what I saw in her eyes. But she nodded, and I followed her out to the parking lot. She offered to allow me to ride with her in the van, but I told her I'd rather drive separately. Out into traffic on 89A, we drove toward Dry Creek Road, and passed the police station. I called Sarras and told him we were going somewhere for a ceremony. He warned me not to drink or eat anything she had, and that he would follow in an unmarked car.

The road twisted and turned, and I couldn't see Sarras behind me. Clarity drove the van off the paved road, past the entrance to Apache Trails. Her van kicked up dust making it hard to see, but I continued on even as she took a side Jeep road and bounced into the wilderness. When she stopped I saw that we had arrived at the northern edge of the wildfire site. Probably arriving via the same route she took that day to start the fire. I looked behind me and no dust flared along the trail from another car. *Have we lost Sarras?*

"I want to be engulfed in the aftermath," she said and trudged through the charred landscape, a canvas bag bumping her hip.

Hard, spiky scents hit my nose, bringing back the flames, the heat, the intensity. Burned sticks and limbs crushed under our footsteps. Soot gathered on the hem of her skirt, the fabric darkened as the wind and her stride stirred all the devastation and death around us.

From her canvas bag, she dug out a book of matches and a bundle of white sage and lit one end. "To purify the energy of this site," she announced. She waved the burning packet of dried weeds.

"How can it purify this?" I asked. "A place of arson, fire that destroyed these trees, plants, animals. Whoever did this has more on their soul than sage can clear away."

She stopped and stared at me as if I were a child not quite capable of understanding the adult world. "Some ends justify the means," she stated. "I know what the radical environmentalists do to new construction is harmful, but the act is a symbol of the earth reclaiming what man has wrongly built."

"What about this?" I waved my arms, wincing in pain when the bandages pulled at my skin. "This is what nature built. What kind of fiend would destroy this? What kind of monster would trap me and Topher in a fire that consumed everything it touched?"

"No one was supposed to be here," she said.

"The fire's purpose was what?" I asked.

"Hawk couldn't have recommended it," she said. "I know he has alliances to his people and their financial future, but look at the ridge." She pointed to the east at the Apache Trails property. "Could you imagine a neon-lit, behemoth of a building attracting every tour bus on their way to the Canyon, calling to every piece of trash on the freeway to come here and gamble away their paychecks?" Her voice rose to a slight squeal. "The night sky would disappear. The sunset would fall behind an asphalt parking lot and a blistered three story box of concrete." She shook her head and walked to the bare branches of a juniper. The delicate burnt twigs crumbled with her touch. "No, no this was much worse than Aubrey's development, although that was the first step. A first step to raping the earth. What Hawk had planned took it further. A casino on that property not only ruined the land, the views, but also the people: the proud, noble Yavapai who would give in to greed, and the poor, ignorant whites who pump quarters into slot machines looking for easy money." She wiped her hands on her skirt leaving black smears along each side. "Hawk wasn't here. Just a warning. The land will re-vegetate. No lasting harm."

Fury brewed in me and I ran toward her, pushing her into the burnt out juniper. It crumbling as our bodies collided into its branches. "No fucking lasting harm?" I yelled in her face. "You stupid bitch. I should kill you right now. I should take a rock and bash your brains out!"

Twisting and struggling, she attempted to free herself from my grip. She tried to kick, to head butt me. The branches pinned her shoulders and scratched her arms and face. My elbows trembled from the force that I clamped her against the trunk. "You killed him. You killed him, and you think it's justified."

"I couldn't let him continue," she said in an even, unemotional voice. "He was never satisfied with what he had. Greed destroyed him, not me."

I relaxed my grip on her, but she didn't move.

"His soul needed to be freed, to escape the confines of the material world."

Aubrey, she was describing Aubrey. My mind shifted, ratcheting down the anger in an attempt to keep her talking. "Why, why did you scalp him?"

"The release," she said. "His energy had to be released from the crown chakra."

"Salvia?" I asked and released my grip on her since I didn't think she was going to escape.

"He was used to Salvia in his tea, and I added Rohypnol to help him relax. I knew it would help him travel his journey. I led him through a death ceremony at the fire pit, then I stopped his breath—a rebirthing passage to another plane. I helped him release his sins and allowed his soul to soar."

"He allowed you to spike his tea with a roofie?"

"No, he didn't know," she said as if she had only brushed dust from his lapel. "The Rohypnol was needed for the ceremony."

Footsteps approached from behind me, and I knew it had to be Sarras. His hand gripped my shoulder and guided me away from her. Two uniformed officers stood with him, and they pulled Clarity from the broken and charred remains of the juniper and slipped handcuffs onto her wrists. The mystified expression on her face told me she didn't believe she had done anything wrong, not in her universe. No, she had taken the only possible route for Aubrey's salvation.

The thought of informing her that her fire had killed Topher occurred to me, but I let it go. She would find out soon enough, and I didn't want to hear her cosmic justifications.

✄   ✄   ✄

"It's something I think he would have wanted you to have," Myra said, handing me one of Topher's paintings. On the canvas, Topher had captured the coolness of Oak Creek's blue waters swirled around rocks and under the towering oaks and sycamores. The bold blues and greens didn't remind me of the reds and oranges of the desert wildfire. This painting would evoke Topher's calm demeanor, a bit detached, a little cool, a James Dean composure. The good *do* die young.

"Thanks, Myra. How are you holding up?" I asked. We sat on the couch in the rental house, now filled with suitcases and a few boxes for my and Ruby's return to North Carolina.

For a moment, Myra just stared at the floor. "It's so hard," she said in a slow, soft voice. "I can't believe he's not here."

"Sarras said that Clarity is charged with first degree murder for Aubrey and arson and manslaughter." I didn't mention Topher's name with the crimes, no need to, and I didn't think I could hold myself together saying it out loud, especially to Myra.

"Bureau of Land Management," Myra began, "is interested in Apache Trails. Will Harris Construction sell their interest?"

"The estate will have to sell the land to pay off the development debts. If we can recover what went into the project, the Board will be happy to get that and get out." I set the painting against the coffee table and took Myra's hand in mine. "If you need anything, please let me or Ruby know. I can catch a flight and be out here within a day."

"Thanks, but I have plenty of friends here I can call on," she said. "Just none as good and dear as he was."

The drive out of Sedona had Ruby squirming in her seat. "I love this place," she said, nose to window, watching the last of the red rocks disappear in the distance. "Just not more than you and the rest of the family. If only I could pick you all up and transport you here."

"You aren't tied to Charlotte," I said. "There are plenty of towns within driving distance. Enough space from the family for peace, but close enough for an afternoon visit, close enough to smack us into shape when needed."

"You're right," she said. "It's just so pretty here."

"Beauty can be found in the simple stitch of thread, a stroke of a paint brush, or the crease in a page," I said.

Her hand felt my forehead. "You okay? Feeling dizzy? That doesn't sound like my Derek."

"A moment of clarity, maybe," I said. Then after the flood of memories washed past me, I added: "Ironic isn't it? She called herself Clarity, but didn't understand a damn thing." *Love and loss, there was no clarity in any of it.*

I reached for my water bottle, but Ruby grabbed it first, twisted off the cap, and handed it to me. "Keep your eyes on the road," she said and patted my hand on the steering wheel.

Greg Lilly

Greg Lilly grew up in Bristol, Virginia, then lived in Charlotte, North Carolina. The rich storytelling tradition of the South captivated him and he began writing. He first turned to creating short stories after plot lines and characters emerged from the technical manuals he wrote for a large family-owned corporation. His first novel, *Fingering the Family Jewels – A Derek Mason Mystery*, grew from those Charlotte experiences.

To escape the city and find a slower pace, he relocated to Sedona, Arizona for several years. During that time, his novels *Devil's Bridge* and *Under a Copper Moon* chronicled adventures of the high desert—present and past.

Scalping the Red Rocks is the next novel in the *Derek Mason Mystery* series and unites the Derek Mason characters with the lead characters of *Devil's Bridge*.

Greg is a freelance writer, magazine editor, and former Arts & Culture commissioner for the City of Sedona, Arizona. Today, he writes and lives in the tidewater area of Virginia.

Readers can reach him through his website: www.GregLilly.com

Acknowledgements

Writing is solitary. An author sits in front of a computer screen and attempts to capture the story in his head. However, the polishing and revisions that make that story a novel require the generous input of many people.

Now that those revisions are finished and before the book ships to the publisher, I have a moment to thank the people who allowed me to tap into their expertise, wisdom, and education. Your assistance is appreciated and treasured.

Thanks to:

- Michelle Moore, Angela McCoy, and Joyice Gere for their enthusiasm and support as my first readers;

- Jayson Coil, Battalion Chief (Sedona Fire District), for guiding me in the right direction on wildfire fuel, behavior, effects, and injuries;

- Sgt. Lucas Wilcoxson, Sedona Investigation Unit (Sedona Police Department), for answering my questions on roles in the department, processes, and special investigations;

- Doris Weintraub, winner of the "Name the Character After Me" contest, for allowing me to use her name in the book;

- Brad Dorris for his direction on real estate and commercial banking procedures and for allowing me to bounce plot turns off him; and

- Kris Neri, my editor, for her keen eye and expertise on plotting mysteries, plus the support that only another writer can give.